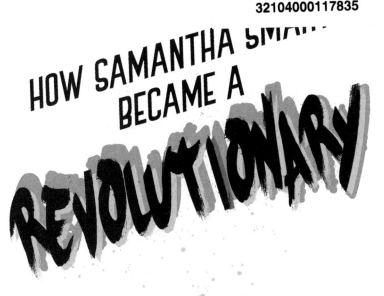

HOW SAMANTHA SMART BECAME A REVOLUTIONARY

DAWN GREEN

Red Deer Press

Published in Canada by Red Deer Press,
195 Allstate Parkway, Markham, ON   L3R 4T8

Published in the United States by Red Deer Press,
311 Washington Street, Brighton, MA 02135

www.reddeerpress.com   rdp@reddeerpress.com
10 9 8 7 6 5 4 3 2 1

Red Deer Press acknowledges with thanks the Canada Council for the Arts
and the Ontario Arts Council for their support of our publishing program.

Library and Archives Canada Cataloguing in Publication

Green, Dawn (Lisa Michelle Dawn), author
How Samantha Smart became a revolutionary / Dawn Green.
First edition.
ISBN 978-0-88995-549-3 (paperback)
I. Title.
PS8613.R42753H68 2017 jC813'.6 C2017-902212-1

Publisher Cataloging-in-Publication Data (U.S.)

Names: Green, Dawn (Lisa Michelle Dawn), author.
Title: How Samantha Smart Became a Revolutionary / Dawn Green.
Description: Markham, Ontario : Red Deer Press, 2017. |
Summary: "In an Orwellian world eerily similar to our own where a close election divides
a nation, an average girl is thrust into the social-media spotlight, labeled a terrorist, and
given the title: revolutionary" – Provided by publisher.

Identifiers: ISBN 978-0-88995-549-3 (paperback)
Subjects: LCSH: Social media – Juvenile fiction. | Political activist – Juvenile fiction.
| Dystopian fiction. | BISAC: YOUNG ADULT FICTION / Dystopian. | YOUNG ADULT
FICTION / Politics & Government.
Classification: LCCPZ7.G744Ho | DDC [F] – dc23

Edited for the Press by Peter Carver
Text and cover design by Tanya Montini
Printed in Canada

For Grandpa Green,
the original armchair revolutionary

Beginning … of the end

What is your name?

Sam: Samantha Avery Smart

Why are you are here?

Sam: Why don't you tell me?

I'm asking the questions. Why are you here?

Sam: You don't want to know about the why. That's not the reason you're here. What you want to know about is the how. Isn't that the million-dollar question? How did this happen? No, how could we let this happen?

It wasn't that long ago when I was "that" girl, walking through the cafeteria door—a bag full of class textbooks at my side, hair up in a ponytail and under a hat because I was up late, studying for a biology test, and didn't have time to shower. Inevitably, I'd be wearing my freshman hoodie, the one with a number 10 on the arm, a fading Trojan team logo over my heart, and a pair of black yoga pants—not because they make my ass look good, or even because I do yoga, but simply because they're comfy. That girl didn't stand out. She wasn't "special." You wouldn't have noticed her unless you were looking for her.

So how did I get here? How did that girl become this—a labelled terrorist and so-called voice of a revolution?

I'm nobody and everybody. My story—this story—is set nowhere and everywhere. I don't exactly know how I got here but I can tell you this: if you're not careful, if you're just living your life, thinking bad things happen to those other people and everything is going to be fine in your world, if you're just going through the motions and not paying close attention to the details, then this story could be set where you live. And my fate could easily become yours.

So, that's why I'm here. That ... and I was betrayed.

1

*"Mark my words, Sam: one day there will be a war
between the haves and the have-nots."*
"But what do they have that the others don't?"
"Everything."
~ Grandpa Smart

NOW

... **MEDIANET NEWS SPECIAL REPORT** ...

Hello, I'm Trisha Weathers, and this is a Medianet News special
report. We have interrupted your regular Medianet programming to
bring you first-hand coverage of this breaking story. Just moments
ago, we received word that Samantha Smart has been captured.

Again, an unconfirmed report that rebel leader Samantha
Smart has been apprehended by the Elite and, as of this moment, is
being transported to an undisclosed location.

No official statements have been released from either side, but
our sources have concluded that ... just a moment ... yes, I'm being
told that we have amateur footage of the Elite escorting a bound and
hooded individual into an unmarked blue van. As you can see, the
video is quite raw, and while there is no conclusive evidence as to
the identity of that person being detained, I have received word from
a reliable source that the hooded individual in question is, in fact,
Sam Smart ... excuse me, Samantha Smart, one of the main faces, if not
the face, of the Wright Resistance.

This could be a great victory for the King campaign and a devastating blow to anyone supporting the Resistance. We will be bringing you more on this story as it breaks ...

At this moment, there are a lot of things I should be thinking about.

I should be thinking about how these tight restraints are beginning to cut into the skin on my wrists. How difficult it is to breathe under the hood over my head. How the hood smells like someone else's sweat and who that someone else was—is he/she still alive?

About the fate of my friends within the Resistance—did they escape the attack?

About where this vehicle is taking me, or, more importantly, about what will happen when I get there.

I should be thinking about all of these things and, to some extent, I am. It's impossible not to. But in truth, my thoughts are mostly, uncontrollably and pathetically, focused on *him*—focused on his betrayal. I wonder what the Medianet lackeys would think if they knew that at this very critical moment, when my fate seems all but sealed and the Resistance might be crumbling, rebel Samantha Smart is thinking about a guy. They'd probably love it, actually. Breaking news.

But it's not really about him. Or me. Or us. I understand that now.

First day of university—Freshman Move In Day. Had I known then how things would play out, I don't think I would have bothered to talk to him, that clumsy jerk who bumped into me while I was on my fifth trip, lugging my life up the stairs. The jolt knocked a heavy box of books I was carrying out of my arms, sending everything tumbling down the cement stairway like a literary avalanche.

He was red in the face, a tall blue-eyed freshman who could have been cut straight out of a teen magazine spread titled *Cutest Boy Next Door*. He stuttered an apology and turned to punch a friend in the arm. His friend nonchalantly muttered, "Good luck, Dude," and then bounded down the stairs and out the nearest door.

"Uh ... I'm really sorry about that. I didn't see you coming up the stairs. I'm Brady, Brady Smith. I'm ... er ... the new quarterback of the football team."

I started to laugh, but not in a flirty way that he was probably used to. "Wow, is that how you always introduce yourself?"

"What? No ... I don't know why I said that. I just ..."

"Does it work? Do most girls just fall at your feet with that introduction? Start begging you to take them out?" I brushed past him, stepping down to grab my books.

"No. I don't usually ..." His face began to match the brick of the building. He ran a hand through his sandy curls and tried to recover. "Can I at least help you pick these up?" He bent down and lifted up a well-read, thin blue hardcover. "Dr. Seuss's *The Sneetches and Other Stories*?! Some classic literature here."

"Don't touch that!" I snagged the book from him. "Sorry, it's just that ... never mind."

"What?"

"My Grandpa gave it to me, that's all." I grabbed the box and started to fill it back up. "Look, you don't have to help me. I'll save you the time and effort and tell you that it's not going to get you anywhere, anyway. Not with me. Go. Join your frat buddies at the bar or something."

Despite my bitchiness, Brady didn't leave. He told me later that it was because he liked the challenge I presented. He stayed to help me pick up every book that had fallen and then carried the box to my room. After that, and with me protesting the entire time, he helped carry all the other boxes I had waiting in the lobby and even stuck around to help me unpack.

At some point, he confessed that he and his roommate Ryan (the friend from the stairwell and a teammate from the football team) had been watching from the window in their room and rating all the freshman girls as they arrived. I almost kicked him out at that point, but there was something about him, about his honesty and nervousness, that I found endearing.

When he first saw me, walking with a box in my arms and soccer cleats wrapped over my shoulder, he made a comment that he thought I was cute. Although he swore up and down that he had no idea Ryan was going to push him, he admitted that our collision in the stairway was no accident.

Unlike many other freshman girls, I had no intention of meeting any guys during my first few weeks of school. "Boys," as my grandpa had warned me on many occasions, "are trouble. They'll distract you from what needs to be done. Keep away." Of course, he told me this when I was only in middle school, but I could still hear his voice in my head as Brady bit on his lower lip and then asked me if I wanted to join him for a coffee. I don't know what made me say yes. Maybe it was fate. Maybe I was attracted to him from the very beginning, something about his innocence. Or it could be that I was simply hungry, tired, and needed a break from all the unpacking. I'd like to think now that it was the latter.

I can't help thinking back on that day and wondering what would have happened if I had said no. What if I hadn't been hungry? What if he hadn't seen me unloading my belongings that day? Would any of this still be happening?

Of course it would all still be happening—our meeting didn't turn the country into the battleground that it is today. But. Maybe. If we hadn't met that day ... I wouldn't be cuffed. I wouldn't be hooded. I wouldn't be surrounded by people who'd like to see me dead.

Maybe I wouldn't be here and this wouldn't be happening.

Not like this.

In truth, I guess you could say I'm not just thinking about the guy, I'm also thinking about the girl. I hardly recognize her anymore. Both of us so innocent, so naïve. How could either of us have known then about the future that is ... now? How could any of us have known? The "what ifs," the "why me's"—none of it matters, anyway. None of it can change anything.

The transportation van begins to slow and a sudden stop jolts me sideways, out of my thoughts, slamming me into the body of a Guard sitting beside me. Two hands grab me around the shoulders and shove me back into my seat.

After a minute, we begin to roll again, slowly, almost carefully. Outside I can hear a dull rumble growing louder as we inch forward. It sounds like a giant flock of squawking birds. Chanting. Lots of it, growing louder as we move forward. Hundreds, maybe thousands of people are outside the van, and they're all yelling about something. Inside, a voice over a radio orders the soldiers to arm themselves and be ready.

For a brief, foolish second, I let myself think maybe someone has come to intercept the van and rescue me. But this is no action movie and I know better. Any false hopes I'm entertaining are quickly dashed as something hard thuds against the side of the vehicle. More thuds, more yelling, and then the van begins to shake as if it's being violently pushed back and forth.

Amidst the shouting, I start to make out some of the words.

"Traitor. Terrorist. Killer ..." or is it *"Kill Her"*?

Angry voices yelling violent words about me, at me, someone they don't even know—not really, anyway.

I try to take a breath and calm my nerves, reminding myself that the anger outside isn't directed at me. It's directed at a propaganda-sized image of me. But under this thick cloth hood, the air is humid and heavy, making each breath a struggle to get any ounce of fresh air.

"Do you hear that?" a voice snarls from behind me. "Do you hear them?"

"Your fans are calling for you," a female voice taunts.

"We should just open the doors and let the wolves take her."

For the first time since it was shoved on me, I am actually thankful that this black bag is covering my face, hiding any fear in my eyes from the Elites around me. I try to swallow a dry lump of thick saliva in my throat, close my eyes tight, and shut out the noise. My thoughts unconsciously drift back to Brady—back to the day we met.

I can't help but think about his smile and the way he laughed at me when I got frustrated because I couldn't do something that should have been simple, like nailing a framed poster onto a wall. I think about how, at the beginning of our relationship, I was surprised he was even into me. A football quarterback is supposed to be attracted to some bottle blonde on the cheerleading squad, not a chestnut-haired midfielder on the soccer team.

I think about his eyes, about the gentle blue that sometimes, in the right light, could look hard and steel gray—the way they did only a few hours ago, when he stood before me, pointing the barrel of a gun squarely at my chest. He may not have pulled the trigger, but I can still feel that bullet embedding itself in my heart.

2

*"Remember, an initial crack is all it takes to
bring some of the world's strongest structures
crumbling to the ground."*
~ Grandpa Smart

THEN

The day before the homecoming game, and the university campus was littered with students buzzing in anticipation. Of course there was excitement, but most of the chatter was about the parties and beer-pong marathons later that night. It was clear from the empty seats in usually full lecture halls, and the number of cheerful yelling bodies scattered around the student square, that the festivities had already started for many.

Exiting class with Kayla, my best friend, roommate, and fellow midfielder on the soccer team, I spotted Brady and Ryan waving to us from the steps of the giant bronzed Trojan horse statue. The horse was decorated with a white bedsheet saddle, and in red, *Go Trojans Go* sprayed across it. As we got closer, Ryan whistled at a crowd of freshman girls and then proceeded to thrust his pelvis into the back of the horse. It had been three years and I still detested him as much as I did the first day we met. Unfortunately, he was Brady's best friend, so I tried to keep my mouth shut as much as possible—which took a lot of effort most days. Looking back, before everything started, his friendship with Ryan was one of the only things we ever disagreed on.

"Ryan!" Brady barked. "Stop being an asshole and get down."

He gave a couple more thrusts before jumping down. "Killjoy."

"Hi, Babe." Brady kissed me on the cheek as I sat down beside him. "What took you two so long?"

"Ask this one," Kayla pointed at me. "She got on a rant during Poli-Sci and couldn't be stopped. Not even when the class was over and people started to leave."

"I said I was sorry." I looked at Kayla. "I don't know what came over me."

"Really? I think it was the TA."

"Well, he's an idiot." I could see Brady grinning. "What? Don't tell me I look cute when I'm angry."

"But you do." His grin widened into a dimpled smile. "What happened?"

"First, we started discussing the election and some of the smear campaigns that both sides are using ..."

"And Sam had lots to say about that," Kayla interrupted.

"... and then," I glared back at her and continued, "we were asked to think about and comment on a quote from Lord Acton."

"Who's Lohd Ahcton?" Ryan asked with a bad British accent.

Kayla laughed. "Some old-stuffy politician."

"Aren't they all old and stuffy?"

"Totally." Kayla and Ryan high-fived.

"What was the quote?" Brady asked.

Shaking my head at Kayla, I turned back to Brady, "Absolute power corrupts absolutely."

"Well, that sounds pretty pessimistic."

"Right," Kayla agreed, "and when our TA started a debate about it in class, our little Sam here went off."

Brady proudly put his arm around me. "Sounds like my girl."

"I didn't want to, but that guy just gets to me sometimes."

"What's so wrong with having power?" Ryan shrugged while tossing a football to himself. "The only people who have a problem with power are the ones who don't have any."

"Oh, don't get her started again," Kayla tried to warn him but it was too late—the hairs on the back of my neck prickled. I'm pretty sure Ryan knew when he was pissing me off and did it anyway. He thrived on confrontation. As usual, I took the bait.

"We're not just talking about power. We're talking about *absolute* power. You think it's right that someone should have that much control over others?"

"Isn't that the way the world works?" he countered. "I tell ya, if I had absolute power, I'd have a fridge full of beer, an oven full of wings, and a harem of hot chicks to serve them to me."

Kayla hit him. "You're such a pig."

"Admit it, Kay. If you weren't so into pussy, you'd be all over this."

She shook her head in disgust. "Ryan, you're exactly the reason why I am so into *vagina*." He cringed at the word. Kayla smirked. "What? Can't handle the real thing?"

"Oh, I can handle it, babe," he tried to counter, but the red blotches on his cheeks revealed how flustered he really was. "Look, all I'm saying is that those that get themselves to the top deserve to be there."

"You sound like our TA right now," I growled back. "So … forget democracy; you think we should all just live in a dictatorship? Be told who, what, when, and where?"

"Sounds a lot easier to me ..."

Like he usually did when it came to disagreements between Ryan and me, Brady threw his hands in the air and tried to play peacemaker. "Okay, whoa. Democracy, dictatorship ... this conversation is getting a little too heavy for a sunny afternoon." He squeezed my shoulder. "We should be partying like everybody else. Big game tomorrow, remember?"

"How can we forget?" Kayla waved at the streamers and painted faces. "You know, we have a big playoff game this weekend, but you wouldn't know it from all the football fever."

"Aw ... is the big boys football team taking away from the little girls soccer game?" Ryan mocked.

"Ugh ... you're such an ass. We're undefeated. When was your last win? Oh, that's right ... four games ago?" Although her comment was answered with a rude gesture, she managed to shut Ryan up, albeit briefly.

Brady nudged me. "Hey? Are you going to be all right?"

"Yes. I know I'm being silly. It's just a class. But some of the things our TA said just ... argghhh."

"Sam, he was just trying get you going."

"Who's the TA?" Ryan asked. "Want us to beat him up for you?"

"Yes, because violence fixes everything," I replied sarcastically.

He shrugged. "It does in football."

"His name is Aaron Mahon, and thanks ... but no thanks. I can fight my own battles."

"Are you practicing today?" Brady changed the subject.

"Yes. Aren't you?"

"Just watching game tape. Can you meet me at the field after practice?"

"Sure. What's up?"

"It's a surprise."

"I hate surprises."

"You'll like this one. I promise." He gave me a quick kiss.

I checked my cell for the time. "I better get going. That stupid TA requested I come by his office before practice."

"Come by his office?" Brady asked. "Should I be weary of this guy?"

"It's wary," I corrected him—an annoying habit of mine, so I've been told. "No, you shouldn't. He's irritating and arrogant and thinks he's right about everything."

"Sounds like someone I know."

"Hey!"

He winked. "I'm just kidding."

"He probably just wants to tell me how wrong I am again." I grabbed my bag and, after a quick kiss and a promise to meet him after practice, I ran across the courtyard, narrowly cutting off a marching band beginning to lead student partiers in a spirited school cheer.

I knocked on the door of the TA's office located in the Political Science wing of Demo Hall, a historic campus building officially titled Demokratia Hall, a Greek political term that translated as "rule by the people." Past presidential busts lined either side of the mahogany corridor. It seemed like a judgmental gauntlet of chalk white faces, critical of today's modern students who walked through the halls, more concerned about checking the "likes" on their social media profiles than taking notes on the history surrounding them.

"Come in," a voice called from inside.

Aaron Mahon sat behind a desk, not bothering to look up from a pile of papers he was grading. The room was small and windowless. Its size and stuffiness made it seem more like a converted janitorial closet than a proper office. Each wall was plastered with photos and posters of political propaganda through the centuries. The largest poster in the room, a stoic looking Che Guevara, caught my attention. As I stood waiting for some acknowledgment from the figure behind the desk, I tried to decipher the Spanish words written across the bottom.

"It says: 'We cannot be sure of having something to live for unless we are willing to die for it.'"

"I didn't take you for a revolutionary."

He grinned back at me. "One can never know they're a revolutionary until they are."

"And who said that?"

"I don't know ... I guess I just did." He smiled and stood up. "Please, Miss Smart, have a seat."

"You can call me Sam." I sat down with my backpack on my lap, preparing for either another argument or a chastisement for my outburst in class.

"And you can call me Aaron."

He seemed much younger than I had assumed. In class I usually saw him from about twenty-five rows up. In the dim light of the office, what I thought was graying hair from a distance now seemed like a sun-touched bronze. The glasses he usually wore were propped on his head, letting me see the amber-brown of his eyes for the first time, and around his face was the faint fuzzy beginning of a finely groomed goatee and long sideburns. Something he was probably growing to make himself look older, or to help him fit in with the faculty. Not that it mattered but, up close, I guessed that he was only a few years older than most of the students.

"What are you thinking?" he asked.

"I was just thinking that you look a lot younger than I thought you were."

"Oh, well … thanks … or no thanks, I guess. I'm not exactly sure if that's a compliment." He squeezed around the mess in the room, carefully avoiding a precarious stack of vintage textbooks, and then half-sat on the edge of the desk, looking down at me, arms crossed. "That was quite the speech you gave in class today."

"I'm sorry. I don't know what came over me. I don't usually …"

"Yes, you do usually. And don't apologize. I thought you were mesmerizing. I've never seen a student get so passionate about politics before and, believe me, that's saying something."

"You're not upset?"

"Why would I be upset? I agree with everything you were saying."

"But why …"

"… did I argue against you?"

I nodded.

"Because that's my job. To push and challenge you. Get the conversation moving. Political lectures should be full of debates."

"Oh." I felt disappointed and slightly manipulated, like my rant in class had actually been the result of a careful orchestration.

"Hey, don't let that take anything away from what you said.

I don't know if you realized it or not but, when you got talking, more than half the class looked up from their texts, tweets, and games to listen to you. It takes someone pretty engaging to do that. It's a gift, trust me. Have you thought about going in for politics?"

I laughed. "Uh, no ... I don't think so. I hate politics. I only took this course as an elective because my best friend Kayla begged me to keep her company. It's totally her thing, not mine."

"Hmmm ... and yet it's usually your voice I hear, not hers. Have you declared a major yet?"

"Yes. Biology. I'm applying to med school."

"You know," he said while getting up and walking toward the poster of Che Guevara, "Che was studying to be a doctor, right before he joined the revolutionary army."

I was starting to wonder why he had asked to see me. "That's ... good for him, I guess."

"It was good for a lot of people. And not so good for others. As it is with all revolutions." He grabbed a stack of flyers from the desk. "Sam, the reason I asked you here was to see if I could convince you to distribute some of these pamphlets to the student body."

I glanced at the front of the flyer. *Make your voice count. Vote.* "Original."

"I admit that we need some help with the marketing. I take it you're planning on voting?"

I shrugged. "I guess so."

"You guess so?" He repeated back to me with a hint of irritation. "I can't believe the apathy of some of you students ... It's only the most important thing you could do. We're electing the leader of our country. I'd say that's pretty damn important." His voice continued to rise. "Are you even following the election?"

"Yes," I countered. It was the first time in my life I was actually following any election campaign. Mostly because it was required for class, but I left that part out.

"And what can you tell me about the candidates?" he asked skeptically.

I took his question for a challenge. I like challenges. "There's Richard Wright. He's a widower who lost his wife to cancer a few years ago. Smear campaigns like to point out that he has spent as much time living away from this country as he has in it. They say it makes him less patriotic. Personally, I think it gives him a worldlier outlook on things. Umm … he's a staunch advocate for the environment, and recently he opposed the Encor Power mining deal that could have destroyed …"

"Okay, and what about John King?"

This was starting to feel like a test. "Well, the only things the media ever really talks about are that he's a celebrated war hero who received some Medal of Bravery, and that while he was away on deployment, his family was in a car accident with a drunk driver. His son died, his wife was paralyzed from the waist down, and he's been fighting for tougher laws against alcohol and drug abuse ever since. According to magazines and hundreds of girls on campus, he's really hot …"

"Do you think he's *hot*?"

"Why does that matter?"

"It's just a question."

I was beginning to get annoyed with all his questions. "Sure, I guess he's good looking. Do I think that should matter? No. Do I think it will matter? Unfortunately, yes."

"I take it you're not a King supporter."

I hesitated before answering. "I don't know who I'm voting for yet." I stood up and hoisted my backpack onto my shoulder. "And I'm not sure it's any of your business."

He smiled and raised his hands in defeat. "No need to get defensive. I was just curious who one of my more engaged students was going to vote for. This election has me nervous."

"Why?"

"There's a lot of conflict in the world right now. Potential food and water shortages, terrorist attacks, pandemics ... it feels like we're reaching an interesting crossroads. I'm not so sure that King is the right person to run a country. He talks a big game, and he has a lot of support, but no one really knows that much about him or his platforms."

"Well, someone seems to believe in him. His campaign is huge."

Aaron raised his eyebrows. "You've noticed that, too?"

"How can I not? I can't walk a foot without seeing a new ad or slogan." I waved my hands in the air to form an imaginary banner. *"John King, the face of leadership. Vote King for a better stronger tomorrow—whatever that means. Or my personal favorite: Because who wouldn't want a King for a leader?* I'm pretty sure nobody does. This isn't the Dark Ages ... and they were called that for a reason, by the way. I mean ..." I stopped myself. "As a TA, are you even allowed to give me your opinion? Isn't that unethical or something?"

"Of course, you're right." He smiled, seeming almost impressed with my tendency to keep challenging him. "I'm sorry. I just figure that none of the students listens to me, anyway."

"Some do." I don't know why I gave in—maybe it was so I could leave—but I reached out and took the flyers. "I'll do my best to hand these out."

"Thanks." He walked back around the desk and sat down. "And Sam, I'm sorry if you thought I was grilling you with questions."

"It's fine."

"Can I ask you one more thing?" Stopping mid-step toward the door, I turned back. "Who do you think is going to win?"

I took a breath. "I don't know." That was a lie. Somewhere, deep down, I knew. "King." Even then, a part of me recognized but didn't want to acknowledge the potential danger that was looming. There were no obvious reasons for feeling that way, just a general unease that this election and his candidacy brought with it. After my conversation with Aaron, I realized I was not the only one feeling that way.

3

NOW

TRISHA WEATHERS—MEDIANET NEWS FLASH

If you are just joining us, then you are learning that the initial unconfirmed reports that the Elite have apprehended Samantha Smart have now been confirmed.

While no statement has been released from the Wright Resistance, leader of the Guard, General Marcus O'Brien, has confirmed that earlier today a secret Resistance base was infiltrated. The released statements reveal that while on a routine check of an area believed to house small pockets of anti-King supporters, the Elite took unexpected fire from the windows of a building. Given no other option but to attack, they stormed the building, shooting and killing many armed and dangerous members of the Resistance.

It was during the skirmish that some soldiers discovered that the building housed the unlikely hiding place of Samantha Smart. One soldier has been quoted as saying, "Once she realized that we had her, she just gave up. To be honest, I expected more from the so-called revolutionary. In the end, she walked out with her hands up, trembling like a coward."

Blurry photos sent to us from an anonymous source show a hooded figure being escorted from a blue van and led into a large unidentified cargo plane. As you can see from the photos, armed Guards and members of the Elite surround the figure believed to be Samantha Smart. At this time, it is unknown where the rebel leader is being taken. We'll have more on this developing story as it comes in.

Now to Bob Goodman for your weather report, Bob ...

Bob: Thanks for that, Trisha. Well, it's going to be another unstable one. We've got clouds and rain moving in overnight ...

4

THEN

When soccer practice ended, I took a quick shower and made my way to the stadium, looking for Brady. The campus was in full festive mode at that point. Loud music, chatter, and buzzing students streamed out from numerous parties in the residence buildings.

I knew something was up because of the way Brady had been acting earlier. He was not only one of the worst liars I had ever met, but being together for three years had given me the ability to read his every expression and emotion. I could tell when he was upset that one of his favorite sports teams had lost a game just by the tone in his voice when he answered the phone, or when he received a low grade on a paper by the furrow in his forehead. It could also be that he never tried to hide anything from me. About a year after we met, and after I had reluctantly given up some of the truths behind my past, I made him promise to never lie to me, even if he thought the truth would hurt. He promised and I did the same.

On my way toward the stadium, I ran into a group of his teammates excitedly talking about the game the next day. Ryan was with them. "Hey, Sam."

"Hey, Sam," a few others nodded.

"Hi, guys. Where's Brady?"

"You mean Romeo?" The group all laughed like they were in on a secret. "Oh, he's back at the stadium."

"He said to tell you to meet him on the field."

"Thanks."

"You two enjoy your night, now!" The group laughed and walked on, whistling and catcalling as they left.

The main gate to the stadium was unlocked and there was a hand-drawn arrow on a piece of paper, encouraging me to go in. Intrigued, I smiled and continued through the tunnel and out onto the darkened field. It felt eerie to be standing in the center of a hollow shell that was so often full of thousands of screaming fans. Walking past the end zone, I thought I could make out something ahead: irregular shadows and lumps on the field. The fall weather had taken a winter turn and, in the crisp night air, I could see my breath evaporate in a soft white haze.

"Keep going," a familiar voice teased from the stadium speakers.

"Where are you?" I yelled out.

"Just keep going."

I obeyed, cautiously.

"Okay ... stop!"

A few main lights buzzed on to reveal a perfectly set up picnic at the fifty-yard line. A large pizza, a container of beer on ice, plates, napkins, and candles were sitting on a red and white checked blanket. If I wasn't impressed enough, Brady sealed the deal when music from our favorite band started to echo over the PA system.

His familiar shadow came running down the stairs of the stands, and as he reached the field and continued his run toward me, I could see him beaming from ear to ear.

"Well?"

"What's all this for?"

He looked down at the picnic blanket. "I know what today means to you."

I kissed him. As uncomfortable as they made me feel, these small acts of kindness were the reason I had fallen in the first place. While most girls were getting angry that their boyfriends forgot momentous days like birthdays or anniversaries, Brady remembered the days that meant the most to me—like that day, the anniversary of my grandfather's death. I didn't have it written on any calendar, and I certainly didn't go around talking about it, but the knowledge and pain of it was still there when I had woken up that morning; Brady had remembered.

I was only weeks into my first year of university when the news arrived that my grandfather had died from a sudden heart attack. It was days away from the home opening soccer game— my first game wearing a Trojans jersey. We had just spoken on the phone the night before and I had told him that I'd set aside one half-line ticket with his name on it. I also told him how nervous I was. As he usually did, he gave me the sage advice I needed and craved. Then he told me how proud he was of the young woman I had become. He ended the conversation saying that he loved me —which I knew, but it was still a rare reveal of emotions for him. My grandpa was everything to me. He'd never had a good relationship with my mother, but he had stepped in to raise me when I was younger, and then again when things with her got worse. I wouldn't be where I was without him.

In the weeks following his death, I felt lost and alone. It's a strange and empty feeling to not have any family; it goes against the essence of being a human being. If it hadn't been for Kayla and Brady, I might have flunked out of school. There were some bad days after he died. Kayla literally helped me to get out of bed, get dressed, eat, go to class, do my homework, go to soccer, and continue functioning. And though we had only been together a short time, it was Brady who helped me to deal with my loss and some past demons. I'm the first to admit that it's difficult for me to let anyone get close. It's who I am. But in those weeks following my grandpa's death, Kayla became a sister and Brady became someone I knew I would eventually love.

"I can't believe you did all this." I leaned forward and kissed him again. "And how did you convince them to let you use the field?"

"Well, Coach felt like he owed me one," Brady said bitterly.

"Oh, no." I pulled back. "He's playing Garrett tomorrow?"

Brady nodded sourly. "It is what it is. But I don't want to talk about it right now. Come on, let's eat. I'm starving."

I tried to give him some space but, halfway through the pizza, I asked the question that he knew was coming. "So, did you tell your dad yet?"

"No." He took a minute to swallow the piece of crust he was chewing. "I was thinking I just wouldn't tell him. Maybe he won't notice."

"Won't notice that his eldest son isn't the starting quarterback of the homecoming game?"

Brady sighed. "I have to tell him. I know that."

"Don't snap at me for saying this but … you don't seem that upset about it. I thought you'd be crushed."

He shrugged. "I knew this was coming. Coach has been riding me for overthinking and playing too soft. Garrett's been playing better than me at practice. He deserves it."

"What are you going to do?"

"I don't know. I could train and try and get my spot back, I guess."

"You guess?"

He picked at a slice of pepperoni. "Sam, I don't know when it happened, but football just isn't fun anymore. It's my Dad's dream. Not mine."

"What are you saying?"

"I don't know. Doesn't matter. Tonight isn't about me." He smiled, wiped his hands clean, and jumped up. "Stay here. I'll be right back."

I could see how conflicted he was, and I wanted to ask him more about football and his dad, but I got the sense that he wasn't ready to talk about it. "Where are you going?"

"Just … stay," he pointed at the ground. "I'll be right back."

When Brady returned, he had something hidden behind his back.

I stood up. "What have you got there?"

He moved his hands to the front, revealing a small black box in the center of his palm. My eyes widened and I started to break out in a cold sweat. Seeing the terrified look on my face, he broke out laughing. "Don't worry, it's not *that*. I promise."

I reached out with a shaky hand and took the box. I opened it slowly, looking up for his reaction as I did. He just kept laughing. Inside was a beautiful silver watch, slightly larger than most female watches and sporty in style. I could tell from the make and model that it came from behind one of those expensive glass cases where you had to ask a salesperson to tell you the price. "What's this for?"

"Turn it over."

On the back was half an "&" sign and the name *Brady* engraved. He held out his other hand holding a larger male version of the same watch. On the back was the name *Sam* and the other half of the "&" sign. The two watches held side by side read *Sam & Brady*.

"Do you like it?"

I nodded. "But Brady, it's too much ..."

"Don't worry about that. You don't think it's too cheesy? Some of the guys on the team said I was being lame, and they ..."

I held up my hand to stop him. "I love it. Honest. Totally my style." It wasn't really my style. I've never been the romantic kind who needs to show my love with grand gestures. And I didn't own anything expensive, anything that I cared about losing or breaking. But he loved it—and he seemed so pleased with himself that I didn't have the heart to tell him it really was too extravagant for my wrist.

"I figured anything more than 'Sam & Brady' would be too ... not us. And I know you're really not the jewelry type, but the watch is supposed to symbolize time, or forever, or something like that. At least that's what the sales clerk tried to tell me."

I put it on and held out my wrist. The shiny silver reflected the bright lights of the stadium. "I love you, Brady Smith."

He put his hands around my hips, pulled me closer, and, under the lights of the stadium, gave me a long, soft kiss. "Right-back-atya, Smart." It was kind of an inside joke between us. The first time Brady had the courage to tell me that he loved me, "right-back-atya" was my response. In fact, it remained my standard response for almost four months. I wasn't making him wait on purpose or playing hard to get, I just had to be sure before I said the L word, that I meant it. And when I finally said it, I did.

"You thought it was a ring?" He grinned.

"No ..."

"Yes, you did. And what if one day it is?"

"Well, then, one day I might say yes." While vague, my answer seemed to satisfy him.

"Do you think you can still love me, even though I'm not the starting quarterback of the Trojans anymore?"

"I don't know," I teased. "I do have a reputation to uphold, and that Garrett is pretty cute."

"Hey." He tickled my side, knowing it was my most vulnerable spot.

"Ah, don't!" I screamed and pulled free, backing away with a hand up to protect myself. He gave a devilish grin and I could see the predator in his eyes. "Don't. Stay back. I'm warning you. I need to pee ..." Brady took a step forward. "Brady, I'm serious. Don't ..."

He jumped after me and I took off running. Our laughter echoed off the empty stands as we zigzagged around the field in a game of cat and mouse. The fresh lump of cheese and bread in my stomach slowed me down, allowing Brady to finally catch me by the wrist and pull me in. He tackled me softly and continued to tickle my vulnerable spots until I couldn't breathe and the threat of peeing myself became real. As I lay voluntarily pinned to the turf and helpless beneath him, he dropped down and kissed me.

A few minutes later, we were lying on the forty-yard line, Brady on his back and me with my head on his chest, both breathing heavily and looking up at the dark sky above.

"Tell me something about you I don't know," he asked, without taking his eyes off the night sky.

"What could I possibly tell you that you don't already know?"

"I don't know. I feel like there's lots you still haven't told me. Something about your childhood."

I suddenly tensed.

"You don't have to talk about the bad stuff. There must be something good. Didn't you have a favorite toy or anything?"

I had to think about what to say. While he knew more than anybody else, there were parts of my past that I had deliberately kept from him. Dark things, things that may have changed how others viewed me, that I didn't feel he or anyone else needed to know. "Okay, but then you have to promise to talk about football and your dad. No more avoiding."

"Deal."

"Don't laugh at me ..."

"I probably will." He joked and I hit him in the stomach. "Owww ... okay, I won't laugh ..."

"When I was little ... sometimes I used to think that my life was a story."

"What do you mean?"

"Like I was a character in a story someone else was reading." I held up my arm and waved it across the sky. "*The Great Adventures of Samantha Smart.* And I imagined someone would be curled up in the corner of a library or in their room, reading all about my life. I used to think about that a lot, especially when things with my dad were ... anyway, it's how I got through it. I knew that if someone out there was reading my story, then everything was going to be okay because stories always have a happy ending. And if it wasn't happy, then it wasn't the end. No matter how bad things got, what kind of trouble I was in, things would turn out okay ... as long as whoever was reading kept turning the pages." I stopped and waited for him to respond. "It's stupid, I know ..."

"I don't think it's stupid. I was just thinking that if someone really is reading your story, I guess that would make me the hero. The dashing prince who comes in to save the day and rescue the princess from the evil clutches of the dragon ... or whoever ..."

"Thanks, but in my stories I was never a princess. And I could always save myself."

"I bet you could," he laughed. "But you know I'd be there if you got into too much trouble."

"I know." I curled over and kissed him slowly. "Thank you. For tonight. For everything." He pulled me closer and we would have continued to kiss if not for the sudden interruption of loud voices, clapping, and cheering that echoed down from the bleachers.

"WOO HOO!"

"GO, SMITH!"

Half of the football team had returned to spy on our evening.

"GET OUT OF HERE," Brady yelled back.

"DON'T LET US STOP YOU," Ryan shouted. "HE ... COULD ... GO ... ALL ... THE ... WAY!!!!"

Brady was my first everything. Our connection, while founded in the security of the university world, felt caring, playful, and strong. For some reason, when I find myself searching for proof, questioning if our love was ever real (which I have been doing a lot lately), I think back on that night as an emotional keystone of our relationship. Little did I know how fragile the foundation actually was.

When did you know things were bad?

Sam: Weren't they always?

Let me rephrase. When did you notice that things were changing?

Sam: It would be easy to say that it was after King was elected, but I think it was right before that. Before the election. Things were unsettled around the country—gun violence, unemployment, food shortages, potential outbreaks, threats of terrorism—people wanted change but they didn't know what change meant, what it would bring. King and Wright both seemed to have the answers.

But for so many, it wasn't just about electing a president, it was about electing their president. Like "theirs" was the one and only option. Maybe it was because of the campaigns, the slogans, the constant bombardment of ideas and platforms, but people started becoming quite fanatical about their choices. In the end, it was obvious, or it should have been—whatever the outcome, some were going to be happy and others … weren't.

Are you saying that it didn't matter who won? That the outcome would have been the same?

Sam: I don't know. Maybe. Yes.

5

NOW

"Are you scared?"

A snarling voice cuts through the thick fabric of my hood. I don't know how long we've been in the air but I estimate a little over two hours. From the hood over my head, my being edgy and preoccupied with my circumstances, to the humming of the engine, it's difficult to know for sure. At some point, I think I heard Brady's voice. Whether that actually happened or I've dreamt it, I don't know.

"HEY!" An open hand smacks me hard on the ear. "I asked you a question!"

Am I scared? The obvious answer is yes, but I think it's better to keep my mouth shut. I know that could provoke whoever is standing over me, but I also don't want to give them any more than I already have. A giant hand grabs the back of my neck and starts to squeeze. The heat from the soldier's breath seeps through to my cheek.

"You think you're better than us, Smart?" The grip tightens.

"Huh? Answer me, bitch."

Suddenly I'm thrown from my seat onto the hard metal floor. With my hands still tightly bound behind my back, it's all I can do to land on my shoulder and stop myself from doing a face plant. Briefly, the hood flies up. The intruding light blinds my one free eye, but a split second later, I can see the blurred images of dark blue legs surrounding me. A black boot steps inches from my nose while another one kicks me in the stomach, forcing the wind from my lungs. Taunting voices begin to yell, egging on whoever is standing above me. I feel the heel of his boot stamp on my collarbone, sending me sprawling onto my back, my hands and wrists crushed under my own weight. The hood has once again been yanked over my head, but I can sense a group of bodies encircling me. I feel like a beetle turned over on its shell, helpless, exposed to the kids who want to tease and poke it with a stick.

"What the fuck is going on here?" A deep voice booms from behind my head. The noise stops abruptly as heavy footsteps clang on the metal floor. The anger behind the tone and the answering mumbles are reminiscent of a parent coming home to find the kids engaged in a wild party. Relief washes over me. I don't know what's about to happen, but I hope I never have to find out.

"Does someone want to explain this?"

"Sorry, Commander," a voice answers. "I heard her whispering something to one of the other prisoners."

It's an outright lie. And there's nothing I can do about it.

"Is that so?" the commander responds. "Get her up. On her knees." Hands grab and pull at my arms, forcefully positioning me on my knees. Two large bodies stand behind me, each with a hand on my shoulders. My heart begins to beat over the rumble of the engine.

"I guess you all deserve to see your catch." The hood is ripped from my head. The light, though dim in the plane, still makes me squint, but I am grateful for the movement of air that cools my sweaty face. My eyes adjust so that I can see a wall of blue uniformed bodies surrounding me like a pack of wolves. The commander (he must be) stands before me. "I give you Samantha Smart—the revolutionary. You don't seem so talkative now." I tense my jaw and focus on the floor of the plane. "Is it true you were talking to one of the other terrorists?"

Terrorists? I hate that word. It's not who or what we are.

The commander's face darkens as he steps closer to me. "Answer me."

"No." It comes out a raspy whisper as I turn my head down and away from his glare.

His hand grasps my chin and forces me to look up. "Are you calling my Elite a liar?"

I do not respond.

"You know, you're much prettier in person."

There is movement to the left of me. With the commander's hold on my chin, I can't turn my head but, glancing sideways, I am positive I see Ryan and then Brady ...

"Commander, we are beginning our descent." A female voice comes over the PA system. "Elites, prepare for landing and prisoner transfer."

I try to look left for a better view, but someone throws the hood back over my head and I'm pulled to my feet. "Saved by the bell, Smart. But not for long." Bodies disperse, orders are yelled out, and I'm taken back to my seat. As I sit in the darkness, waiting for what's coming, one image flashes over and over again in my brain—Brady's eyes, looking past the barrel of a gun, no longer full of happiness or love, but anger, hurt, and regret.

6

*"When there is right and wrong,
there can be no in-between."*
~ Grandpa Smart

THEN

Brady and I sat in a car parked in his parents' driveway. A rusty basketball hoop with a torn net, just barely hanging on by a single frayed string, stood in front of a large yellow house with white trim and white picket fences to match. Every time we pulled up to his house, with its perfectly landscaped yard and freshly cut lawn, I imagined the typical suburban life that Brady had grown up in. Sunday afternoons spent shooting hoops in the yard with his younger brother, Dad dutifully cutting the lawn, while Mom made freshly squeezed lemonade and baked cookies in the kitchen.

Brady noticed my discomfort. "What are you thinking? Don't tell me you're nervous." He reached over and held my hand. "You've been here before. You've met my parents a hundred times already." A hundred times was a bit of an exaggeration but he had a point. This wasn't my first visit and there really wasn't any reason for me to be as nervous as I was.

"It's just that every time I come to your house, I'm reminded of how different we are."

"We're not that different. We just have different pasts. Relax. They love you." He tightened his grip on my hand. "Come on. If anyone should be nervous, it's me. My dad still hasn't spoken to me since the homecoming game."

The front door opened just as we stepped onto the porch. Mrs. Smith wiped her hands on a tea towel and then greeted us with smiles and open arms. "Honey, welcome home." She kissed Brady on the cheeks and hugged me next. Her embrace always felt like a mix of warm bread and fresh-cut flowers. "Samantha, you look lovelier than ever. Come in, come in."

As we stepped inside, I was hit by a waft of warmth from the fire burning in the living room, mixed with the smell of turkey roasting in the oven.

"Sorry we're a little late, Mom."

"Oh, don't worry at all. Your father and brother just sat down. And Samantha, we're just so excited you decided to come home for the holidays with Brady this year. When he said you were thinking of staying to work on campus I just said no—no way you're going to let that girl stay on campus all by herself. Between my two sons and my husband, I could use a little extra estrogen around here."

"Well, thank you for having me." I took off my jacket and followed Brady into the dining room. Jackson smiled when his big brother came in, but his father's lack of expression was noticeable; he didn't waste any time conveying his true feelings.

"Finally, if it isn't my oldest son, back-up quarterback for the Trojans football team." He raised a glass of wine in the air as a mock toast.

"Honey," Mrs. Smith scolded her husband, "you promised to leave it alone."

I didn't need to look at Brady to sense every muscle in his body tensing. I reached over and squeezed his hand. "Jackson, you look so much bigger than the last time I saw you."

"Hi, Sam." He jumped up and gave me a giant bear hug. "I should—I'm a senior this year. Plus I've been hitting the gym since last spring."

"Jackson just won three first-place medals in his last swim meet," Mrs. Smith proudly boasted. "Jack, why don't you fill them in on everything while I grab the rest of dinner."

"Could have grabbed dinner an hour ago," Mr. Smith said under his breath.

Mrs. Smith hesitated on her way to the kitchen and wiped her hands on her apron. "Well, things have been ready for a little while because I wasn't sure if the power was going to stay on, what with these roaming power outages. However, I did manage to get one of the few turkeys the store could bring in."

"Few?" Brady asked.

"Oh, it's just those darn food controls causing people to go crazy and stock up. I've never seen the store like that before. Another lady in the checkout line even offered to buy me two pumpkin pies in exchange if I would give it up. Anyway, it's not big but it should be tasty."

"Would you like some help?" I asked.

"No, Sweetie, thank you. I think it's best you stay here and … uh … try your best to be the referee."

Over the course of the evening, the tension between Brady and his father continued to build. It felt like air being blown into a balloon that was already too full. I knew it was going to pop eventually but couldn't predict the exact moment.

For most of the meal, the only sound that could be heard was the clinking of cutlery on china. I tried to break the uncomfortable vibe by asking Jackson questions about girls, school, and swimming. But eventually, toward the end of the main course, Mr. Smith, who had remained silent since we sat down, gruffly interrupted.

"So, Samantha, I hear that congratulations are in order for your soccer team."

I swallowed a mouthful of mashed potatoes. "Yes, thank you."

"And for you. Not only captain of the championship team but tournament MVP." What he was saying should have sounded like a compliment but came out like a calculated jab at his son.

"Yes, it was a good couple of games for me. I got lucky a few times."

"It wasn't luck, Sam. You were amazing." Brady looked over at his father in defiance. "She deserved it."

"Sorry we didn't make it out, Sam, but I couldn't miss watching my son's ass warm the bench at his game."

POP!

"Honey," Mrs. Smith jumped in, "that's enough. It's the holidays ..."

"No, Mom. It's okay. Dad can say what he wants. I know he thinks I'm a failure. And you know what, Dad? Maybe I am. Maybe your son is a loser."

"Brady ..." Mrs. Smith pleaded.

"No, hon, let him finish." Mr. Smith directed a challenging glare at Brady.

"I'm finished, Dad. And you know what else? I'm not sure I want to stay in university right now, either. I don't even know what I'm doing there. I'm barely passing my classes. I'm sitting on the sideline at practice. If it wasn't for Sam, I'd probably already be gone." His chair screeched across the floor as he got up and left the room. A door to the outside slammed shut, leaving a deathly silence around the dining room table.

I kept my eyes down on my half-eaten dinner. All I wanted was to get up and run after him, but I also knew that when he got like this, he needed space. There were plenty of times in my life when I wished I had grown up with a bigger, more normal family; this was not one of them.

"Did you know about his wanting to quit school?" Mr. Smith barked it like an accusation, not a question. Brady had spoken about his father's quick temper before, but this was my first experience of it.

I shook my head. "No."

He glared at me, not giving up.

"Really, he's never said anything before," I said.

"WELL, HE CAN'T DO IT!"

Every muscle in my body clenched.

"I won't let him." Mr. Smith began to stand up but his wife reached for his arm.

"Honey, please. Let him be for now. He'll come back." When he sat back down, she looked over at me. "Sam, how is school going?"

"Uh ... good."

"Are you still thinking of med school?" Mr. Smith asked, glancing at the door Brady had slammed when he left.

"Eventually, yes. But I'm also taking some electives in anthropology and political science that I find interesting."

"Smart girl," Mr. Smith said approvingly.

"That's what they call me," I answered, hoping to lighten the mood.

"Political science sounds interesting," Mrs. Smith continued. "What are your thoughts on the coming election?"

"Umm ..." I hesitated. The last thing I wanted was to talk politics with anyone, especially the Smiths. Conversations with Brady led me to believe that their political views differed from my own. Thankfully, Mrs. Smith kept the conversation going so I didn't have to respond right away.

"Well, we just love that John King—don't we, honey? There's something about him ..."

"You just think he's hot." Jackson looked up from his second plate of food.

Mrs. Smith's face matched the red of the cranberry sauce. "Hot? Well, no ... though he is quite debonair, I'll give him that. I just think he has the right idea when it comes to this country. What do you think, Martin?" It was clear Mrs. Smith was trying to pull his focus away from their son, and bringing up the election was, unfortunately, the only topic that could do it. Mr. Smith took the bait and looked away from Brady's empty seat.

"I think this country needs a man like King. The man's a war hero. He's seen the other side of things. He's tough, honest, and knows how to keep this country from slipping, unlike so many others."

Even though a voice inside my head told me to stay quiet, I just couldn't keep my mouth shut. It was a problem, and still is. "You don't think he's a bit extreme? Some of his ideas, I mean?"

"We live in extreme times. Extreme times call for extreme measures, and he's not afraid to say it or act on it. That's to be respected."

"But some of the ideas are ..."

"Needed." Mr. Smith would not let me finish my sentence. "Tighter security measures. Tougher laws. And that Immigrant Reorganization idea of his is something this nation sorely needs. If those trying to live in this country cannot live up to certain standards, they need to go back where they came from. We need to focus on supporting ourselves before we support others. And don't even get me started on the undocumented ones ..."

"We used to stand for opportunity and freedom. What King is proposing, spying on citizens, hunting down people without documentation, taxing others, creating harsher immigration policies ... it's just going to make us more divided." I tried to tone down my temper but I could feel self-control quickly slipping away.

"You can't deny the stats. The majority of terrorist attacks are coming from outsiders infiltrating our country through our borders and online. We're being overrun. And as for the legal ones, why should I pay for them to come into my country and take my job?"

"It shouldn't be about money. We used to say: bring your ideas, your knowledge, your labor, your optimism ..."

"That was a different time. Hell, I admit that even my family were immigrants at one time. But these days, optimism doesn't put food on the table. Money does. This country can't afford to take care of those who can't take care of themselves. Water rationing, food restrictions, medicine hoarding, they're all signs of things to come. And it's only going to get worse. There's not enough to go around. Why should we share what we don't have with those who don't deserve it?"

"Some people aren't fortunate like others." I could hear my voice rising.

"Look, Sam, I understand where you're coming from with this. You've had to earn your keep. I'm not attacking people like you. I'm saying the ones who aren't like you, the ones who don't belong here and live off the backs of others ... we have no room for them anymore. Times are tough everywhere. The economy is weak. Energy shortages are happening on a global scale. Soon there won't be enough for everyone and King realizes that. He's willing to make the tough decisions for the ones who deserve it. At least he's got the balls to say what everyone is thinking."

Mrs. Smith stood up, directly between Mr. Smith and me. "Who wants dessert?"

"I do," Jackson nodded eagerly.

"Yes, please," I smiled and stood up to help clear the table, but mostly to leave the room and the conversation.

"Oh, no, dear. Jackson will get that."

"I will?" Jackson looked up at his mother's stern expression. "I will," he nodded and, like a good son, began to clear the table.

Only Mr. Smith and I remained in the room. "I take it you're not a King supporter?" There was a dangerous tone to his voice.

"I ... I don't know who I'm voting for yet." It was a lie. I had made up my mind weeks ago, but something told me that my vote was not welcome in this house. I could tell that Mr. Smith was searching my face for a real answer, so I continued. "There are a few things I like about both King and Wright."

"Like what? What do you like about King?" This wasn't really a question. He was trying to call my bluff.

"I think that when it comes to some of his proposed restrictions on weapons and drugs, even alcohol consumption, he's got the right ideas. I mean, I feel for the man with what happened to his wife and son, and I understand where he's coming from."

Mr. Smith nodded in agreement. "And did you tune into the debate this past week?"

"I did."

"And what's your take on this planned Beliefs and Values Program? Personally, I like his position that everyone should be more tolerant."

"Yes, tolerance is good ..."

"But ...?" he pushed.

The last thing I wanted was to enter into an argument with Brady's father. My next words needed to be chosen carefully. "Well, I'm not exactly sure why he thinks it's a good idea to have to declare one's personal beliefs, or really how tolerant it is to tell everyone: believe what you want but just don't express it around others. Some might consider that an attack on freedom of expression, and I think it's a slippery slope."

"He's not telling people to hide their beliefs. In fact, he's saying everyone should identify with one. They can believe and pray to who or whatever they want. He's just saying we shouldn't be flashing it around. He's creating unity."

"Unity or uniformity?"

"You say it like it's a bad thing."

"Umm ..." I hesitated. If this kept going, it was not going to end well. I looked at the front door and then scanned to the kitchen, hoping someone would interrupt us soon and save me. No luck, and Mr. Smith was waiting. "To be honest, I think our beliefs are personal and I'm not a fan of religion in politics ..."

"Sam's right, Dad," Brady had finally walked into the room and sat back down at the table. "Religion shouldn't have a place in the state when it comes to how we're governed." I breathed easier with Brady at my side. Under the table, his hand reached out and reassuringly rested on my thigh. A gesture to let me know what I already knew—he had my back.

"Well, look who's returned with an opinion that's not his own."

Brady's jaw clenched and his hand tightened on my thigh.

"So, you're with Sam here? You don't agree with King's policies?"

Suddenly I felt like I was being positioned between Brady and his father; at least, it felt like that was where Mr. Smith was placing me.

"No, Dad, it's not like that. I actually like a lot about King. But there's a lot I like about Wright as well."

"Like what?"

Mrs. Smith entered the room with a still steaming apple pie in her mitten-covered hands. "I think that's quite enough serious talk for one day. Now, who wants ice cream with their pie?" It was evident that she wanted the subject changed completely. Her family was back at the dinner table together and she seemed determined to keep it that way.

"I'll take some." Mr. Smith held out his plate but his eyes remained on me. What lay behind them was discomforting, challenging.

One after another, everyone held out their plate for a scoop of vanilla and, as forks were put to mouths, the topic quickly jumped from politics to the highlights from the weekend sports games. I decided to keep my head down and eat my dessert quietly, nodding in agreement when someone commented on a great play. While I was grateful that the mood in the room had changed, with lighter topics and conversation, I couldn't help but notice a shift, however subtle, in Mr. Smith's attitude toward me. I knew that evening, long before Brady would come to realize it, that his father no longer felt I was right for his son.

7

THEN

TRISHA WEATHERS—MEDIANET NEWS

Good evening, viewers, and welcome to our Medianet nightly newsflash.

It's only been a few months since President King narrowly claimed victory over Richard Wright, and already his presidency has met with multiple protests and objections from Wright supporters who are quickly growing in numbers.

An online poll taken just yesterday shows that, since the election, Wright's numbers have risen slightly while support for King has dwindled. A spokesperson for President King has said that the King camp expected some backlash from such a close race, and they suspect things will begin to settle in a short time.

General Marcus O'Brien, the President's advisor, was quoted as saying, "It doesn't matter what the numbers show. We won. The people who take issue with that need to get over it so this country can move forward in the direction it needs."

Meanwhile, Richard Wright has released a statement denying

that he or any members of his group have had any involvement in the current protests, saying: "The 'What's Wright' campaign is simply a peaceful way for the citizens of this country to voice their concerns over where we are headed."

As of today, the "What's Wright" campaign has filled the Mediaverse with online demonstrations, blog blitzes, and flash protests. The latest to jump on the "Wright" bandwagon seems to be a countrywide university and college campaign, gathering students to protest impending tuition hikes and heightened interest rates on national student loans. This comes on the heels of the government announcement that there will be changes in the mandated curriculum for high schools and first-year university students that will be implemented as soon as next semester.

Even though the King camp has been bombarded with questions from multiple groups, there has been no further explanation as to what that curriculum will entail. As expected, the student response to these impending changes and fee hikes has not been well received. Tomorrow, peaceful demonstrations are predicted in all major cities across the country, and we are advising citizens to be prepared, as it will disrupt some major traffic routes. Be listening for traffic advisories as you commute in to work tomorrow morning.

Earlier today, five people were arrested in relation to the shooting at Sundown Mall last week and, as first believed, police are now confirming that these attacks have terrorist ties. President King has denounced the attacks and, in response, has announced the experimental launch of his proposed King's Guard program. This program aims to, as General O'Brien declared, "create better vigilance and help the citizens help themselves."

People who sign up for the King's Guard will receive training, benefits, educational funding, and support in return for servicing their communities.

Critics of the proposed program question where the funds for such a program are coming from and believe there needs to be more regulations. Many fear that a program of this nature could lead to neighbors spying on neighbors. King has responded to those critics by defending the program:

"The Guard will not only create jobs but it will also create a better sense of security. The fact is, people want to feel safer. Our local police and national forces are facing a growing invisible enemy that lurks behind computer screens and in the shadows of our everyday life. The King's Guard is just another tool in the fight against terrorism that will make the people feel safer."

This has been your nightly newsbreak. Make sure you tune in tomorrow for updates on the student-led demonstrations and more comments as we take to the streets to hear your thoughts about the King's Guard.

I'm Trisha Weathers. Goodnight.

8

THEN

Asleep and snug under my down duvet, I was rudely awakened by the thud of a backpack dropping on my bed. Kayla plopped herself down beside my feet and started to tie up her boots.

"Ugh … what time is it?" Looking out the window, I could see that it was still dark outside.

"Six twenty-seven!" she responded eagerly. I let out a groan, slipped a pillow over my head, and turned over. It took only seconds for Kayla to smack me on the ass.

"Ughhh … what?"

"Aren't you coming today?"

"Coming to what?"

"The student protest."

"Another one?" I grumbled. "You've dragged me out to enough. I'm tired. I'll go to the next one."

"This is the last one before school lets out. It's supposed to be the biggest one." She nudged and poked at the blanket cocoon I had wrapped around myself. "Come on. Please. I promised to recruit as many students as I could."

"Well, then, they won't miss one tiny me."

"Everybody counts—as in *every body*. You know that."

"Kay, I was up late, finishing a final paper for Anthro. Just let me sleep."

"Nope." She grabbed my pillow and pulled my warm cocoon away. "Up you get—let's go."

"Hey!" I shrieked at the intrusive cold and folded into the fetal position to conserve heat. "That's not playing fair."

"You can come back and nap after. Let's go." She hit me with the pillow.

"Ughhh ..." I rolled over in defeat. "Fine. You're such a pain in the ass sometimes."

"But you still love me. Here, I washed both our shirts." She held out a red shirt with white writing that read *Students Support* on the front and *What's Wright* across the back. A few weeks earlier, I had been roped into helping screen-print the shirts along with a small group of eager Poli-Sci students looking to stretch out their vocal muscles in protest. The raise in tuition was the perfect cause for so-called rebellious youth. It didn't take long for the shirts to start making a fashion statement on campus and then spread to others across the nation. Grudgingly, I took mine and put it on.

When we got outside, the morning air was crisp. The clear blue morning sky foreshadowed a nice day to follow but, in this moment, it was still quite nippy and I slipped on my soccer hoodie to cover the goose bumps. "I'm hung—"

"Here." In anticipation of my whining, Kayla held out a breakfast bar and a banana. After living with me for three years, she knew her best friend well. I admit that I am no fun when

I'm tired and hungry—the soccer team complains that I give "hangry" a new meaning. Kayla thought she could fix at least one problem with the snack. "And we'll grab a coffee on the way."

"A mocha?" I asked hopefully, my mouth half-full of banana.

"Yes, a mocha."

"With that chocolate whipped cream?"

"With the chocolate whipped cream," she confirmed.

"And you're buying?" I was pushing it, but Kayla just smiled.

"Yes, my treat."

As we made our way down the road to the university's main gate, other silent protesters joined in the march. It was like a scene out of those walking-dead zombie movies. Hundreds of bleary-eyed students dragging their feet toward the main city center.

"Thanks for the food." The caffeine and sugar were perking me up.

"Thanks for coming."

"Would you have let me sleep?"

"Probably not," she admitted.

"You really think any of this makes a difference?" I waved my hand at the others walking around us.

"I don't know. But don't you think we have to try?"

"What do you think any of this is going to accomplish? We march and protest. No one cares what we think. No one who matters. They're going to do what they want and we just have to take it with a smile and a 'Please, sir, can I have another.' The whole lot of us are drawing the short stick and there's nothing anyone can really do about it."

"What's gotten into you?"

"Nothing."

"Nothing? Sam, it's me. The pepper to your salt, remember?"

Salt and Pepper were nicknames we had been given as freshman soccer players. It was an obvious allusion to our skin tones but, even more, it was a reference to how our quick passing plays in the midfield complemented one another and propelled us both to lead the league in assists and goals.

"It's nothing. Really." I looked away so she couldn't see the lie. "I'm just grumpy and tired."

"Sam." She stopped me. "Tell me."

I let out a dejected sigh. "I lost my scholarship." My voice was loud enough for others walking to turn their heads and look over.

"What? What do you mean?"

"Yesterday the coach called me in and told me and a couple others that because of certain restrictions, the economy, fee hikes, and other administration blah, blah, blah ... they are being forced to cut costs. Athletic scholarships are the first to go. Can't say I blame them. I mean, I really should have seen this coming."

"They can't do that to you," Kayla replied in disbelief. "Half our team has some kind of scholarship."

"They already did. I'm still a student here and I'm still on the team. I have the summer to come up with next year's tuition. And if I work a couple of jobs and apply for student loans, I might be able to come up with it."

"That's it?" Kayla snapped. "That's all Coach had to say."

"No ... she said ... she said she was going to do what she could to get our funding back but ..."

"But?"

"But it seemed like a lost cause. She did provide one option, though."

"What?"

I pulled out a wrinkled blue pamphlet from my back pocket and handed it to her.

"You've got to be kidding me!" Kayla swiped the pamphlet. "Join King's Guard? That was her suggestion?"

"Not her suggestion. It came as an option from the university administration. Says if we sign up for the Guard, they'll cover half the tuition and forgive any student loans we take on. The longer we stay on, the more the government will forgive. It's not a bad deal."

"And Coach was pushing this?"

"Not really. She seemed pissed about the whole thing."

"I bet." Kayla looked at me seriously. "You're not actually considering this?"

"It's not like I have a lot of options ..."

"Oh, this is ... this is ... bullshit! I can't believe you're thinking about ..." She paused when she saw the grin on my face. I couldn't resist playing with her and I was enjoying how flustered she was getting. "You think this is funny?"

"Relax, Kay. I'm not doing it," I laughed.

"You're not?"

"Hell, no. I may be desperate and I want my degree, but I'm not going to sell out to get it. I've already got jobs set up at the library and a campus café. Coach said the least she could do was get me free room and board for the summer to help me save."

"I thought you were going on a road trip with Brady?"

"That's kind of out of the question now."

"Does he know?"

"No. And don't you say anything, either. I'm going to tell

him at the party tonight." I could see a worry line forming in the middle of Kayla's forehead. The only time "the line" came out was during final exams—that, and overtime shootouts at soccer. "It's going to be okay." I tried to reassure her but, to be honest, it was difficult to believe my own words. Nothing about any of what was going on felt okay.

She hugged me. "You scared me. I thought I was going to lose you."

"Lose me? Even if I decided to join the Guard, I wouldn't be going anywhere. You're acting like they would ship me off to sea or something. It's not that bad. In fact, I think they're doing some good things."

"Whatever. The whole idea of it still scares me. It's like some kind of organized cult, and they're growing in numbers. King's Guard ..." she shook her head, "... more like his army!"

"It's not his army."

"Well, it could be. She squeezed her fist in anger and let the bold letters of the *King's Guard* pamphlet crumple together.

"Well, it's easy to understand why they're growing." I took the pamphlet back. "They don't leave many options out there. If I couldn't find a job over the summer ..."

"Don't say it." She held up a finger to stop me. Her eyebrows arched high. When Kayla had that look on her face, I knew she was thinking something crazy. It was the same look she had when she got the idea to toilet paper the locker room of the boys soccer team. When our coach found out, we ran laps for three straight practices.

"What is it, Kay?"

She grabbed the pamphlet back. "You have to talk about this today. At the rally."

"What?" I shook my head. "No way. I don't want to ..."

"Sam, you have to alert the other students to what King and his side are trying to pull."

"His side?"

"Well, whatever. They can't get away with this."

"If you're so upset about it, you talk. I'd rather pull my eyelashes out than speak in public. You know that."

Kayla thought about it. "This doesn't affect me like it does you. I'll talk about it but it would be better coming from you."

"From me? Why, because I'm the one who stands to lose something here? Because I don't have a family who can support me and my education like you do?"

"Well ... yeah." She nodded. "Plus if I speak, they'll make this about my color and not my words. And no one wants to hear from some privileged-private-schooled-daughter of a lawyer, anyway. You're more ... relatable."

I laughed at the half-insult. "Well, thanks for that, I guess."

"Sam, you know what I mean." She reached out apologetically.

"Yeah, I do." I stepped away. "Kay, you pulled me out of bed. I'm here to support this protest but I'm not talking. There's no way." I started to march at a brisker pace, joining in with a now swelling red river of students flowing toward the city center. She could tell her words had stung.

"Sam, don't be like that. Sam! I'm sorry!" She called out an apology but I was already too far away to hear her, or at least I pretended I was.

Later that evening, a large group of students huddled closely together in an off-campus living room. Red plastic cups were raised high in the air as Ryan stepped up on the table. "We raise our glasses to the end of another year, another season, the end of final exams, final papers, final projects ... and to the end of another semester of good friends and GRRREEEAAATTT TIMES!!" A loud cheer erupted, cups tapped together, drinks splashed, and everyone began to drink away the stresses of finals week. "The drinks are cold, the friends are plenty, there's a heated pool outside, and any loser who thinks they can beat me in a sporting game of beer-pong is welcome to try out on the deck. NOW LET'S PARTY!!" Ryan jumped down off the table as loud music began to thump from the surround-sound system.

Outside, I sprawled on the plastic pool furniture with Brady, Kayla, and other school friends, reminiscing about the top moments from our sports seasons.

Becca, a defender from the soccer team, took over the conversation and pointed at me. "I still think the highlight of the year was Smart over here. Championship semi-finals, tied 1–1, seconds from OT, she gets bulldozed down in the box—should have been a red card on that girl, by the way—but it didn't faze our Sam here. In the same moment, she gets up out of the mud like some creature from a swamp movie and dives, from her knees no less, to head the ball past the goalie into the net, sending us to the championship game. Awesomest play I've ever seen—and, yes, I know 'awesomest' is not a word, but I'm making it one just for Sam. Oh, and the look on that chick who thought she'd taken you out ... man, that was the best part." Becca started to laugh at the memory.

Brady knew me well enough to know how uncomfortable I felt with the attention, but he decided to continue anyway. He put his arm around my shoulders and hugged tight. "That's my Sam. Just when you think she's down for the count ... BOOM, up she gets ..."

"My hero," Kayla gushed. "The awesomest!"

"OKAY, enough ..." I pushed Brady's arm off. "What about Kay?" I tried to divert the attention away from myself. "Anyone else hear her speech at the Center today?"

"At the Center? Did you go to the protest today?" Brady turned to me with a hint of concern in his voice.

"I didn't really have a choice. Little miss fight-the-power practically dragged me there in my pj's."

"Were there a lot of people?" Becca asked.

"At least a few thousand," I continued. "And Kay just marched up to the front and started spouting off about King making bad choices and how his tactics are going to lead this country into despair ..."

"Disarray," Kayla corrected. "I didn't say despair."

"Whatever." I waved her off. "You were still pretty amazing up there ..."

"You guys were lucky nothing happened. You shouldn't have gone there today ..." Brady's serious tone dampened the mood.

"What's wrong with ..."

Before I could finish, he took out his phone and pulled up some images. "Didn't you see the Medianet flashes? One of the student protests in the North got out of hand. The police moved in with water cannons and teargas. It started a full-out riot. Some people were hurt, others arrested. Look." He held out his phone and the group scanned through images. Students wearing red shirts, similar to those Kayla and I were still wearing under our hoodies, could be seen running from armed police officers. There was smoke, broken glass, blood. The scene sent a shiver up my spine.

As Brady tried to scroll through more images, the screen went black and a caution window popped up that read: CONTENT UNAVAILABLE.

"That's weird. I was looking at this site earlier." He tried to find more but the same message kept popping up. "Oh, well. Maybe the Medianet's glitching again."

"And maybe someone doesn't want you to see what happened there," Kayla piped up.

"That's a bit extreme."

"Is it?" she shouted back. "They don't want us to know the truth."

"And what's that?"

"That this is all part of a plan. First they start to monitor the Medianet, and then they'll want to control it. This is just the beginning. There's a bigger truth out there—they just don't want us to know about it yet."

Brady laughed. "Okay, conspiracy theory. Settle down."

"Did they say what happened?" I asked Brady and simultaneously gave Kayla a look that told her to cool off.

"Not really, just that some people, new members of the King's Guard, came to hand out some flyers to the protesters, and one thing led to another. You're just lucky nothing happened at the city center today. I think people need to stop with these protests, anyway. I mean, the people elected King and now we all need to accept it. Move on."

"I didn't elect him." Kayla scowled. "And he only won by two percent. That doesn't exactly say the country elected him."

"Whatever—he won."

"Did you vote for him?" It seemed like an accusation, not a question.

"So what if I did? It's not really any of your business who I voted for."

"Can you two just relax?" I interrupted. "It's a party. It's the final time we get to hang out before everyone leaves for the summer. Can't we all just ... chill?"

Kayla stood up. "Yes, let's *chill*. Let's not worry about the fact that because of this government, you lost your scholarship and might not get to come back to school, or if you do, you might have to learn something the government plans to force feed us with some new curriculum, or that immigrants are being pulled out of their homes and, if they can't pay enough, are being forced to evacuate and live in tent cities, or that tax hikes are forcing foreclosures, or about the food and energy shortages ..."

"What?" Brady looked at me. "You lost your scholarship?"

Kayla shook her head. "After all I just said, that's what you're worried about?"

Brady ignored her. "Did you?"

I glared at Kayla. "Thanks."

"Well, he was going to find out sometime." She snatched up her cup and motioned for others to leave with her. "Come on, let's go beat Ryan off the beer-pong table." She was still heated but mouthed a quick "sorry" before leaving.

"What's going on?" Brady asked me.

"Let's go for a walk." I downed my drink and stood up. "I need to get out of here."

Brady followed me down a gravel path that led to a park bench overlooking a small campus pond. The light from the moon reflected over the water and the rhythmical croaking of frogs filled the night air. I reached over and took his hand in mine.

"It's true." I finally breathed out. "They're taking away all inconsequential athletic scholarships."

"What does that mean?"

"It means that, like everyone else, the university is being forced to cut costs and they are picking and choosing where to cut the fat. Women's soccer doesn't exactly rank high on the list of priorities."

"Can they do that?" he asked angrily.

"It seems so." I paused. "The thing is, as mad as I am, I can't say I blame them. It is just a sport. And it's always been just a sport to me. I mean … I love it. I remember when I was in my first year of high school and my coach told me that I was good enough to get a scholarship. The idea that playing soccer could actually get me something, somewhere better—just thinking that was possible changed everything for me. Soccer was my passion, but it was always just a means to an end. I can also remember running home to my mom and telling her what the coach had said." I stopped.

Brady squeezed my hand. "What did she say?"

I stared out into the darkness, lost in a memory.

"Sam?" he asked again. "What did she say?"

"That the coach was probably just trying to sleep with me, because men only gave women compliments like that when they wanted something else." I turned and looked at him. "She didn't even know that my coach was a woman. She didn't know because she had never come to see one of my games." I knew that listening to me, to my past, Brady felt helpless. I could feel his tentativeness, wanting to reach out and hug me, not knowing if he should. My past always created this uncomfortable barrier between us—which is why I didn't talk about it very often.

"Grandpa told me that she only said things like that because she was scared of me leaving her all alone. She knew I would one day."

"I'm sure he was right."

"He usually was," I said quietly.

"So, what now?"

"Well, lucky for me, I only have a year of school to worry about paying for, and I've calculated that if I work a couple of jobs over the summer and through next year, then apply for a student loan, I might just be able to pull this off."

"Over the summer?" His tone suggested that he knew what was coming next.

"I can't go on a road trip with you. Not this summer, anyway." Brady let go of my hand and looked away. "Hey, it's not that big a deal, is it? One more year ..."

"No," he shook his head. "It's just that I really need to get away. I need something ... I don't know, different. I'm not upset, I totally get it. I was just looking forward to us camping out, eating bad gas station snacks. Maybe ..." He turned back with a bit of hope in his eyes.

"What?"

"Maybe I could lend you the money?"

"No," I said firmly.

"... and then you wouldn't have to work ..."

"No way."

"... and then we could be together. My family wouldn't ..."

"Brady," I snapped. "NO!"

"You know, one day we could be married and then you'll have to take whatever I give you."

"But that day is not today." I smiled.

"It could be." He quickly slipped off the bench and onto his knees.

"Brady!" I shouted. "Get up ... right now ..."

"Samantha Smart, will you ..."

"Oh, my God." I covered my eyes with my hands.

"... kiss me?" He stretched his head toward me and stole a kiss, then pulled back, laughing.

I hit him in the arm as he sat back down. "That wasn't funny."

"I thought it was," he winked. "I'm a little buzzed but I'm not that drunk. No road trip this summer. That means my dad is going to want me to work for him again. He'll probably make me train for football. He thinks I can win my starting spot back."

"You told him that you don't want it?"

"Doesn't matter to him. So, you're going to stay on campus and work?" I nodded. "Well, I'll just have to come up and visit you lots, then." He leaned in for another kiss.

"You better," I whispered between lip locks. At that moment, the frogs stopped croaking and the night fell dead silent. As I looked out at the pond, a shiver ran through my body. "I hate it when the frogs stop like that. My grandpa used to say it was a sign that something was coming."

"Something bad or something good?"

"Never said."

"But he was usually right."

I couldn't hide the apprehension in my next words. "Almost always."

9

"Whether or not we realize it,
life is constantly preparing us for all the battles
we have yet to face."
~ Grandpa Smart

NOW

So far, being a prisoner is not how I had imagined it. I had envisioned rusty shackles, dark cells with bars on the windows, maybe even rats running around damp floors. Clearly, too many classic novels and action/adventure movies have influenced my ideas of captivity. Yes, I'm trying to make light of a dark situation, but I know this isn't just some story; it's my life and, at this moment, it all feels very real.

Aaron was always warning me what would happen, what they would do to me if I ever got caught. There were rumors floating around the Resistance community, stories from people who had been taken by members of the Elite. Designated locations where anti-government activists were being interrogated. The first stories spoke about over-the-table interviews, isolation rooms, sleep deprivation tactics, but then we started hearing about starvation, beatings, various forms of physical torture ... The progression and severity of these tactics were chilling in their own right; however the reality that the methods were being enacted by humans against fellow humans (people we called fellow countrymen) was almost unfathomable.

Aaron asked, practically begged me, to take this Resistance thing seriously and forced me to sit in on some information sessions he and Wright had organized for new recruits. They put together everything from *Understanding the Mind of Your Enemy*— an informative lecture taught by a professor of psychology—to *Self Defense for the Political Activist*. That class was a good workout and I also found it kind of fun.

There was also *Unbreakable: How to survive if you are captured*— taught by an ex-soldier who was trained as a professional interrogator.

When the King's Guard program had more members than our nation's police and military, O'Brien initiated a unification of forces. The idea was that one entity would be cost effective and easier to manage. Initially his plan was met with anger and opposition from within the other forces, but King did what he always does and went ahead with what he wanted. Thousands of police and soldiers who disagreed with the move and did not want to be unified with the Guard quit their positions, which ultimately became a boost for the Resistance when many ended up joining our cause. The ex-soldier leading the interrogation lecture was one of the many who had defected.

Aaron dragged me to sit in on his session, warning me that I needed to be prepared for anything. He even sat beside me to make sure I didn't leave—maybe he knew something that I didn't. In a way, I felt like I was back in my regular university classes with him acting as my TA, and, with everything going on, I craved the normality of it.

When it came time for the question period, he asked things

like: "Do they handle men and women differently?"—and then looked at me to make sure I was listening.

I always was a good student, something Aaron was counting on, and I remember the ex-soldier's response, "Yes. I have personally found that women are pretty good at withstanding physical pain, but easier to break when they are attacked on a personal, emotional level ..."

I can still hear the icy disconnected tone in his voice. "I have personally found ..." like it was nothing more than recounting his findings on a tax report. Of all the things I took away from those sessions, what stuck with me most was the demeanor of the interrogator. He was like a robot. There was no emotion or remorse behind what he said or did. He talked about people as if they were units. Aaron had wanted the tutorial to scare me and, although I never admitted it to him, it had its desired effect.

I'm thinking of Aaron now. In the past, I understood he was only trying to scare me because he cared ... maybe cares too much. As my level of notoriety increased, so did his worry that one day I could be captured or killed.

What is he doing and thinking now? At this point, he must have heard about my capture. How much time has gone by since they black-bagged and threw me in the van? How long has it been since I arrived? How long have I been standing here?

I'm trying to focus. I'm trying to think.

But I'm so tired.

My eyes are dry and burning. I just need a little shuteye. A few seconds, that's all. My eyelids start to close and slowly the weight of my head becomes too much for my neck ...

WHACK!! The loud crack of a long bamboo stick hitting a metal desk snaps my head back up. A severe-looking woman wearing a dark blue skirt and crisp white-collared shirt with the emblem of the Guard Elite—a bold GE inside a tilted pentagon outline embroidered on each collar—stands up from behind the desk. "Close your eyes again and this cane won't be hitting the desk to keep you awake."

Keep you awake—I thought that was why they had kept me standing in the middle of this empty room, but "Stick-up-her-ass" or "Stick Bitch," as I have affectionately named her, has just confirmed it. This whole time I have been made to stand with my hands bound behind my back, in the middle of what I guess used to be a classroom of some kind, I've wondered if it's because they're waiting for someone to arrive or if it's an interrogation tactic. *They will try to disorient you by depriving you of sleep*—part of the lesson I am remembering. But how did he say to combat this? I try to think of his advice but all I can focus on is Stick Bitch, currently pacing back and forth at the front of the room.

Mid-forties, I'm guessing. Sort of pretty, in that ice-bitch kind of way. Her chin-length blonde hair reveals much darker roots that says it must have been dyed months ago. I wonder if the roots bother her. It's clear from her perfectly pressed shirt and flawless makeup that she takes pride in how she looks. She probably hates her roots. It must have been difficult to find a hair salon since the revolution started. I must be a bit delusional from my lack of sleep, because it takes everything in me to contain a rising giggle.

"What the hell are you smiling at?" she snarls and I quickly tighten my lips. "You won't be smiling as soon as O'Brien and King get here."

My reaction must reveal too much because it's Stick Bitch who's smiling now.

"That's right, sweetheart. They should be here any minute."

At that moment, the door opens and we both jump. A Guard enters and whispers something in her ear. I can't make out what they're saying but, by the annoyed glance she sneaks at her watch, it's obvious that they haven't arrived yet. I let out a breath that I didn't realize I was holding in. As the Guard turns to leave, he hesitates and looks at me like he's seeing a two-headed circus freak for the first time. Since my capture, this has been happening a lot. Heads turned in nervous disbelief as I was escorted down halls and led into this room. I've even caught Stick Bitch staring at me every now and then.

Stick-up-her-ass … Stick Bitch … Stick-for-brains … Miss Sticky … I try to amuse myself and think of different names—anything to keep my mind busy.

I shift my stance ever so slightly. My feet and knees are aching. My eyes continue to burn. The restraints around my wrists have made my hands go numb, and the cramps in my stomach are making me seriously regret skipping lunch the day before. What was the last thing I ate? No, I shouldn't think about food right now. Bad idea. What was I thinking before? Right, so far, being a prisoner is not how I imagined it. Well, not all of it. In fact, it's kind of starting to feel like I'm in some evil afterschool detention nightmare. Fitting, given the location.

Once they had taken me from the transport and finally removed my sweaty, itchy hood, it only took a few minutes to recognize the location—worn-down hardwood floors, red brick walls, wooden staircases, and a circular clock mounted high near the foyer ceiling. At first I thought they had brought me to a military base. That would have made sense. But as I was led down halls and through different areas, I saw lines of green lockers, rooms piled high with desks and chairs, and signs pointing routes to the gymnasium and theater. By its size and architecture, it is (or was) some kind of private or boarding school. And judging by some of the posters and student work still up on the walls, it's only recently been converted into an Elite interrogation facility—an ingenious location, actually. The Resistance has been scanning military bases, police stations, prisons, and even hospitals to discover where the Guard is training future soldiers and holding detainees. I personally led a group exploring what remains and can be recovered from the now government controlled Medianet, deciphering maps and editing documents to uncover Guard and special Elite locations.

The room I'm standing in has been cleared of almost everything that once made it a classroom. All that remains is one large metal desk and its chair at the front, empty chalkboards on the walls, two armed Guards standing in opposite corners, Stick-up-her-ass, and me. It's the perfect facility, multiple rooms and secure location— made even more secure by the metal blinds that cover the windows. No, they would never think to look for me here.

Here. How did I get here? How long have I been here? The plane landed. I was pulled off and hurried into another vehicle. I estimate that we drove for maybe another four hours before arriving at this place. It's a definite guess, because it could have been two hours and it could have been six. I realize now why the black bags are so effective. Without visual references like trees, buildings, roads, and light, the only other practical sense a person has to go on is touch and sound.

I saw the clock in the main entrance when they took my hood off. At the time, everything was blurry; as my eyes adjusted, I tried to take in all of my surroundings. In truth, I wasn't taking in anything, I was looking for him. Pathetic.

Don't start thinking about him again. Think. Remember. What time was on that clock?

Four something? Maybe … yes, definitely four something. And it was light out, not the light of early dawn, light like it was late afternoon. And if it was four something, and I was captured just after seven the night before, that means it hasn't been twenty-four hours yet. It's a small, personal victory, but I'm happy to figure something out.

Now, what happened next? They brought me into the building and removed the hood. I looked around—did not see Brady—but did see three other hooded prisoners standing in a line with me. I could tell by their clothes that they were Maya, Matt, and Jose. I hated seeing them in restraints but I'm relieved to know that they are still alive, and comforted to know that I'm not completely alone here. The front of Matt's shirt was caked with dried blood that was almost black in color—I don't want to think about how it got there. I was still looking at the blood on his shirt when a long polished stick touched my cheek and forced me to look ahead. That's when I was introduced to Stick Bitch.

"I just had to see for myself." Even in heels, she was still a couple of inches shorter than me. "And here you are." She reached out and gently pushed my loose hair behind my ear.

It was a casual gesture, a power move, and it pissed me off.

"Mmm ... my, you really are quite tall. The news and magazines don't fully do you justice, do they?" She stepped back and addressed the commander from the plane. "Well done."

He nodded proudly, as if capturing me had been his accomplishment. "O'Brien arrived yet?"

"No," she shook her head. "He's escorting King here as we speak. He seemed very keen to meet our guest." She smiled and glanced over to see my reaction. "There's food for you and your crew in the hall." She barked her next orders at the Guard soldiers. "Put those three through orientation and then to the East Wing. O'Brien's orders were clear: do what needs to be done to get information from them. He wants results before they arrive." She turned to me. "This one is coming with me."

Two Guards roughly grabbed me on either side and forced me down a long, dimly lit hallway. We walked down two flights of stairs and down another couple of halls until we reached a large change room with individual white-tiled shower stalls. The Guards shoved me into the middle of the room, removed my restraints, and moved to either side of the door, blocking the only exit that I could see.

Stick Bitch moved confidently in front of me. "That's a nice watch."

I stopped rubbing my sore wrists and looked down at the watch Brady had given me. "Remove it," she snapped. "And everything else, too."

"NO." My response flew out of my mouth without thought, and before I had time to react, the stick flew up and whipped me across my upper thighs. "Ahh ..." A yelp of pain escaped from my mouth. For such a skinny little stick, it hurt—a lot. I reached down to rub the area and another blow came fast and struck the knuckles on my hand. "Ouch ... fuck you ..." Shaking off the sting, I took an angry step forward, but both Guards jumped from the door and slammed me against a set of lockers lining the wall. The back of my head hit the metal with a clang.

"Get the watch."

"No." I knew it was a losing battle but I struggled anyway. A Guard turned me around, shoving me into the lockers and twisting my arm behind my back with so much force, I thought my shoulder was going to pop free. He held my body still while the other removed the watch and handed it over.

Stick Bitch examined the engraving and smirked. "'And Brady.' How cute."

I continued to struggle, managing to land a hard blow to the side of a Guard's face. A fist thrust into my stomach, knocking the air from my lungs, causing my legs to give out and my body to double over onto the ground. I got to my hands and knees. I was struggling for breath. A hard boot kicked me in the side, sending me sprawling into a wall. I was sure I felt a rib or two crack.

"THAT'S ENOUGH!" Stick Bitch commanded. "O'Brien's orders were clear. He wants her relatively unharmed before he and King arrive."

The Guards backed away.

"*Relatively*," she hissed, stepping closer to me. "STAND UP." I slowly struggled to my knees, holding my throbbing ribs. "This is not some game, Samantha Smart. And if it was, you're not playing it very well. In case you haven't noticed, you are at a disadvantage. Words can't help you here. Now, take off your clothes and get into the stall for cleansing or I'm sure these Guards would be more than happy to do it for you."

I contemplated fighting back. How much mercy could "relatively" buy me? I thought I could definitely get in a few good blows before they subdued me. Maybe I could even get out the door and make a run for it ... but to where? The halls they had brought me down were like a maze. I wouldn't get far. Everything in me said to fight—but then I thought back to a private conversation I'd had with the interrogator.

After his class, he had come and introduced himself to me, and I took the opportunity to ask him the only question on my mind. "What advice would you give to those you interrogate ... about surviving, about not revealing what they know?"

He took a minute to think before responding: "Stay as strong as you can as long as you can. Choose your moments to fight and only pick the battles that truly matter."

As I knelt on the floor thinking about what might be coming next, I thought about those words. This battle was not worth it.

"Fine," I whispered.

"What?"

"I SAID, OKAY," I growled and gradually stood back up, using the wall to hold my weight. The Guards moved back to their posts, keeping a close eye on what I was forced to do next. Once I'd removed my clothes, I stepped into the cold, exposed shower stall. *They will try to make you feel weak and vulnerable*, another lesson from the interrogator. *They want to break down your defenses*. This wasn't about me getting "cleansed"—it was about humiliation, and I wasn't going to let them make me feel ashamed.

Shivering, I stepped out of the shower and tried to cover my parts from view. Stick Bitch handed me a large plastic bag that contained a sports bra, underwear, and a fire-red jumpsuit with *RESISTOR* printed on the back.

After the shower, they led me back upstairs and into the room where I am currently standing. But I wasn't ready for what happened next. The two Guards pulled me over to the desk and forced me to kneel on the ground. They grabbed my right arm and laid it out flat, pulling up the sleeve to reveal my inner forearm. Realizing what was about to happen, I started to struggle again. I had met other Resistance fighters who had escaped their prisons—or were let out as warnings to other resistors—and they had all come back with a souvenir, a small, four-inch brand forever identifying them as *Resistance.*

I yelled and tried to fight them off but a third Guard came in and overpowered me. They slammed my head down on the desk and held out my arm, while Stick Bitch held a rectangular metal device centimeters above my skin.

"Fight and it will only hurt more."

With my cheek flush to the table, I gritted my teeth and was forced to watch as the metal stamp burned into my skin. What started as an initial hot sting grew into an unbearable searing pain. After a few seconds, the tool was lifted away. The smell of my own burnt flesh made me feel like I was going to pass out.

"Good for you. Most resistors usually scream." Before I could look at the mark, they pulled my two hands behind my back and restrained my wrists again. "Stand her there. And. Don't. You. Move."

The middle of the room is where I still stand, have been standing for hours. My legs are shaky, my throbbing inner forearm itches where they marked me, and I can feel certain nerves on my body twitching involuntarily. But I am still standing, and now it has become an internal battle. I can tell that Stick-up-her-ass is hoping I will give in and crumble, and I will not let her win.

I closely examine the woman sitting behind the desk and question what she did before all this. Has she always been this bitchy? Maybe a neglected housewife with a chip on her shoulder? An administration assistant to an unruly boss? An unruly boss? A clerk at the DMV? What had she done before that allowed her to become this? Or was this always who she was? Had the revolution changed or revealed her? These thoughts are always bothering me. I wonder about everything that has happened and how this revolution has changed people. How it has changed me.

Stick Bitch catches me staring and stands up. She grabs her trusty side stick and walks around the desk, stopping within an arm's length. "What the hell are you looking at?" She glares, daring me to speak.

I can tell that she gets off on this little power trip. "Nothing."

Her grip tightens around the stick and my body tenses. "That's right, nothing." She turns to walk back but stops abruptly as I dare to speak again.

"I was just wondering … what you did before all this?"

The Guards take a step from their posts but she lifts her hand to stop them and turns back. I flinch and prepare for another blow to come. "I was a flight attendant." She seems as surprised to say it as I am to hear it and, for a brief moment, her hard exterior softens, maybe remembering her life before—but only for a moment.

I push a little more. "How did you end up here? Doing this?"

But I've pushed too far and a swift backhand slaps me hard

across the face. "Let's just say I saw an opportunity for career advancement and I took it." The woman composes herself and calmly sweeps her hair behind her ear. "Do not speak again." She sits herself back behind the desk and stares icily ahead. My cheek throbs from where the slap struck me, but knowing a little more about Stick Bitch is worth it.

After a few minutes, I drift back into my thoughts, trying to total up how much time it took for my so-called orientation. Probably over an hour. And how long have I been standing? At least four or five hours. Maybe more. Probably more. It must be some time in the middle of the night—which means that I have now been awake for over thirty-six hours.

Thinking about my orientation makes me think about the others, especially Maya. Do the others know it's my fault they're here? Do they blame me? I blame me. Of course they knew the risks involved with being in the Resistance, but they had been captured because of me. I worry about Maya and what they will do to her ... what they are doing to her. I haven't known her all that long, but it's amazing how close people can become when they fight for the same cause.

Three times Stick-up-her-ass leaves and comes back, each time ordering the soldiers to punish me if I move more than an inch or fall asleep. In that time I let my thoughts drift back to Brady. Is he here? Does he know what I'm going through? I'm not sure I really want to know the answers.

A chair squeaks as Stick Bitch gets up from behind the desk and walks around to the front. When did she come back in the room? I look at the Guards and notice that they are different from the ones who brought me in. When did they change? I've experienced this before. The loopy, almost drugged, sensation from lack of sleep. Having to pull some all-nighters in order to finish term papers for class the next day, I have gone more than twenty-four hours without sleep a few times. Who would have thought that university could have trained me for sleep-deprivation interrogation tactics? Maybe everything in my life has trained me for this. I'm not one to believe in astrology or destiny, but something my grandpa once told me is starting to make a lot of sense. Or maybe this was all happening to me because I deserved it, because of my past. For some reason, I find this thought amusing. Was this my past, or ghosts from my past, coming back to haunt me now? I laugh ... In my head? Out loud? I don't even know anymore.

My eyes are heavy ... too heavy ...

My knees are too weak ...

My feet ...

I fight with everything I have but I can't do this anymore. Luckily—or not—for me, I no longer have to. At that moment the door clicks open. The Guards stand at attention. Stick Bitch flattens her skirt and straightens her hair.

King has arrived.

10

THEN

TRISHA WEATHERS—MEDIANET NEWS

Hello to everyone tuning in out there. I'm Trisha Weathers with your morning newsflash.

In our top story, yesterday's march protesting the Encore Energy Controls and Essentials Allocation Act went from a peaceful demonstration to a passionate confrontation between protesters and King supporters. The march, organized by intense Medianet campaigns, came into contact with a large mass of King supporters who began their own march in order to intercept the protest. Within minutes, fights broke out in the street and police, along with members of the newly formed Guard, had to intervene with riot gear.

Footage taken by our own news crew in the heart of the action shows the officers using tear gas, water cannons, and physical force in order to subdue the protesters.

(A woman on camera) **Olivia Turner—a protester:** We only came here today to have our voices heard. It's our right, as

citizens of this country, to speak freely. I will not be bullied by those who disagree with what I have to say. I don't agree with the way John King is running this country. I ... we want him gone ...

(An older man on camera) **Mark Duncan—King supporter:** I'm tired of all the losers whining about everything they don't agree with. How is King supposed to make decisions when the Opposition acts like spoiled children? Don't do this and we don't like that ... Well, too damn bad! I think King needs to get tougher. If they want to act like children, crying because things don't go the way they want, then the government needs to step in and be the adults.

(Young woman with her face blurred) **Bystander—nonpartisan:** I don't know what to think anymore. Yesterday I saw a man punched and thrown out of a café just because someone overheard him speaking against the King's Guard. No one did anything to help him. No one.

As you have seen and heard, there are varying opinions on the matter, and with marches planned for the coming weeks, it doesn't look like the protests are going to die down.

In a related story, you'll recall the extremist group that admitted to releasing the "Robin Hood" virus that crippled the banking industry two weeks ago by deleting the financial records of thousands in substantial debt. Well, the group has struck again, this time in the area of real estate. They have sent out thousands of eviction notices to employees residing in government-subsidized estates. These notices claim that all government-granted housing allowances have been revoked and those employees affected will have to vacate or be charged with unlawful residency. The prank created a mass panic with workers who have been given sizeable living allowances. Spokespeople for King have had to do damage control on many fronts, assuring employees that the eviction notices are simply an extremist joke created by cyber-terrorists. In response to questions from the Wright Opposition, King staunchly defends the program that provides bonuses for those working in specialized areas of the government.

General Marcus O'Brien has released an official statement saying that there will be stricter Medianet controls and demanding any and all information leading to anyone involved with the extremist group calling themselves "The Truth Tellers." The government says it is currently in the process of tightening online controls and creating an official "Suspected Enemies of the State" list. They are asking all loyal citizens to submit names of anyone they suspect of anti-national activities.

In other news ...

11

THEN

It had been fifty-two days since classes had ended, since I last saw Brady—not that I was counting. I'm much too independent to admit to counting the days I've been away from my boyfriend, but this was the longest we had ever been apart. And I missed him.

Twice he had promised to come and see me and both times things "came up," preventing him from visiting. I'm not the jealous type. Really, I'm not. And I knew if Brady said he couldn't make it, he must have had a good reason for it. Although his last two excuses of "my dad needs me for something" and "I can't get out of a work thing" were a little suspicious. It was mostly the tone of his voice that was suspect. I felt like something was up but I didn't press the issue.

We talked and/or texted almost every day and I kept myself busy enough working at the library and picking up extra shifts in the café. Combined with soccer workouts, this gave me barely enough time to relax. Yes, relationships work both ways, and I could have gone to see him, but my last meeting with his father had me thinking that it was best to keep my distance.

Today Brady was due to arrive, and every time the bell rang at the door to the café, I found myself peeking over the espresso machine, hoping that the next order walking in would be him.

"Well, don't you seem impatient about something!" a voice playfully teased from behind the counter.

"I'm sorry?" I asked absentmindedly.

"Or about someone? Ah, that's right. Isn't today the day Mr. Samantha Smart is coming for a visit?"

I looked over at Aaron as he leaned on the counter and sipped an extra-foam chai-latte. He had taken another TA job, working at the university over the summer, and had made it a regular routine to come in and grab an afternoon drink from his favorite barista. He usually preferred soy but, with the recent food regulations, all the café had to offer was normal milk; from the rumors about food shortages in the south, I think we were lucky to have that.

"Yes. He's supposed to be here sometime this afternoon."

"Should I go, then?"

"Why?"

He returned my question with a stare.

In one of our many phone conversations, I had told Brady about Aaron coming in to get a drink and how he usually stayed a while to chat. The campus was slow in the summer and there were not many students remaining that I knew. It was nice to see a familiar face and I enjoyed his company. I kept up with current events, but it was usually Aaron who filled me in on the news and engaged me with challenging conversations about King and where the country was headed under his leadership. I liked that I could talk openly with him. It was getting difficult to have any real conversations with Brady. Since he had returned home, living under his father's roof, I had noticed him starting to defend King's actions and policies more and more. It had gotten to a point when anything politically oriented came up, one of us would soon change the topic to something trivial like the weather or sports scores.

During one of our last chats, I mentioned something Aaron had said to me—advice on a class I should take in the fall—and Brady erupted in a way that I had never heard before. He went on about how I talked about Aaron too often and he didn't like how Aaron always came in to see me. Without his actually saying it out loud, I felt as if he was accusing me of cheating on him. It was one of the worst fights we have ever had and I felt physically sick after. He called later that same evening and apologized for things he had said, blaming how much time we had spent apart and his dad for putting a lot of pressure on him lately. He made a promise to come and see me as soon as he got a free couple of days.

"Brady knows there's nothing between us." I deliberately turned to wipe down a counter so I could not see Aaron's response. "I told him we're just friends and he needs to accept that."

"Still, I think it's probably better if I take off before he gets here. I don't really need to witness the lovers reuniting."

"Are you sure?"

He nodded. "But, hey, I want to give you something before I leave." He reached into his bag and pulled out a book.

"Leave?"

"That's what I wanted to tell you. After tomorrow's class, I'm going down to work with a friend in the West. He has a link to

Wright's Equality Organization, and I think it's time I stopped talking politics and start taking some action."

"What about your TA job?"

He shrugged. "I don't know. I'm starting to feel like it's all kind of trivial. There's just too much going on out there with the riots and protests. And now there are rumors of a secret force knocking on doors of suspected enemies of the state, people being detained ..."

"Detained?"

He nodded. "I think the worst is yet to come and I just can't sit on the sidelines any longer."

"Nice sports reference." I was always making fun of his lack of sports knowledge.

"Did you like that? I've been working on it. Does it make you feel like maybe you want to join me?" His eyebrows raised hopefully.

"Aaron ... I can't. For a million reasons, I can't. You know I need this money."

"Just thought I'd put it out there." He handed me the book in his hand. It was tattered, with folded pages and coffee ring stains.

I read the cover. "Che Guevara?"

"It's about his life, his personal thoughts, his journey to becoming a revolutionary. I think you should have it."

"So much for subtlety."

Clipped to the front cover was a handwritten note. *Sam, I don't know why, but there's something in you that reminds me of an early Che. I've highlighted things you might find interesting. Thanks for the intellectual stimulation! Aaron (Your TA)*

"Did you have to add 'your TA'"?

"Just in case you forget who I am."

"I'm going to see you in the fall ..." His look said the opposite. "Aren't I?"

He shrugged. "I don't know. If the rumors are true ..."

"Rumors. That's all I hear about. But rumors are rumors, not fact."

"Maybe. You're probably right. I'll be back. Either way, I'm sure we'll keep in touch. I hope we do."

As he turned to go, I felt a sudden finality about his leaving. "Well, wait." I came out from behind the counter and stood before him. Not knowing what to do next, we embraced in an awkward hug. "Thanks ... uh ... for the book."

"You're welcome. And, hey, if things get ... well, if you need a place to go, you're always welcome to join me." He hugged me again and then waved a final goodbye as he disappeared out the door.

I stood alone in the café and looked down at the book. Flipping through the pages, I saw yellow highlighter and written notes scattered throughout. I knew that Che Guevara had been a Communist revolutionary leader in South America, and I knew that he had been killed a long time ago. Other than that, I didn't know much about him, but it was intriguing to hear Aaron say that I reminded him of Che. I placed the book on the counter and glanced down at my watch. Brady should have been arriving any minute.

I continued to glance at the time as a few more students came in and ordered drinks, chatted, and read their books. I did my best to distract myself with cleaning and organizing but, as the light outside started to fade, I became worried and a little agitated. I checked my phone but saw nothing. Finally, as I was turning off the lights and locking up, I decided to call him. No answer.

I texted: *Where are you? Closing up shop and going back to the dorm. See you soon???*

When I arrived at the top step of my dorm floor, there was a lone figure slumped over by my door at the end of the hall. My heart sped up—Brady had gotten my text and decided to meet me here. But as I got closer and the figure looked up, I recognized Kayla's long, braided hair.

"Don't get too excited to see me," she said sarcastically and stood up.

"No ... I just thought ... Brady's supposed to be coming today. He should've been here by now. What are you doing here?" We hugged. "Of course I'm happy to see you." I looked down at a suitcase and backpack next to the door. "Training camp doesn't start for another three weeks. Why all the luggage?"

Kayla grabbed her bags and joined me in the room. She noticed how clean everything was, that my bed was made, and that candles had been strategically placed. "Shit. I've interrupted something. You planned a whole romantic night with him, didn't you?"

"It's okay." I slumped onto the bed and checked my phone. "I don't even know if he's coming."

Throwing her luggage on the bed, Kayla collapsed and sat on the floor facing me. "I can sleep on the common room couch tonight." She hugged her legs into her chest and rested her chin on her knees.

Something was wrong. "What's going on, Kay? Why are you here?"

"I don't want to wreck whatever you had planned ..."

"Kay?"

She took a deep breath. "You know how I told you that I've been joining in more and more protests. Nothing big—just a few demonstrations, a sit-in at the library—stuff like that."

"Yeah." I replied, sure there was more to come.

"Well, last week I was at that march, the one against the Encore Energy Controls ..."

"The one on the news?" I asked. She nodded her head. "That looked pretty scary."

"It kind of was. And I don't know how it got so out of hand so fast. We were just walking down the street, holding signs, yelling protests: *Give Power to the People, Enough of King's Corruption* ..."

"All the typical protester stuff."

"Exactly. But peaceful, nothing aggressive or violent." She paused. "I didn't see the other group show up. I was too far back, I think. All I knew was that something was going on. I heard people shouting, then everyone started pushing each other—I didn't know what to do so I booked it out of there. Some of those Guard rent-a-cops tried to stop a few of us but we just ran right past them. I might have knocked one down ... by accident. I was just trying to get by."

"Okay." I waited. She was holding something back.

"There has been some talk. Mostly online. People are saying that some cops and a special Elite unit of the King's Guard are going around knocking on doors and interrogating anyone who might be involved in the protests."

"An Elite unit?"

"Like a freaky secret force. I don't know if it's true or not, but I heard from this girl I met at the last rally that her sister has a friend who was super-involved with online protests and stuff ... and that he's just disappeared. No one knows where he is or anything."

"So, this girl you just met has a sister who has a friend that's gone missing?"

"Yeah. They think this private high-up Guard force took him."

"Took him where?"

"I don't know ... AWAY!" Kayla was getting angry.

"Okay, calm down."

"Don't tell me to calm down, Sam. This is serious shit." She stood up and started to pace the room. "I didn't really believe it, either. I mean, that stuff just doesn't happen here, but yesterday I went out for a run and, when I was on my way home, my dad pulled over in a car and told me to get in. My brother was with him and he had a bloody nose. Apparently this Guard Elite came to my house ..."

"WHAT?"

"That's what I'm telling you. This shit is for real. They asked my parents if I was home, and when they said no, they asked where I was. My dad didn't like the way they were asking, so he didn't want to tell them that I was out for a run and I'd be home soon. Instead, he told them that I was up north visiting my grandma."

"You don't have a grandma."

"Yeah, well, they didn't believe my dad, either, so they asked to come in, and when he said no, they forced themselves in. My brother tried to stop them and he got hit in the face. They searched my room for evidence that I was an activist. They took my journals, my laptop, my phone, pictures of friends. They gave my parents this card." She handed me a card with a phone number on one side and *Do Your Duty, Protect the Nation* on the other. Under the slogan, there was a small pentagon logo with the letters *GE* in the middle—the first time I had seen that. "They told them to call the number and tell them when I got home. They even said that if I called and turned myself in, things would go better for me."

"Turn yourself in for what?"

"I don't know. Running into that stupid rent-a-cop? Being at the protest?"

I kept turning the card over in my hand. "So you came here."

"I didn't know where else to go. My dad was pretty freaked out. He said that the guards that came to the house weren't anything like the ones King is advertising. They were trained and had serious weapons. Definitely a special force. He thought it was best if I went to stay with someone other than family. I'm sorry ..."

"Kay, are you kidding me?" I could see tears pooling in her eyes and I felt a sudden and overwhelming surge of anger, a need to protect her from anyone who would try to hurt her. I hugged her and let her cry onto my shirt. "You know you can always come to me. Salt and Pepper, remember? You're the only sister I've ever had."

"My mom thinks this is all an overreaction to the protests and that Truth Teller group. She thinks the government is just trying to put a stop to things before they get crazy, and that this will all blow over soon. She actually wanted me to turn myself in. She thinks it's all a big mistake and they'll realize that, once I call them. But my dad disagrees. He thinks I should lay low for a while."

"Well, you can stay here as long as you want. No one knows I'm here and Coach said my being here was off the record."

"Thanks."

My phone started to vibrate and both of us jumped at the sound. We let out a nervous giggle. "It's Brady," I read from the phone while changing from my work shirt into a hoodie. "He's just pulling into campus. I'm going to go meet him downstairs."

"I'll move into the common room. I don't want to wreck your night with him."

"You're not going to wreck anything." I turned to her before leaving. "Are you going to be all right?"

"Oh, yeah. My mom's probably right. This will all blow over soon."

The smile on my face faded. "One thing I'm wondering, though. How'd they get your name and address?"

"I was thinking about that, too. I don't know. It could have been that video of me speaking at the last school protest. Or someone probably saw me on the street. They knew I pushed a cop or something." She pointed to the window, "For all we know, they probably have secret drones flying around. Who knows … go, your boy is waiting." She waved me away and started to unpack her clothes but, before the door closed, I saw her looking out the window and got a glimpse of that worry line on her forehead. She was scared and I was scared for her.

"Hi, Babe." I opened his Jeep door and leaned over to give Brady a hug and a kiss as I got in. I hadn't even closed the door before I sensed that something was off. There was very little embrace in his hug and his lips stayed hard and still as we kissed. I pulled back and looked at him. His hair was much shorter than I was used to and he looked … guilty. "What's going on?"

Gripping the steering wheel and looking away, he didn't even try to deny it. "Sam, I have something to tell you."

All of a sudden, I felt very claustrophobic sitting in the car. "What?" I could barely get it out.

"The whole way down here, I thought about not telling you until after, when I had to leave. But I just can't keep this from you anymore."

Anymore? I thought back to his distant tone, his anger, and realized he had been holding something back for more than a few weeks now. I prepared for the worst.

He turned to look at me. "I'm not coming back to school."

"What?"

"I just feel like I'm wasting my time here. I've felt like that for a while, you know that. Football's not the same. School doesn't feel right ..."

"For how long?" I snipped.

"I don't know."

"What do you mean, you don't know?"

"I don't know, Sam. I really don't."

"Are you sure about this?"

He nodded.

"What ... I mean ... what did your dad say? Have you told him?"

"Yes, and he agrees with me." I found that hard to believe and tried to make my disbelief known through my raised eyebrows "We made an agreement." He looked away from me again.

"What does that mean?" I asked sharply.

"I joined the Guard." His words were a hammer crashing down. He looked at me, waiting for a reaction, but I didn't move. "I only signed up for a year. And they're going to train me in all kinds of things. You should hear about the benefits and ..."

"Why, Brady?"

"My dad. It's what he wants from me and, to be honest, I don't think it's such a bad thing. Even Jackson is going to defer his college admission for the year. It's a good résumé builder and the connections you can make are amazing." He sounded just like the promotional video. "I like the way they're helping the country. And Ryan's doing it, too. Actually, it was his idea in the first place."

"Of course it was." I couldn't hide my anger or disappointment. I didn't try to. "Ryan's exactly who they would want."

"What's that supposed to mean?"

I ignored the question. "Ryan, Jackson, your dad ... is this what you want?"

"Yes. It's what I want." There was no doubt in his mind or his tone. "And I was thinking ..." He reached over and held my wrist. Our matching watches were inches apart. "Why don't you do this with me?"

"What?"

"Think about it. It would help you pay for school, and it could give you a lot of contacts for work after. And we could do it together ..."

"What about my school? What about soccer?" I pulled my hand away. "I like it here. I know what I'm doing here. I'm not just going to put it on hold ..."

"You don't have to. They have part-time Guard options. You could still stay in school. You should see everything they give us—there are a lot of privileges. Guard members have access to food and supplies that others don't. You have to admit, Sam, these days school isn't really that important. I mean, even with a degree, where are you going to work? At least the Guard is a start."

I could see Brady's desperation. His eyes were pleading for me to join him, or at least to give him my approval. "Brady ... I can't. I won't. It's not just about school. And it's not about you. I don't agree with what the Guard is. I don't like how they bribe people into joining them. I don't like that they get special privileges and benefits that others don't. How is that right?"

"Well, we deserve it for what we do ..."

"WE?"

Brady didn't respond.

"Look, I don't support King, and this would be like joining his ... side." When the word came out, I actually started to see and feel the divide that I had been trying to ignore. But it was there. Right in between Brady and me. We sat in silence for the next few minutes, each contemplating what this meant.

"You already signed up?" I asked, hoping it wasn't final.

He nodded. "I've been through orientation and the first part of training."

"Training?"

He nodded. "And I'm pretty good at it. You should see me. They say I'm a natural."

I scoffed. "A natural what?" Again, he didn't—or couldn't—respond. We had always shared everything about our lives, but Brady had been holding this back for a while, and it felt worse than if he had been lying. "I just don't get it. I thought you didn't like the Guard, either. You didn't even vote for King."

His look told me everything.

"Wow ..."

"I didn't tell you because I knew you didn't agree with him, but my whole family supports him and what he stands for. My *whole* family, Sam. I didn't want it to be a big deal between you and me."

"It is now. I wouldn't have cared who you voted for, but you made me believe you agreed with me and then you voted for King?"

"I should have told you. I don't know why I didn't."

"Because you never say what you actually want. You're always trying to please everyone around you. Including your father." I knew what I was saying would hurt but it had to be said. "Did you know that King is trying to put through a censorship law called *Civil Minds and Civil Mouths* that would affect our freedom of thought and speech?" I sounded like Aaron now.

"Well, maybe not everyone should have a say," he snapped back. "Some don't deserve to have a say."

"Do you hear yourself right now? Did they teach that to you in Guard Training 101?!" I was yelling. "I can't believe this. I can't believe you." I got out and slammed the door. Brady jumped out of the car and ran around to follow me.

"Sam. Don't. I don't want to fight. I didn't come here to fight. I love you."

His words disarmed me but only for a brief second. "No, you came here hoping I would join the Guard with you. Did you know that there is some secret guard force taking people away who are against King? Knocking on doors and pulling people out of their homes?"

"What? Where did you hear that?" He sounded genuinely surprised.

I was about to say "Kayla," but I stopped, feeling that saying something would betray my best friend in some way. "I just heard it."

"From that TA?" he hissed. "He's probably the one filling your head with all these lies."

"What?" I whispered furiously. "Don't tell me you're jealous."

"Should I be?"

I folded my arms over my chest. "You should go."

"Come on, Sam, I just got here."

"I don't care. I can't be around you right now."

"Because of the Guard?"

"Because of you." I felt hot tears in my eyes.

"Sam ..."

He walked over and tried to put his arms around me. I had missed his embrace but, in this moment, his presence repulsed me and I pushed him away.

"Go, Brady."

We stood, both quiet, under the beam of a single streetlight. It felt like forever before one of us dared to speak.

"What does this mean?"

"I don't know."

He waited for more but, when I refused to give it, he turned and walked back to the driver's side door. "I don't want to leave it like this."

I didn't respond.

"You know ... I didn't sign up for the Guard for Ryan, or for my father. I did it for me, because I want to be someone that you deserve. With this year, and how things have been going ... I needed this. I hope you can understand that. And I think, in time, you'll see that the Guard and King aren't as bad as you make them out to be. I'm proud of you, Samantha Smart. I just want to be good enough for you."

"It was never me you needed to be good enough for."

"Can I at least call you later?" he asked hesitantly.

A nod was all the response I could give.

I stood outside and watched the red taillights of Brady's Jeep all the way down to the exit where they turned out of sight.

At the sound of the common room door opening, Kayla looked up from watching a Trisha Weathers newsflash. "Can you believe this? King's 'Enemies of the State' list. Creating a fucking witch-hunt is what he's doing. I told everyone that this was going to happen. I said there was a bigger truth, a larger agenda behind ... What's wrong? Where's Brady"

I walked over and slumped onto the couch, resting my head on her shoulder. "When did things get so messed up?"

Kayla squeezed me and rested her head on mine. "I don't know."

12

*"Remember, Sam, the offense can only play as well
as the defense lets them."*

~ Grandpa Smart (Cheering from the sidelines)

NOW

Two seconds before President King walks into the room, I feel the atmosphere shift—a thin fog of fear fills the air—and it isn't only coming from me.

I wish I could be the fearless, iron-willed revolutionary that the Resistance campaign has made me out to be. But the reality is I'm just me, Samantha Smart, and I'm as terrified as anyone else would be.

King enters, wearing a navy-blue suit that suggests elements of the Guard Elite's uniform. He has been wearing items with the insignia of the Elite ever since his announcement that the Guard would be assuming complete security control over the entire country; his secret Elite force was a secret no longer. The bizarre and truly terrifying thing was that no one questioned it; the country just seemed to quietly accept it.

He's smart and clean-shaven, and his salt and pepper hair is combed into a perfect salon-styled wave. I remind myself that this clean-cut look makes it easier for his followers to believe his lies. Behind him follows an entourage of personal security guards and Marcus O'Brien—entering with his signature blood-red cane.

King deliberately avoids looking at me and walks over to greet Stick Bitch. It's O'Brien's bald head that briefly turns in my direction, eyes glaring. I'm sure I see an evil half-grin twitch at the sides of his lips. King might be the leader of the country, but it is and always has been O'Brien who gives me the creeps.

Within the Resistance, I heard rumors about O'Brien's tactics. He's ruthless and follows his own unique moral code. Watching him give interviews and sound bites on the Medianet news feeds, Wright believes—and I agree—that the existence of the Guard, and many events that have happened since the election, are results of O'Brien's manipulation. But I also suspect there is more to it than that. As Kayla liked to say: "Dig deeper—if there's slime on top, there's something worse underneath."

King turns and faces me. I adjust, try to stand taller, stronger—in order to appear less vulnerable. He notices and smirks. It's undeniable. He's good-looking, in a classically handsome way. There is almost a movie star quality about him, like someone has groomed him behind the scenes. Every one of his actions, speeches, and smiles seems rehearsed, calculated. It's an act. Fake. He's a politician after all, but there's more to it than the regular political placating, something much more sinister and choreographed behind his eyes and voice that I can't quite nail down.

"Leave us." His order is meant for the entire room. Everyone looks at me and then slowly makes their way out. I can't tell if their looks are of disappointment or sympathy. Only O'Brien is left, leaning on his cane, waiting to see what happens next. "You, too." King is exerting his authority. O'Brien doesn't move. It's a small power play, but I notice, and O'Brien sees me notice. "Go. Get the Guard prepped and ready for the reveal."

The reveal?

O'Brien stands an extra second longer, glaring at me while holding something back. He reluctantly nods at King, glares one last time, and limps out of the room.

With the click of the door closing, King and I are alone. I think I always knew that at some point we would be.

"I hope I haven't kept you waiting long." He takes a deliberate pause to study my reaction to his presence. "You're ... taller in person." For a long awkward minute, he stares at me. I do my best to maintain eye contact until finally I break.

"Nothing to say to me?" He goads. "I'm not taller in person? Shorter? Better looking? You must be thinking something." He waits for my response. "Come on. You, me, the entire nation. We've all been anticipating *this very moment*. We all knew this time would come. And now we finally come face to face—and here the girl of many words is speechless? How *anticlimactic*." He stops and his eyes assess me as if he is searching for something. "Tell me, though, because I really am curious: how are you feeling? Right now? In this moment?"

I give him nothing. I'm afraid that if I say anything, I'll reveal everything.

"Come on. Say something. It's a simple question. They will get harder, I assure you. What's going on in that mind of yours, Samantha Smart?"

My body recoils as he begins to slowly walk in a circle around me. He's studying me—I can feel it.

"Samantha Smart: The heart of a revolution. That must feel

pretty neat." He stresses the T in neat. "That's what you are to everyone. That's how they all see you. Wright may be the brains— well, what he has of them—but you ... well, you ... you're what keeps this incessant thing going, aren't you. They tolerate Wright but they love you—defender of the weak." He says the word as if he despises the very letters in it. "But you're not like the ones you defend, are you? You're strong. You do what you have to do when it's needed." He stops and leans closer. "Like what you did to your daddy when he came home that night."

My head snaps in King's direction. I'm sure he can see the shock in my eyes. The surprise attack of his comment goes straight to my core and achieves his desired effect. He has disarmed me. Angry with myself, my jaw tightens and I try to look away quickly. But it's too late; I have already given him what he wants.

"Oh, there she is." He claps once. "That got your attention, didn't it?" I can hear a hint of satisfaction in his voice. "Yes. I know all about you. *All about you, Sammy.* I don't usually conduct these interrogations myself. I find them tedious and predictable, and I usually leave the grunt work to O'Brien. But with you, I'm making an exception."

"Lucky me." The sarcasm rolls off my tongue.

"She speaks." King stops directly behind me. His hands land on my shoulders and I shudder at his touch. I can tell that he enjoys how uncomfortable he's making me; he gets off on power and control. Squeezing, ever so lightly, he leans down and speaks next to my ear.

"I understand you were quite close to your own grandfather, so you'll appreciate the fact that mine used to say, if you want to really understand someone, you need to crack open their story at the beginning. Yours was a harder one to uncover, but we did. And I have to say, I find it and you ... quite ... *intriguing.*"

I hate, *hate*, that he mentions my grandfather. "You don't know me."

"Oh," he whispers, so close I can feel the heat of his breath on the back of my neck, "but I do. Granted, you're not like the average mind-controlled Mediaverse freaks that post ten selfies an hour and feel they have to broadcast or comment on every single detail of their mundane lives, right down to their latest meal. You're much more guarded than that. Of course, you have reasons to be, don't you? It was almost fun trying to uncover your hidden secrets. And I guarantee it will be fun finding out the rest." I try to squirm away but he tightens his grip. "You're going to give me three things, Samantha Smart ..."

"I'll give you nothing."

"ONE: all the dirty little Resistance secrets and projects that Wright has you working on. I'm going to know everything you know ..."

"No." I try to sound strong, speaking with as much courage as I can fake.

"TWO: the names of all your co-conspirators and base locations."

"I won't." I shake my head.

"... AND THREE—and this one really is non-negotiable—you're going to admit that Wright and those connected are responsible for the O2 attack, and that given more solid information and facts, you find yourself no longer supporting the Wright Revolution. You, who helped to make it *stand*, Samantha Smart, are going to be responsible for bringing it to the ground."

I speak through gritted teeth. "Never. Going. To happen."

An unexpected kick strikes the back of my legs and I fall hard to my knees. King grabs me by my hair and looks down at me; there is something animalistic in his gaze. "That's better. The great Samantha Smart, on her knees, before her King."

"You're disturbed. Is this why your wife left you? She realized the monster you were becoming? Or did she just outlive her usefulness. You got elected, so who needs a crippled wife anymore." There is a momentary flash of anger in his eyes that readies me for the hit. A blinding pain on the side of my head sends me to the ground. A second later a large boot kicks into the small of my back. As I lie gasping, I can see King pacing at the front of the room, adjusting his uniform and trying to collect himself. I taste something warm and salty and know his blow has cut the side of my lip. The taste makes me think about when I was younger, and the memory ignites an inner fury. With my hands still bound behind my back, and my legs feeling like jelly, I gather the remainder of my strength and do my best to stand.

"I know all about you, too, John Alexander King. *All* about you. In some twisted way, you actually believe that what you and O'Brien are doing is right. *United We Stand, Divided We Fall*— twisting and manipulating it to your advantage. You label it survival but you're taking away our freedoms, our right to think, to speak, to live without fear."

At any moment, I think he's going to react or stop me, but he doesn't, so I continue.

"I've known people like you. Ones who need to bully in order to feel some sense of control, some sense of power. But it's not even your power, is it?"

For a split second he flinches and I can see that I have struck another nerve.

"You're the weak one. You're just a puppet."

King smiles. "Oh, you're good. But you'll see. Soon that mouth of yours is going to betray you."

The door opens and O'Brien walks in. Two members of the Elite follow. He looks at King and then over at me, assessing the situation. "They're ready."

King adjusts the cuffs on his jacket and uses his hand to comb through his hair. "Gag this bitch and bring her out."

O'Brien nods. "Gladly."

King exits the room, leaving O'Brien and the Guards. I can see a roll of duct tape and a black bag in O'Brien's free hand. The look on his face, like a predator about to devour its prey—no, more like a predator about to play with its victim first—makes me feel uneasy and sick. He motions to the Guards. They move in unison, each grabbing me by an arm and holding me firmly against the wall.

O'Brien's cane strikes the linoleum floor and echoes off the bare walls as he makes his way toward me. He stops close enough to reach out and touch me. I'm not exactly sure what it is about him that makes him so unsettling. His cane definitely adds to his overall creepy-old-man character, but it's more than that. He's much older than King, heavier set and bald. A defining scar he received in the service spiders out from his left ear. It looks like a web of thick pink veins crawling up to the top of his scalp and down underneath his eye. He is the opposite of King, whose movie star smile and debonair persona fool the majority of his supporters. Not only does O'Brien look like pure evil, he seems to take pride in playing the part.

He pulls out a piece of tape and tears it off with his teeth. Sticking it over my mouth, he holds his hand firmly on my face. I turn my head from him and squirm to get free. The Guards tighten their grip.

"I've been waiting to do that for a long time," he snarls. His breath and body odor smell like a combination of strong coffee and onions. "King's not the one you should be afraid of. But you know that already, don't you?"

I don't have to nod, I'm sure the fear in my eyes gives him everything he wants to see. "Smart girl."

Another bag is placed over my head and I am led through various corridors and up a flight of stairs. I can hear the tap-tap-tapping of O'Brien's cane a few feet ahead and, even under the hood, I can still smell the sour stench of him. From somewhere in the distance, I begin to hear King's voice. He is giving a speech. Every word is said slowly and with purpose. His voice gets louder the closer we get. He says something about honor, sacrifice, and victory, and suddenly a raucous cheer rings out, and I realize that whatever he is saying is being addressed to an extremely large crowd. And they're getting closer. The cheering begins to die down at the same time that the cane stops tapping. A hand grabs my shoulder and holds me in place.

"Guards, Elites," King's voice belts out, "I need to commend all of you on the excellent work you have done for your country. The people of this nation owe you their gratitude for your services and the manner in which you conduct them. This day is a day we celebrate a great victory over the Wright Rebellion—or should I say the 'Wrong' Rebellion ..." The crowd begins to laugh, clap, and whistle. "... OKAY, OKAY ... I may have used that one a few times before ..."

It feels strange to be standing so close to King as he speaks. I have seen and heard him hundreds of times on the news flashes, but it's different hearing him give a speech in person. He's disarmingly smooth and personable. Making jokes, laughing, and acting so casual he makes it difficult to believe he's the same man who was standing over me just minutes ago, the same man responsible for attacking and murdering thousands. This is how he has convinced so many to follow him.

"Guards: be proud. Be proud of the change that you have helped to create, the change that this country so sorely needed. It wasn't long ago that we were weak. Weak because we let ourselves become complacent. We cheered on diversity and, in doing so, became more divided. We said freedom of speech is good and we developed platforms to let everyone speak. From the intellects to the uneducated, voices tweeted—but in the end, did we really hear anything? We gave an A for effort and cheered on the weak and less deserving in the name of fairness. I ask you—is it really fair to nurture the weak and not the strong when it is the strong who lead us, who defend us? Darwin never wrote about survival of the weakest. We cultivate weakness and we become weak ourselves. We cultivate strength, together, united, as one, and we become strong, powerful—indestructible from within, against the parasites that don't deserve to thrive on our success, and from the outside forces that would try and destroy us. You are the strength of this nation, and it is you who will lead this country into greatness. WE ARE ONE."

The crowd cheers and then begins to chant in unison. "WE ARE ONE ... WE ARE ONE ... WE ARE ONE ..."

My body breaks out in a cold sweat and my stomach turns

in knots. I start to feel dizzy and nauseous as the chanting grows and echoes like thunder. And then, and as suddenly as a rolling summer storm, it stops and everything is eerily quiet.

King continues, "Not everyone agrees with what we are trying to accomplish. There are individuals in the Wright Rebellion who still selfishly believe that freedom of thought and speech are what this country needs. That we should go back to the way things were—letting the individual rule with his or her thoughts, beliefs, and free love. They are weak. We are strong. They foolishly fight against the inevitable. They resist us and say it is because they are fighting for freedom ..."

Without warning, I am thrust forward and pushed to walk. When I am stopped, hands turn me around and steady me to stand in position. The hood is ripped from my head and a bright light temporarily blinds me. It takes me a few seconds to realize it's a spotlight and that I am standing on a stage in a large gym, packed wall to wall with dark-blue-uniformed members of the Guard and Elite. King stands at my side, but does not take his eyes away from his audience.

"This ..." King shouts, putting his hand on the back of my neck and forcing me forward, "... this is the face of the rebellion that thinks they can *stand* against us ..."

Angry jeers and hate-filled boos erupt from the crowd. The light makes it difficult to see into the darkened audience, but the fury and hate targeted at me is palpable. I'm suddenly grateful to be standing on stage, to have any distance between me and this rabid crowd, but I worry that King could easily push me over to be devoured and torn apart like a piece of meat thrown into a ring of starving dogs. King turns and nods at O'Brien.

"And this is their fate ..."

I don't see O'Brien swing his cane from behind me, but the sickening crack and sting that comes from the force of it hitting the side of my knee makes me crumple like a stringless marionette. The tape over my mouth muffles a scream of pain. Angry, approving cheers roar out but they almost sound muffled to me. In my years of playing soccer, I have had sprained ankles, torn ligaments, and broken bones. None of that comes close to the pain I'm feeling right now.

King bends down and pulls me from the ground to my knees. He has to hold me in place just to prevent me from falling over. I breathe in heavily through my nose, gasping for the extra air that my mouth has been denied. And no matter how desperately I try to prevent it, I cannot hold back a hot tear that slips from my eye and down my cheek. I wonder how many in the crowd saw it. I'm giving King everything he wants and I hate myself for it. I hate him.

A hand reaches down and, before I can ready myself, the duct tape across my mouth is painfully ripped off. King tightens his grip on the back of my neck. "What do you have to say now, Samantha Smart?"

Why ... How did you come to be a member of the Resistance?

Sam: I used to have a bag of marbles when I was little. It's not a popular game now. It wasn't even popular when I was little, but I found this particular bag in my grandfather's closet. He didn't have any use for them so he let me have them. I didn't really know how to play with them. To me it was just a bag of round colorful rocks, really...

What's your point?

Sam: Have you ever dropped one?

One what?

Sam: A marble. Because if you have, you'd know that those little suckers can go anywhere. They are unpredictable. It all depends on the bounce and roll.

You want to know how I came to be Resistance? I'll tell you. Get a bag of marbles and a piece of chalk. Find some flat pavement somewhere. It's important that it's flat. Take the chalk and draw a line on the ground. Then, standing with your feet straddling the line, hold that bag of marbles out in front of you, turn it upside down, and let them fall—every last one. At first it's kind of pretty, all the colors, the bouncing, it can be really distracting, but don't pay attention to that—the action is not what you're there for, it's the outcome. When it's over and the last marble has stopped rolling, that's when you want to look down. What you will see is different marbles on different sides, for no good reason other than the first few bounces and the roll they took. And the thing is, you can do it again and again and again, and you'll always have the same outcome—different marbles, different sides.

I don't understand.

Sam: Me neither.

13

*"When you get to be my age, you'll look back at your life
and only remember flashes—mere moments, the ones that changed
everything. Sam, I want you to remember this—you can let the
moments define you, or you can define the moments."*
~ Grandpa Smart

THEN

"Sam? Sam? Earth to Samantha Smart? Helloooo … are you there, Sam?"

Kayla's voice snapped me out of my foggy daze. I turned to her and saw a silly face with two straws sticking out of her nose. "You're such a dork," I laughed.

"Aw," she smiled while snorting the straws out, "that's why you love me so much. So what do you think?"

"About what?" I asked absent-mindedly.

"So glad you were listening. I said we should get our faces painted. What do you think?"

"Oh. Sure. Why not?" I looked down at the all-dressed hot dog on my plate and lost myself in thought again.

It was October 2, the first weekend of the month, and that meant it was the opening day of the professional football season. Besides the championship finals, this was the most anticipated game day of the year. Like the majority of the fans, we had decided to arrive a couple of hours early, stop at the tailgate party in the parking lot, and grab a bite to eat. Usually food didn't last very long when it was placed in front of me but, today, with everything going on, I sat at a bench rearranging barbecue chips around a hot dog on my paper plate. Even with the escalating food shortages, game day hot dogs and snacks were in abundant supply, and no one was questioning where it all was coming from.

With the recent anti-King protests and rising clashes with the Guard, many believed that the league could be suspended and all opening day games canceled. The government surprised everyone by announcing they would allow the games to go ahead and that they would provide Guards at all venues to ensure public safety. Taking it a step further, President King—an avid sports fan—was expected to make a public appearance at Hickory Stadium to cheer on his favorite team, the Marauders. With his expected visit, the number of Guards and local police stationed around the stadium had substantially increased. As I glanced around, it seemed like the area was preparing for battle, not a friendly sports match.

Not everything was friendly. On the way to the stadium, we had walked by a park where a couple of thousand anti-King protesters had taken the prospect of his arrival as an opportunity to set up camp. An onlooker might have thought it was a giant picnic instead of a protest. There were no chants or painted signs, only people in red T-shirts walking around and handing out flyers that denounced King as president. Each of us willingly took a flyer and signed a petition calling for a new election.

As I was signing, a commotion broke out behind us when a group of fans scrunched up and threw their flyers to the ground. They physically pushed aside the young man who was handing them out and started yelling that they just wanted to watch a game.

As they left the area, they started chanting King's popular slogan: "WE ARE ONE, WE ARE ONE, WE ARE ONE!" Emotions were reaching a boiling point everywhere and it gave me an uneasy feeling.

Going to the game was the last thing I felt like doing. Since the start of the new semester, I hadn't done much, other than work, run, train for soccer, and go to class. I was just going through the motions. Doing what I always did because that's what I— and everyone else—was supposed to do. Keep things as normal as possible. Pretend that what was happening throughout the country wasn't actually happening.

It's surprising how easy it was to ignore the obvious. People never see what they don't want to see. University enrolment had dropped by almost a third. Students had either joined the Guard, joined the growing Wright Resistance, or simply disappeared. Or as in Kayla's case, they only appeared to have disappeared.

Kayla had intended to return to school with everyone else. She had foolishly hoped that the Guard's initial interest in her would blow over and they would leave her alone. But a week before classes started, a group of Guards had shown up at soccer practice during an optional pre-season training session. Kayla was notorious for taking her time in the change room, something the team razzed her about endlessly because it usually meant we would have to run extra laps. Luckily for her, being late that day was an unintended blessing in disguise.

Three Guards arrived in a blue Jeep and marched their way onto the field. Our head coach loathed it when anyone other than the team walked onto the field during her designated field time. She was so well known for her on-field rants that most athletes and students stayed out of sight when our soccer practice was in session. It didn't matter that the Guards were armed; true to form, Coach stormed out to meet them at centerline, yelling at them to get off her field.

Amused by watching anyone try to negotiate with our irate coach, the players all stood on the sideline and tried to eavesdrop. We all heard Kayla's name, and then heard the coach deny that she was back at school. I was the first to see Kayla emerging from the locker room tunnel and I quickly waved her to stay hidden. Seeing the Guards, she didn't take long to realize what was happening and wisely stayed out of sight.

With the Guards walking closely behind her, our coach approached the team. "These gentlemen here are looking for Kayla but, as I've already told them, she hasn't returned to school yet." Her eyes fell heavily on each player, making sure we *understood* her. We were a team, so of course we understood her.

A Guard stepped forward. The darker blue tone and collared uniform made him easily recognizable, but it was his confident and arrogant attitude that made him stick out as an Elite. "Ladies, can you please line up on the sideline?" He asked nicely but it came out as more of an order. The team obeyed while a soldier lifted his communication device to eye level and walked slowly by each of us. As he got closer to me, I briefly saw the headshot of Kayla on his screen.

"We'd like to speak with Kayla Marchette. Have any of you seen or heard from her?"

One after another, each member of the team looked confused and shook their heads. Some shrugged and others mumbled the word "No," or looked at the person next to them and asked if the other one had seen her. If the Guard could tell that the team was hiding something, he didn't show it.

"Kayla Marchette has evaded our questioning for more than a few weeks. She is officially being placed on the Guard Watch List."

"What's that?" Becca asked with a hint of attitude.

The Guard ignored the question and continued. He pulled up another image on his screen and began to visually scan each one of us. My stomach balled into a tight fist. I instantly recognized the photo from Kayla's friend-posts online, a shot of her and me on the beach our first spring break together. He stopped searching our faces when he reached me, looked down at his com-device and then back again. He moved toward me. "Are you Samantha Smart?"

"Yes," I answered nervously.

"Isn't Kayla Marchette your best friend and former roommate?"

"She is. And yes, we lived together."

He took a step closer and looked skeptically at me. "And yet you have not seen or heard from her since ..."

"Since before the summer started, I think." The eyes of my entire team were on me.

"You think?"

"No ... I know," I said in an effort to sound convincing.

"I find that hard to believe. We have recent evidence that you supported and reposted a few of her posts and statements on a public computer profile. You really expect me to believe that you, her best friend, haven't seen or heard from her in months?"

"I ... umm ..." I stuttered to form a response.

The two Guards behind him stepped closer, closing in on me.

"And did you or did you not attend a student rally with her on ..."

Coach intervened. "I'm confused. Is it Sam or Kayla you're looking for?"

The Elite asking the questions was surprised that our coach had dared to interrupt him. "We are looking for ..."

Coach took another step forward and raised her voice. "Because I have a practice to run and you three have put us behind ten minutes. As we have already told you, Kayla Marchette is not here, nor do any of my players know where she is."

The Guard looked back at me and seemed to be contemplating his next move. It was clear that he and the other two were inexperienced at dealing with an irate coach. Reluctantly, he put his com-device away and took out a card. "I hope you understand that it is your citizen's duty to alert us if Kayla Marchette turns up." He turned to me, "And I expect that you will encourage your team to do the same. Good day."

Coach waited until they were almost off the field before crumpling the card and tossing it to the side. "Assholes," she mumbled loud enough for the team to hear. "OKAY, LADIES, I WANT FIVE LAPS. LET'S GO!" As the team started to run, Coach grabbed me by my jersey. "Smart, as soon as these guys are gone, I want you to peel off and check on Marchette." I nodded. "Good, now go catch up with the others. And, Smart ..." I stopped. "I'd be careful if I were you. Watch your back."

"So you want to do it?" Kayla asked wide-eyed.

"Do what?" I asked.

"Helloooo ... get our faces painted. Geez, where are you right now?"

"Sorry, just thinking about stuff."

"What time are you meeting Brady?"

I shrugged. "He said he was being posted by Gate 11. I guess I'll see him when we go in."

"I still can't believe you haven't broken up with him yet. I mean, what if he turns me in?"

Her unwanted comment made me freeze. "Kayla, I ..."

She put her hands up in defense, "I know. I know. You've been together for three years and you're not going to break up just because he joined the Guard. I get it. Still, I would have ended it the night ..."

"Kayla! Enough. I don't want to talk about this. It's between Brady and me. And do you really think he'd turn you in? Brady!?"

"Fine. You're right. I'm sorry. I don't want to fight."

"Thank you. Me, neither." I wanted to change the subject and went back to her earlier question, hoping it would be a good distraction. "Yes, let's get our faces painted."

"Really?" She jumped up and smiled.

"It's probably a good idea, considering ..." I nodded at a group of Guards near the parking lot entrance.

Kayla looked around. Guard and Guard Elite were peppered throughout the crowd. "Not this again. You worry too much. They're here for President King and the game. Look around. Look at how many people are here. No one's looking for me here. No one's looking for anyone in this."

"I worry too much?" I replied. "You've been sleeping on a foamy in my dorm for months. You barely leave the room and, when you do, it's always wearing one of my hats or hoodies." I shook my head. "I never should have agreed to this game. I think I'm more nervous than you."

She looked hurt. "You said you didn't mind if I stayed with you."

"I don't. At all. I love having you close by. I'm just worried about you."

"Don't be. I'm fine. They're going to realize that it's all a misunderstanding and that I've got nothing to offer them. Sooner or later, they'll give up on me. Maybe they already have. My mom said she hasn't seen them drive by the house in weeks. Come on, Sam. Lighten up. Not only am I the one on the list, but I'm supposed to be the paranoid one, remember. If I'm always hiding out in the dorm, then I'm kind of letting them win. We gotta live."

Considering all news and media footage reporting on a developing riot, increased food shortages, or reported deaths from sickness in the growing tent cities, it was easy to start feeling down and depressed. For everything she'd gone through, Kayla tried to remain upbeat and keep me feeling that way, too.

On the day the soccer team was told that school sports were going to be suspended until further notice, I came back to my dorm room to find it decorated with strings of Christmas lights. Kayla had even risked being seen and snuck out to buy my favorite gummies. She was always worrying that her being there was putting me in danger, but in truth, I was thankful to have her around. Lately, with Brady so dedicated to his Guard activities, it felt like Kayla was the only person in my life.

When she had heard that the pro-league opening day games were still on, she weighed the risks and then pleaded for me to go with her. It was a tradition that Brady and his football buddies had started; recruiting a group of friends to dress up in Thunder gear, pregame party, and march down to the stadium together.

I didn't feel much like doing something that Brady and I used to do together, something that felt so normal when things were anything but. Agreeing that Kayla needed to get out of the small dorm and have some fun, I gave in. It was an easier decision to make when Brady told me that he would be there, too.

After the bomb he dropped on me that night in his car, it was more than a week before we spoke, and two weeks after that before our conversations felt comfortable again. I was still hurt and upset that he had joined the Guard without even discussing it with me, but I never considered breaking up with him over it. Not then. There was still some part of me that thought—that hoped—we could get through it.

Guard training had kept him so busy that we only spoke on weekends. He was allowed twenty minutes to chat, and we easily filled the time telling each other what was going on in our lives and saying how much we missed being together. I could hear the enthusiasm that he had been lacking coming back. He felt like he had a purpose, like he was needed. He was happy and I was happy for him. But I'll admit that it made me slightly jealous, knowing he was getting that from the Guard.

Those initial conversations always ended with him asking me the same stupid question. "Why don't you leave school and join up? Then we can be together."

In the beginning, it was just something he said, knowing I would respond with some deflection or joke, like, "Well, I can't join now. That would make you my superior, and we both know I'd never listen to anything you told me." Then we would laugh and move on to something else. But he kept asking and, at some point, I knew it wasn't a joke and that he actually hoped I would say yes. I think it was at that point I started to clue in that this "Guard thing" was not some silly whim of his, and it was definitely not short term.

It was no secret that from the beginning I took issue with King and almost everything he stood for. To my mind, government regulations were creating a bigger divide in society. Those that supported King were being given special privileges that included access to better health care, job access, and even food supply. He was cutting social funding for some of the less fortunate, reasoning that people needed to learn how to help themselves and that handouts only led to more handouts.

More unbelievable was how many people, including Brady, supported him. Only once had he and I tried to talk about King's policies, and that conversation resulted in another heated argument. Our phone time elapsed before anything could be resolved and before either of us could apologize or even say goodbye. It was another week before I spoke to him again and it was one of the worst weeks of my life. Even Kayla struggled to cheer me up.

I desperately wanted Brady to see what I saw in King, and he wanted the same thing from me.

Opening-game day was the first time I would be seeing him since the night he had told me about joining the Guard. Although neither one of us would admit it, I knew we were equally nervous about seeing each other. Maybe it was because we were afraid to see how much each of us had changed. And maybe it was because we knew that actually seeing each other face to face would make us confront an ugly reality.

After Kayla and I visited the face-painting station, we joined the long line at Gate 11 to enter the stadium. We each had decided to get our faces painted green with a white lightning bolt cutting diagonally down the middle. It wasn't really a mask but, with our faces covered, I started to feel more relaxed about Kayla being out in public and near so many armed Guards.

From the back of the line, I stood on my toes and looked for Brady. I finally saw him—and Ryan, which was an unwanted surprise—with other Guards, doing security checks as people entered. His hair was a little shorter and he looked ... there was something different about him, though I couldn't place it. The blue uniform definitely gave him an air of authority, but it wasn't his outward appearance that I noticed first. He was carrying himself with more confidence. He seemed edgier and strangely more attractive.

"Do you see him?" Kayla looked up ahead.

"Yep." I stretched to see past another person.

Kayla noted my concerned tone. "What is it?"

"I don't know." I dropped back down. "He just looks ... not like himself."

"What do you mean?"

"I don't know. He's just different. Ryan's up there with him, too."

"He is?" I could hear the trepidation in her voice. While I was confident that Brady would never turn Kayla in, I wasn't so sure where Ryan's loyalties lay. I could tell that Kayla shared my concern.

"You sure you want to do this?" I asked again.

She nodded. "It's almost like old times."

"Almost," I whispered under my breath.

The line continued at a sloth-like pace.

"So," Kayla said, trying to make small talk, "who do you think will win the game tonight?"

"Does it really matter? This is all just a distraction from what's really going on."

"I know." She couldn't argue. Even though she agreed, she also welcomed it. "I'm just happy to finally get out of the dorm. I think I've read all your class texts two times now."

I smiled and tried to cheer up. Poor Kayla had been stuck in a room with no phone, no school, and no soccer since the day the Guards had shown up on the field. I knew how much she had been looking forward to a night out, a night where things felt normal again. I didn't want to be a downer. "So, you wanna get some popcorn, maybe a slushie?"

She clapped excitedly. "Oooh, a blue-raspberry slushie, for sure. You think they'll still have them?"

"I think it would take an apocalypse for them not to have blue slushies. And even then, they'll probably still be around," I joked. "What do you want to do after?"

"I don't know. It's not going to be the same without the gang, but we could go to The Sideline for an after-game libation."

"Libation?" I laughed at her. "Wow, you have been reading too many textbooks."

Kayla laughed with me. "I know. I'm studying more now than I ever have." For a brief moment, we were back to our old carefree selves.

As the line pushed forward, I saw her smile slowly shift into a look of serious contemplation. "What is it?"

"It's nothing."

"Kay, it's something. What is it?"

"I was going to wait until after the game to tell you."

"Tell me what?"

"I think I should go ... out west. Maybe join up with Aaron and the Wright campaign."

"The Wright campaign?" My voice carried and a few people standing in line turned and gave us dirty looks.

"Sssshhhh ..." She pulled at me. "You can't say that stuff too loudly."

"Okay ..." I lowered my voice. "But really?"

"I've been thinking about it a lot lately. You have to admit, I've had a lot of time to think. And it's just ... well, you know ... I can't just keep living in your dorm forever."

"You just said that you didn't think all this was going to last much longer." I couldn't hide my disappointment. Selfishly, I didn't want to lose Kayla, too.

"I know but ..." she looked around at all the Guards, "I mean, really, who knows how long this is going to last? And I have to do something." She lowered her voice to a whisper. "I'm already on the GWL; I might as well do something to deserve it. You should come with me." She flashed a hopeful smile.

For a few seconds, I actually entertained the idea, but then I shook my head. "I can't do that. I'm almost done school. And ..." I looked up at Brady, "this is my home." It was scary to think about leaving the comfort of everything I knew, even if it was changing.

"But you'd be with me."

"I know."

"Will you think about it?"

I nodded. "I will."

"Bag?" Brady's gruff voice ordered without looking up.

"What, not even a hello kiss first?" I teased.

He instantly recognized the face behind the paint and couldn't suppress a smile. A spark of the Brady I loved shone through his tough Guard shell. He quickly contained himself and took me by the arm. "Come here." He turned to another Guard. "Watch my post." The guy nodded and stepped in. Brady guided me behind a corner and, as soon as we were out of sight, he kissed me.

At first the ferocity of his kiss surprised me. I was expecting a reaction but nothing this enthusiastic. I quickly let my defenses down and returned his kiss with equal force. I can't be sure but I think, looking back, Brady's kiss was meant to prove (to him, to me, to both of us) that the love between us was still there. When I pulled back, I could see traces of green face paint outlining his lips and I carefully wiped it away with my thumb. He hugged me. "I missed you."

"Me, too." I rested my head on his shoulder.

We held tight, as if just holding on could stop or slow time— anything to make the moment stretch a little bit longer. But Ryan's head popped around the corner, interrupting us. For a split second, I swear I saw a hint of resentment in his eyes. "Okay, lovebirds. I've been covering for you long enough. Let's go."

Brady kissed me again.

"Look who I found." Ryan walked over with Kayla. "Almost didn't recognize her. And look what she had on her." He held up the red flyer that we had taken from the protesters.

Brady's eyes widened and, from the exchange of quick glances between him and Ryan, it was obvious that they knew about her being on the GWL. I could see them contemplating what to do next. Seeing their faces, I felt an uneasy tension among the four of us that had never been there before. It seemed that Kayla had yet to pick up on it.

"What's wrong with the flyer?" she questioned innocently. "Some guy gave it to me at the park."

"And then you signed the petition," Ryan said. "You both did."

"How did you—" she started to ask but I interrupted.

"Because it wasn't a petition, was it?" I looked at Brady. "It's a list."

Kayla must have realized what I was saying. "You mean … that protest is bullshit? Those are Guards?"

"Not all of them," Ryan boasted. "We have orders to check for flyers and take names …"

"Ryan!" Brady snapped. "Never mind. It's Kay and Sam. Let it go." He turned to me, his serious Guard persona back. "You two should leave. Now."

"Brady?"

Ryan stepped in. "He's right. You can't be around here."

"What you really mean is that we can't be around you."

Brady held my shoulder. "I don't want to argue. I've been looking forward to seeing you all week."

"It's true. Couldn't stop talking about it," Ryan rolled his eyes.

"It's not safe for you, Kayla. Or you, Sam, if she's found with you. And if they find out that we didn't report it …"

"Unless you want to turn yourself in." Ryan said. Kayla and I both shot angry glares at him. "I'm just saying that they'd probably go easier on you."

"What *would* they do to me?"

Brady and Ryan exchanged another look.

"You don't even know, do you?" I said.

"She'd go in for questioning."

"And they'd probably send her to one of the CIP's."

"What the hell's a CIP?"

"Citizen Improvement Program," Ryan boasted. "It's a pilot program, putting high-risk resisters to good use."

"*Citizen Improvement Program?!*" I used air quotes for emphasis. "Did they get that straight from the Orwellian playbook? We're talking about Kayla. She's not a high-risk anything."

Ryan stepped toward me. "She's been attending rallies, avoiding questioning ..."

"Because she's scared!" I countered and moved forward, intentionally getting in Ryan's face. "Not because she's hiding something."

"Well, how do we know that?"

"We? Meaning you and Brady? Or *we*, as in the Guard?"

"Sam! Enough." Brady stepped between us. Ryan and I didn't budge, our eyes remaining locked, each of us refusing to be the first to back down.

"Guys, please." We finally turned away when Kayla spoke up. "I don't want it to be like this. I don't want us to fight. You were right, Sam. This was a bad idea. Let's just go."

"NO!" Brady shouted. "Don't go that way. They're doing ID scans. Here ..." he opened a door at the side. "Go this way."

Ryan looked around nervously. "We shouldn't be doing this, man."

"Dude, relax," Brady reassured him. "It's the girls."

Kayla shot an obvious glare at Ryan, nodded a thank-you to Brady, and then snuck in through the door. I wasn't ready to say goodbye but, looking at Ryan, I knew we had worn out our welcome. I reluctantly gave Brady a peck on the cheek and then had to wipe away the faint outline of my green and white lips. "Will I see you later?"

"Exit through Gate 7 after the game. I'll be there. We'll find each other." At the last second, he grabbed my arm and pulled me back for a final kiss. "Gate 7."

"Gate 7," I repeated. After a quick half-hearted wave at Ryan, I slipped through the door.

I think back to that moment now. That exact moment when I left Brady and went into the stadium. With Kayla and Ryan, things had felt intense, but we had all gotten through it. Nobody turned Kayla in, and Brady and I acted semi-normal together. I left, believing that even though we didn't see eye-to-eye, we were still Sam, Brady, Kayla, and Ryan, and we would always be able to work it out. It may have just been wishful thinking but I left feeling a sense of hope.

It was the last time I ever felt it.

14

THEN

... We interrupt your regularly scheduled programming to bring you this breaking news. If you were following any one of the broadcast games, you already know shots have been fired and there have been a number of explosions at Hickory Stadium. It is unconfirmed but word is coming in that this could be a planned attack from a terrorist organization. The explosions came during the late stages of the second half when The Thunder was making an unprecedented comeback against The Marauders.

As in other cities around the country, tens of thousands of fans turned out for the opening-day games of the professional league. They were in the middle of cheering a late scoring drive when the first explosion erupted from under the stadium seating. The Guard, already on hand to provide extra security for President King, began ushering fans to the exits when gunshots rang out and another two explosions occurred. Live game tape shows how the events unfolded. We caution that the images you are about to see are graphic in content ...

It is unknown if President King was the intended target of the alleged terrorist attack or what his status is at this moment. The number of casualties and wounded are also unconfirmed, but it is being estimated that at least 5,000 people have been killed or wounded by the explosions. At this time, all emergency crews, including paramedics, police, and the Guard, are moving in to help the wounded.

We are tapping in to the stadium cameras and are going to pull you to a live feed. What we are seeing looks to be complete and utter chaos. It appears that fans are desperately trying to escape through an opening in the side of the stadium caused by the first explosion. I am receiving reports that clashes between the alleged terrorists and the Guard have broken out. While police and the Guard are doing their best to control the scene, the situation seems to be escalating. An armored squad is now on scene and it looks as if they are using teargas to calm the mayhem.

... I'm sorry, it's hard to describe what we are seeing here ...

What happened?

Why did we lose the feed?

I apologize to the viewers at home but it appears that we have lost the image. While we work to get it back, we ask that you remain calm and stay off the streets. We have a news crew enroute and should have a camera on the ground in minutes.

No other stadiums have reported bombings at this time, but games in other cities have been halted and evacuations are underway. Our thoughts and prayers are with anyone caught up in this unbelievable disaster right now ...

15

THEN

A thick cloud of ash and smoke blurred my vision and my ears were throbbing with a high-pitched ringing. Somewhere in the distance, I could hear the faint sound of people yelling—screaming—crying.

"SAM? SAM?!" A hand fell on my shoulder.

"I'm right here." I reached down for Kayla. "Are you all right? Can you stand up?"

Kayla nodded and took my hand. "I can't hear anything. I can barely hear you. It's all muffled. SAM! You're bleeding ... from the side of your head." She pointed.

I felt the side of my forehead. When I pulled my hand away, red blood mixed with green face-paint left a sticky brown goo on my fingers. "It doesn't hurt. I don't feel anything."

Kayla looked around at the surrounding destruction. "What happened?"

"I think there was another explosion."

We had been chanting with the crowd when the first blast

rocked the stadium wall to our left. It sounded less like a BOOM and more like a low rumble followed by a huge crash. Kayla was thrown from her seat, but I grabbed her by the back of the shirt just as she was about to tumble down over the rows in front.

It was difficult to register what had happened. Did the floor collapse?

Had there been an earthquake? Would an earthquake do that?

Through the smoke, I started to make out a giant hole in the side of the stadium. I could see right through to the cars in the parking lot. Chunks of debris were still falling to the ground ... and then I focused, and the horrific realization set in: what I was seeing wasn't chunks of debris falling. I was watching bodies cascade down from their stadium seats. The high rows had nothing below them for support. People were hanging, clinging to their seats, to bars, to each other. Before I could point out what I was seeing, someone yelled out: "BOMB!"

... and then all hell broke loose.

"Come on, Kay, we need to move."

I started to pull Kayla through a maze of seats and people. We reached the field and were sucked into the flow of panicked spectators moving toward the opening in the stadium wall. Not the way I wanted to go. All I could think about was getting to Gate 7. To Brady. I needed to know if he was okay, and I knew he would be wondering the same about me. I looked around for a gate or exit sign, but with all the commotion and dusty haze, it was impossible to tell where we were.

POP—POP—POP—POP—POP—POP ... Heads turned toward what sounded like fireworks going off. Then, more popping, more screaming, and in the distance, toward the back of the stadium, a blur of bodies started to avalanche and cascade down the side of the stands.

"IT'S AN ATTACK!" someone yelled.

"TERRORISTS!"

"IT'S TERRORISTS!"

At that moment, an invisible switch controlling all rational thought flipped over and everyone's panic mode revved into hyper-drive.

I had once watched a scene in a horror movie where thousands of rats charged through a subway tunnel, trying to escape a fire. Their little black eyes bulged out as survival mode made them go rabid, climbing over and killing each other, ultimately overtaking and eating through the villain of the film just to get to freedom. For the viewers, it was a visually gross but fitting ending that gave me nightmares for weeks. Eventually I managed to forget about it—until this moment. Spectators in the stands were no better off than the trapped rats. They wanted out, and they didn't care who they had to get through or what they had to do to get to freedom. As legs kicked and arms pushed and punched, fights began to break out all around us.

Was this really happening? Just minutes ago, we were waiting to stand and raise our arms in the air as a stadium wave rolled its way closer to our section. Everyone was laughing and having a good time. I had accidentally spilt the cheesy nachos I was sharing with Kayla when she jumped up and cheered for the Thunder scoring on an unbelievable trick play. Then this ...

Kayla's hand tightened around my wrist. "I'm scared, Sam."

Me too, I thought. "It's going to be okay."

"WHAT? I still can't hear you. Were those gun shots?"

I turned so Kayla could see my face and read my lips. "I said it's going to be okay. Hold on." She nodded. Calling on all of my athletic training, I thrust forward with the crowd. I found holes to sneak through, shoved three-hundred-pound men to the side, and dodged flailing arms and legs.

A few feet in front of me, I saw a little girl fighting to stay on her feet, but the pull of the mob was too much and she disappeared, swallowed under the weight of the horde.

"Kayla, look." I pulled her forward and tried to move the mass of bodies. It took all my strength to hold off a push from behind and haul the little girl to her feet. "Are you all right?"

The girl, about ten years old, I thought—it was difficult to tell with tears streaming down her dirty face—nodded back. I couldn't hold off the force from behind any longer, so I scooped her up with my free arm and kept her moving with us.

"Where are your parents?"

"I don't know," she sobbed, "I can't find them."

"I'm sure we'll find them when we get out. What's your name?"

"Annie."

"Annie, I'm Sam. And this is Kayla." Kayla gave a feeble smile. It was her best attempt at not looking scared.

A few seconds later, we crashed into bodies as the group suddenly ceased moving forward. People continued to surge from behind, making us feel like we were being squeezed between four constricting walls. "Why aren't we moving?" Kayla asked.

I strained to see over the wall of heads in front. There was a large group of armed Guards forming a human blockade. It looked like they were trying to filter everyone into smaller lines, sifting through them as they went. The weight of the bodies behind us pushed harder. People starting yelling louder. Anger was flaring, tensions were rising, and the panic that had already settled in bordered on mass hysteria.

"Take her." I gave Annie's hand to Kayla. "Hold on to me. I'm going to try and get us out to the side." It was difficult maneuvering, but with Kayla and Annie linked behind me, I guided us through the crowd and to the side of the field, near the lower seats and away from the middle of the push.

When we reached the side of the field, I climbed up the railings to the first few rows of seats and helped pull Annie and then Kayla up with me. With the majority of people on the field, being in the stands offered us an almost clear path to the opening in the stadium wall.

"This way." I pointed for Kayla to follow and then led us forward. Above us, bloody and unconscious (or worse, dead) bodies were scattered throughout the upper stands. My mind refused to believe what my eyes were seeing. People were dead and dying right in front of us.

I turned to Annie, hoping to distract her from the horrors a few feet away. "Look in the crowd for your parents, okay?"

Annie nodded. The roar of panic from the crowd was deafening. Everyone was frantically shouting for a loved one or yelling for people to move. The closer I got to the gap in the wall, the louder I could hear a voice booming out from a handheld megaphone. The Guard behind the voice was trying in vain to calm the situation and get people to settle down.

With the three of us, it was a struggle, but we finally managed to climb and crawl our way down some of the loose rubble and reach the opening to the parking lot. As we descended the final hill of cement chunks and stadium debris, I could see a thick wall of armed Guards blocking any exit to the outside. The panicked horde of fans trying to run from the stadium was yelling and pleading with them to let everyone out. People were slowly being filtered through; some filed toward waiting paramedics, but as some were being let out, others were being hauled to the side and made to kneel with their hands on their heads while Guards inspected them and their belongings.

Kayla stopped with me to survey the scene. "What are they doing? Why aren't they letting people out? Why aren't they letting the paramedics in?"

I looked closely at the people kneeling. Red flyers were being pulled out of bags and pockets and thrown to the ground. The Guards inspecting them were yelling and corralling a large group toward a secure area where other heavily armed Elites surrounded them. "They're pulling out anti-King supporters. They must think this was an attack, that someone was targeting the President."

"Oh, my God, the President? Do you think that's what this is? Do you think they got to him?" Another large section of stadium cracked and crumbled to the ground, creating a giant plume of gray smoke. Annie screamed and grabbed at my arm, clawing at my skin with her nails. The crowd erupted in terrified calls for help and started shifting forward toward the barrier of Guards. People were starting to fight and climb over one another to get to any exit or opening they could see.

Kayla frantically turned to me. "We have to get out of here."

"I agree." We each held on to one of Annie's hands and started pushing forward with the rest of the people at the front of the group.

"EVERYONE STAY BACK!" a megaphone voice bellowed down.

"WE ARE HERE TO HELP. STAY CALM. STOP MOVING OR WE'LL HAVE NO CHOICE BUT TO USE FORCE. STAY BACK!"

A wall of Guards began shifting away from the irate mob. Others were shouting orders for them to hold their ground—to arm themselves—to get ready. Shields were raised, black batons were lifted, and cans of teargas were hurled high in the air.

The teargas hissed as white clouds rose up, enveloping the unsuspecting crowd. Annie started coughing and tugged on my jacket. "My eyes are stinging ... I can't breathe."

I pulled the T-shirt neck under my hoodie over my mouth. "Do this," I ordered Annie and motioned for Kayla to do the same. "Hold on to me. Try to keep your eyes closed."

"PEOPLE, STAY BACK!"

The man with the megaphone pulled out a gun and pointed it in the air.

"STOP! STAY BACK! BACK!"

We continued to walk forward with the group, trying desperately to get clear of the teargas now burning our eyes. Through the smoke, I could see the dark-blue wall of Guard uniforms getting closer. I was close enough now to see the same fear and panic in many of their eyes that were in the eyes of the fans moving forward. They were all just as scared as we were.

"LET US THROUGH!" a voice shouted.

"MY WIFE IS HURT!"

"WE CAN'T BREATHE!"

"WE NEED TO GET OUT!"

"EVERYONE WILL GET HELP. WE'RE HERE TO HELP YOU. STOP! STOP! STAY BACK!"

If you asked me now, I would say that I sensed what was going to happen even before it did. I think if you asked anyone, from the fans to the Guards to the spectators watching reports on the news, every one of them would say they felt the weight of that single split second just before their world was changed forever—86,400 seconds in a day, 31,536,000 seconds in a year, an unfathomable amount in the average lifetime, and yet it only takes one to change the world that you know forever.

My feet froze in place. I reached to stop Kayla and Annie, but Kayla, who must not have heard the orders, must not have seen the guns, continued to walk forward. "KAY, NO! WAIT!" I reached out and tried pulling her back. The rest happened like a slow-motion action sequence, a nightmare I couldn't (and still can't) wake up from.

Kayla looked back at me just as the Guard with the megaphone fired his gun in the air. The CRACK of the shot silenced everyone. A second went by and no one moved. It felt like the whole scene had been frozen in time, and then ...

CRACK—a gun fired.

CRACK—another gun fired ... and another ... CRACK ... CRACK ... CRACK ...

Multiple shots rang out as I crouched to the ground and held Annie tight in my arms. I closed my eyes and could hear people screaming and scuffling everywhere. *What was happening? Was any of this real?*

"STOP ... HOLD YOUR FIRE ... HOLD YOUR FIRE!" A frantic voice boomed out from the megaphone. The shooting stopped and everything went eerily silent. "HOLD YOUR FIRE. LOWER YOUR GUNS."

I opened my eyes and loosened my hold on Annie. "Are you all right?" She was crying and I could feel her body trembling, but other than that she seemed unharmed. "Kay, you okay?"

There was no answer.

"KAY?" I yelled louder, thinking that she just couldn't hear me.

I looked around Annie—and there, about three feet in front of me, Kayla was slumped on the ground in an awkward and unnatural position.

"KAYLA!?" I lunged toward her and reached out to grab her shoulders. When I pushed her back, I could see a large red stain slowly seeping out and expanding on the front of her shirt.

"KAYLA!" I gently laid her down on the ground and held my hands over the blossoming wound. Warm streams of blood began to ooze through my fingers.

"NO, NO, NO. KAYLA! COME ON, KAY!?" But there was no response. Her eyes remained closed. Her body limp. I held her tightly and looked around for someone, anyone. Annie stood over us, eyes wide, looking down, frozen in shock.

"KAYLA!!" I cried out. "HELP! SOMEBODY HELP ME!"

But the world around us had shattered into complete chaos. People were fighting against the Guard, using anything they could—cement debris, bags, shoes, fists—as their weapons. Teargas continued to be hurled toward the group. Armed Guards, wearing black helmets and riot gear, attacked at random, using metal batons to subdue anyone near them. It had broken out into a full-scale riot ...

... and in the middle of it all, I crouched on the ground, holding a motionless Kayla in my arms. Black boots stomped by me. Screams filled the air. I felt like I was outside my body.

How could any of this be happening? We had just got our faces painted. We were laughing. Cheering. Sipping slushies. Eating nachos ...

"Kayla?" I shook her. "Come on ... No, no, no ... NO! COME ON."

Trying to remember what I had learned in a first-aid training course a few years back—a course I had taken with Kayla when the two of us got a job working at spring-break soccer camp—I felt for a pulse and then began compressions on her chest. I may have been trained in CPR, but I had never been trained for this.

"Please, Kayla ... please ... Salt and Pepper, remember? I need you."

I listened for a breath.

"Please ... No ..."

I held her close and cradled her body. I pleaded over and over again for her to open her eyes. It was clear that no one was coming to help. I didn't know what else to do. There was nothing else to do.

Slowly, I struggled to my knees, then to my feet, holding her in my arms. Annie was still glued to my side, trying to stay as close to me as she could.

"Is she okay?" Annie asked. "What's wrong with her?"

I couldn't answer. I no longer felt fear, anger, or sadness ... I no longer felt anything.

"Use your shirt and cover your mouth," I ordered. "Close your eyes and hold on to me."

Annie nodded and did as she was told.

My eyes and lungs were burning from the gas, but I took a step forward and then another, walking steadily toward the area where I had seen paramedic vans stationed. Figures were running back, trying to escape the smoke and the Guards, but I continued forward, untouched and unbothered by anyone around me, slicing right through a wall of Guards too busy battling fans to notice or care about a trio of wounded girls.

A paramedic van finally came into view and figures wearing white and black ran toward me. Annie was pulled from my side and Kayla lifted from my arms. I watched them set her down on a stretcher and attach a clear mask over her mouth and nose. Hands and arms started compression on her chest. Words were shouted about critical condition, gunshot wound to the chest, no response …

Another black and white suit pulled me to the side of the van, sat me down, and squirted water into my eyes and over my face. Voices were talking to me, asking me a million questions. *Was I hurt?* No. *Was I sure?* No. *Could I feel anything?* No. Pressure and a bandage were applied to the wound on my forehead, but I moved the hand away from my head and pushed the body in front of me out of my line of sight. I needed to see Kayla. The paramedics were doing everything they could to help her but I already knew—I had known it from the moment I cradled my friend's body in my arms—they were too late.

It was all too late.

16

THEN

A blue backdrop. Two chairs. Trisha Weathers and President King.

Trisha Weathers: First of all, Mr. President, I'd like to start off this interview by saying: thank you for being here. We all know what you've been through and how incredibly hectic your schedule must be with everything at the moment.

President King: (No answer—just a stern nod)

Trisha Weathers: It's been three weeks since the tragic events of October 2. What many are referring to as the O2 Attack. How are you doing?

President King: Like most people, I was shaken, in shock from this senseless act of terrorism. But I am recovering and trying to repair the damage to the country. Focused on guiding us forward.

Trisha Weathers: Are you still resolute in your decision to declare martial law and give absolute security power to the newly formed Guard Elite?

President King: Absolutely. The Guard Elite might be newly formed, but they are well trained and fully prepared to protect this country from its enemies at home and abroad. As long as terrorist threats continue, riots continue to break out, protestors continue to storm the streets, and Wright continues to build his so-called rebellion against this government, the Guard Elite, led by General O'Brien, will continue to maintain control.

Trisha Weathers: There are some who say that the Guard lack proper training and that all this is occurring because of the ill-advised decisions made during O2. What is your response to them?

President King: Who are they?

Trisha Weathers: (Stumbling) Certain critics.

President King: Well, again, I'd like to know who these "certain critics" are. To them and to everyone else, I say that they need to open their eyes and look around. O2 was an act of terror. It was an attack. Not just on me but on the people and the security of this country.

Trisha Weathers: So the government is firm in its stance that this was an attack?

President King: Not just an attack. What occurred at Hickory stadium was one of the many symptoms that have been plaguing this country for a long time.

Trisha Weathers: A symptom?

President King: Of the tragic failure we have let this country become. This is exactly what I ... the government and the Guard ... are trying to fix.

Trisha Weathers: There are many who criticize the Guard ...

President King: (Raising his voice) What everyone needs to understand is that the Guard was and continues to be on duty to protect the citizens. As we have now confirmed, the bombs were set by an insurgent group within the Wright Rebellion ...

Trisha Weathers: Has that been confirmed? Do you have the evidence?

President King: I'd appreciate it if you didn't interrupt me while I am speaking, Miss Weathers. O2 was an unfortunate day in this country's history. I managed to survive, but thousands of people were killed or wounded because a small group of individuals disagree with our nation's policies. That's a fact. These ... terrorists must be stopped—at all costs. The Guard was on duty that day to provide safety to the people. They had undisputed information that the terrorists who set the bombs were still in the stadium. They had to be thorough in order to catch those involved.

Now, was there miscommunication? Should the Guard have done things a little differently? Well, that's not for me to decide and what's done is done. It was a day that nobody was prepared for and, unfortunately, many, including members of the Guard, were wounded or killed. It's important that we, the media included, keep our focus on the real threat here.

Trisha Weathers: But do you agree that the Guard should have shot into the crowd?

President King: I was being ushered out of a different area of the stadium at the time. I don't know what exactly went on that led to that specific shooting incident, but I can tell you that having experienced a war first-hand, I know things can get messy. In the heat of the moment, people make quick decisions and mistakes are made.

Trisha Weathers: Messy? Those mistakes cost innocent lives.

President King: (Glaring at Weathers) Not all lives lost were innocent, I assure you.

Trisha Weathers: But some were.

President King: This country is in the midst of a revolution. Innocent lives are being lost every day.

Trisha Weathers: But some are saying that one of the main causes of this conflict can be attributed to the Guard's actions during 02 and if you had just admitted to their mistakes, instead of defending their actions, this country might not be where we are today.

President King: Again, I'd like to know who, exactly, you are referring to, and I'd like to remind them that it wasn't the Guard who set those explosions. Look, that day, while tragic, was also chaotic. Bombs exploding, gun shots being fired. The Guard's main objective was to preserve public safety. And they did their job.

Instead of spending time criticizing the actions taken by the brave men and women who protect the nation, I think they ... I think we all need to shift our focus and energy where it belongs—stopping the terrorists, the riots, and any future attacks on the people of this nation. It's time we started to put right what's wrong.

Trisha Weathers: (Looking at a piece of paper) You said in a speech last week, "If you are not with us, you are against us." That was a pretty absolute statement. Do you still stand by these words?

President King: I don't think I need to give you an answer to that question. The critics of this government need to understand our ultimate goal here. In an unstable world, a world with terrorism, mutating viruses, impending energy and resource shortages, a world outgrowing itself, we are trying to create a better, stronger, more stable future. A future in which we not only survive but, as a country, we thrive. In order to do that, we need to become one.

Trisha Weathers: But what does that future look like to you?

President King: I'm not ready to comment on that until we have taken care of our present situation.

Trisha Weathers: You have limited people's access to the Medianet, created tough restrictions on the use of personal communication devices, ordered a public curfew, and taken a lot of criticism for announcing a law that gives the Guard Elite power to listen in and spy on all forms of communication. Do you really feel that all these measures are necessary? Doesn't this all seem a bit extreme?

President King: Extreme? (He laughs) Look, every order and decision that this government makes is done with public security in mind. What's "extreme" is what has been happening in this country and in the world, for that matter.

Supporters of Richard Wright and anyone else involved with insurgent groups opposing this elected government must be stopped before other innocents are harmed or killed. Those who choose to criticize the tactics we are implementing are the ones who have something to hide. And we will find out what they are hiding. We will do whatever we have to in order to maintain public safety and ensure this country remains strong. I make no apologies for that.

Trisha Weathers: Since 02, it seems that the Wright opposition, what has now become a Wright rebellion, has grown in numbers. Many are attributing that growth to one individual …

(Holding up a photo: The image is of Sam carrying a bloody Kayla in her arms with Annie holding on to her shirt and following behind. Sam is standing amid the smoke and chaos while members of the Guard are fighting with batons and shooting pepper spray into a nearby crowd. With a green and white painted face, dripping tears, and with blood down the side of her head, Sam walks into a sea of armed Guards. Under the photo, in bold, it reads: STAND UP, STAND AGAINST)

Trisha Weathers: ... It is now common knowledge that the girl in this photo is known to be Samantha Smart, and the girl in her arms, her best friend, although there is some speculation they were more than friends, is Kayla Marchette—shot by members of your Guard during O2.

President King: Supposedly shot by members of the Guard. That is unconfirmed.

Trisha Weathers: Within minutes of this photo hitting the Medianet, the image spread through hundreds of thousands of social media sites around the nation. Some say that it was this photo that sparked the subsequent O2 riots and that Samantha Smart, the girl who stands against you, is rumored to have joined the Wright Rebellion. What are your thoughts on this image and the fame around Samantha Smart that it has created?

President King: First of all, Kayla Marchette was not some innocent bystander. She had been placed on the GWL weeks before the O2 bombings occurred. And Samantha Smart, the so-called O2 heroine, ran from the stadium as Elite Guards moved in to question her. In my experience, innocent people don't run. Their names were identified on a list of Wright supporters, anti-King propaganda found in their bags, along with footage of them sneaking through an unauthorized access hallway at the stadium, and we have reason to believe that both Marchette and Smart are linked to insurgent groups involved in the bombings. For all we know, Samantha Smart is one of the terrorists.

Trisha Weathers: But you have no proof of that?

President King: I am not at liberty to comment on ongoing Elite investigations.

Trisha Weathers: And at this time, you do not know the whereabouts of Miss Smart?

President King: Again, I am not at liberty to comment. What we do know is that the media has grossly glorified exactly who this girl is. Samantha Smart is not a hero. Her father was an unemployed alcoholic who froze to death in a passed-out stupor. Her absentee mother died of a drug overdose, and she spent some of her youth on the street, in and out of juvenile detention and state care before being taken in by her grandfather. The girl has a troubled past and is looking to cause more trouble. She is a danger and part of the extremist society that this government is trying to control.

Trisha Weathers: Is it not true that she was also an honor-roll university student with a full scholarship and captain of her soccer team?

President King: Your point?

Trisha Weathers: Well, my point …

President King: Samantha Smart is a perfect example of the filth that survives on the outskirts of the model society that this nation was built on—she's a symptom. Without work and rehabilitation camps, these types of people can fool us but will eventually always revert to their radical ways. She and others like her are the problem, and we cannot move forward toward a better, stronger future with people like her dragging us down.

Trisha Weathers: But Mr. President, with all due respect, Samantha Smart …

President King: Miss Weathers, I am done talking about and hearing about Samantha Smart. The public, the media—you included—are giving this girl far more credit than she deserves. I suggest you place your focus on other more pressing areas. This interview is over.

17

"There's never an easy way out, Sam. Sometimes, when the going gets tough, you simply have to get through it."
~ Grandpa Smart

NOW

"You are causing a lot of problems, Samantha Smart. *A lot* of problems." King stands before me, hands on his hips. It's his signature pose, one used to resemble a superhero in his past ad campaigns, and one that certain satirical media outlets have dared to mock. He waves his finger in a patronizing manner. It makes it seem like he's scolding a child, which, I suppose, is his intention.

"There are others, much more dangerous than myself, others you should be truly afraid of, and they are not too happy with your actions." King paces back and forth. It's painfully obvious how much he enjoys hearing the sound of his own voice. "What's almost amusing is that I told them early on to watch out for you, but they didn't agree with me. They didn't see the threat in you. I, however, could tell you were going to be trouble even before you knew it yourself."

I know by the sharp, controlled tone in his voice that he is still pissed at me for what happened on stage. Things had not gone exactly the way he'd planned, I'm sure, and now I'm going to pay for it.

When he held me up on stage, ripped the tape from my mouth, and taunted me to speak, he must have assumed, like everyone else, that I would stay silent—that I wouldn't dare defy him.

Truth be told, I had no intention of saying anything. I was just going to keep my mouth shut, let King use me, humiliate me, and wait for the nightmare to be over. Even the worst things in life end at some point. But then I saw *his* face—near the back corner of the gym. He wasn't cheering with the rest of them. He wasn't enjoying what was happening on stage like everyone else. He looked apologetic, almost sympathetic. And seeing him triggered something.

"I used to know you," I said, staring directly at Brady.

The fact that I had actually accepted King's challenge and opened my mouth shocked the room into silence. Even King seemed interested in where this was going.

I struggled to stand up on shaky legs, my knee throbbing painfully from where O'Brien had smashed it. I turned my head and nodded at an anonymous female Guard. "And I used to know you, too, and you … I knew all of you. Sons, daughters, brothers, sisters, friends, students, teachers, servers, clerks … you used to get together in bars and at friends' houses, watching the Sunday game or binge-watching your favorite series.

"You'd go for five-dollar lattes at the local café, help your neighbor by cutting their lawn, taking out the garbage, or lifting a heavy box of books into their house. I used to know all of you.

"What do *I* have to say? What do *you* have to say?"

I would have continued but, before any more words could escape, O'Brien threw the black bag over my head and had me hauled off the stage. I hadn't said much but it was something, enough to silence the room and incense King. To make matters worse, for King and ultimately for me, someone in the gym had been recording the scene and leaked it to Trisha Weathers and the Medianet newsflashes.

O'Brien swiftly discovered and dealt with the mole, a Wright sympathizer whose daughter had been arrested and sent to the work camps during the early stages of the Resistance. He didn't even try to deny what he had done; in fact, he was proud of it. They made an example of him, quickly found him guilty of treason, but, as the triggers were being pulled, he shouted out a final defiant statement: "I stand with her and against you."

I know all this because they made me watch him die.

King wanted me to know that the "traitor's" death was on me. He boasted about how his Guards had managed to track down, erase, and destroy all video posts of my mini-speech. That's what he thinks. But I know that trying to completely erase something from the Medianet is like trying to hold a snowflake in your hand. It may seem to disappear, but it's still out there somewhere, just in another form. I know how this media game is played better than most.

At first I was an unwilling participant but, after a time, I was taught to use the media as a tool in order to strengthen Wright's campaign and weaken King's government. It's small consolation to know that, even in captivity, I've managed to cause some trouble for King. Truly, the only thing that matters to me is that the video has been seen, which means Aaron and Wright will know I'm still alive. But, judging by the look on King's face right now, I'm not sure how long that will last. I've seen a look like this before. He wants, needs, to hurt me. And I know that no matter what I do or don't say, he's going to.

We're in the basement changing rooms of the school, the girls' changing room, judging by the lockers, showers, and faded pink tile lining the walls and floor around me. The large open shower space has recently been converted into an interrogation facility. There's a stench of mold mixed with body odor, and traces of fresh red blood staining the grout from whoever had been held here before me.

Following O'Brien's orders, I was dragged directly from the execution, stripped down to shorts and a sports bra, and made to kneel on the floor. My wrists were tied to two black cords attached to the ground on either side, making it impossible for me stand. The sharp grooves in between the cracked tiles feel like razors cutting into my skin. I've tried shifting to ease the pain but nothing seems to help. I'm so tired I feel delirious and I can't even remember the last time I had anything to eat or drink. The sound of dripping shower faucets next to me is a cruel tease. All of this is racing through my mind, but I try to keep my expression as stoic as possible. I give King nothing.

"Aren't you going to ask me how I knew you were going to be trouble?" He takes off his jacket and slowly starts to roll up his sleeves.

He's playing with me.

"How did you know?" I think it's better to play along—for now.

"I could tell from the look in your eyes in that photo—you know the one I'm talking about. I've seen that look before in the eyes of enemy soldiers who have lost their families and loved ones. It's a look that says: I have nothing to left to lose. I've learned over time that those people can be the most dangerous. Because they're reactionary. They don't think about the consequences. Like you. You weren't thinking about standing and facing off against the Guard that day, were you?"

"I was just trying to save my friend."

"Your *friend*? I think we both know she was more than that." Stick Bitch enters the room and hands King a glass with ice. "Did you find it?"

She nods as she very deliberately holds up and opens a bottle of ... no! It can't be. A tidal wave of nausea hits me as I instantly recognize the purple horned devil on the label—an image seared into my brain at too young an age.

Like the practiced flight attendant she was, she pours the amber liquid until King motions for her to stop. He holds the glass out. "Would you say that's half-full or half-empty?" He smiles and takes a long sniff—eyes glued to my reaction the entire time. "Doesn't matter," he sips, "it tastes like cheap garbage all the same."

I hold his gaze but can't control the increased pace of my breathing and heartbeat. How does he know?

He turns to Stick Bitch. "You can leave us now."

She deliberately glances at me before leaving. For a brief moment, I swear I see a slight hint of something vaguely resembling compassion in her eyes.

King looks back at me. "You were just trying to help Kayla ..."

"Don't say her name," I utter through gritted teeth.

He continues, "How could you know that someone was taking a photo and that that photo was going to, as they say, go viral and give you your five minutes of fame?"

"I didn't know any of that was going to happen. I didn't want any of that to happen."

"But you liked it, didn't you? Admit it. You like the attention. You like being *Samantha Smart.*"

I keep my mouth shut, curious where King is going with this whole charade.

"You don't have to say anything. I know the answer. See, that's what's wrong with this society. Giving hero status to a girl they don't even know, based on an inflated image with some catchy hashtag underneath."

"You think marketing and social media are what's wrong with us? I didn't want this. Any of this. I was a student. I was playing soccer. I was happy and then ... and then you and your fucking government came along and everything changed."

"Oh, sweetheart, things had changed long before we came along. It's just that nobody wants to admit that. It's interesting, though." He pauses and stares down at me, his eyes studying, looking for answers I can't give him. "If I hadn't come along, if that picture hadn't been taken, you wouldn't be here. You wouldn't be 'Samantha Smart the Revolutionary.' Or would you? Because I think it's who you are, who you've always been—you just didn't know it. We can't know who we really are until we're pushed to our limits. So, in a way, you can thank me."

"Thanks," I hiss with contempt. The purple devil is staring at me from the bottle at King's side. "What is this? Some of your twisted psychology training?"

"I see you did your research on me." He smiles and takes another sip from the glass. "I didn't expect anything less from you. In fact, I'm quite glad that you're everything I expected you to be, because I would have been really disappointed if you hadn't lived up to the legend."

He steps toward me and holds the glass within reach.

"Where are my manners? You must be terribly thirsty."

I involuntarily swallow and cringe at the smell as I turn my head away. All of my inner alarms are sounding in warning, urging me to do what I can't—run.

"Oh, that's right. You don't like this particular brand of rum, do you?" He violently grabs me by my hair and holds the glass to my mouth. "Drink it."

"Fuck you."

He tightens his hold on my hair, holds the rim to my lips, and forces a small amount into my mouth. The majority of it runs over my face and dribbles down my front, but a small quantity begins to burn my throat. I spit back at him what I can.

He grins, pleased with himself. "It is believed that the sense of smell can trigger the strongest memories. Tell me, *Sammy*, what are you thinking about? What are you feeling right now?" His questions sound clinical. This is more than an interrogation to him.

I spit out the rest. "I'm feeling like I want to smash that glass on your face and I'm thinking that you're a sadistic asshole. And don't call me Sammy."

I try to stay calm, even, but whatever game King is playing with me, he's winning, and he knows it.

"Interesting. I don't care for this particular brand myself. I find it quite *cheap*. But we both know who used to drink it. And I bet, by the look on your face, you're wondering how I can know all this."

He raises an eyebrow and looks for me to confirm his statement. "Information is everywhere. Hell, we don't even have to look hard anymore. People willingly give up the tiniest details of their life. If they've had a bad day—hashtag-worst-day-ever, insta-pics of where they went for their vacation, who they went with, what they ate, their favorite cat videos, sports teams, what brands they support, who they know, what they know, how they know it, every minute detail right down to the way they like their coffee ..." he pauses and snaps his fingers, "... don't tell me ... medium skim-milk mocha with chocolate whipped cream?"

I don't confirm it. I don't have to. King hasn't actually touched me, yet I feel violated in a way I can't explain.

He smiles, knowing he's getting to me. "You see, it's all out there. Things we don't even know about ourselves. Things people don't think matter, until they do—until it matters to someone else. I have to say, unlike most of society, you are a bit of a closed book. But that just got me thinking that maybe you had something to hide."

He walks over to a bench and picks up a faded manila file folder. I instantly recognize the tattered corners. King opens it and flips through the pages.

"Not an easy file to dig up, by the way. Only one hard copy existed. You could say that psychology is a bit of a hobby of mine. I find what makes people tick quite fascinating and with you, well—tick-tock tick-tock—interesting stuff. There are evaluations from when you were just four years old."

I suddenly find myself transported to a small beige room. Children's toys and stuffed animals are scattered about to make it feel less sterile. A white-haired woman seated across from me places a blank page and crayons on the table, encouraging me to draw out my feeling and emotions.

"It says here that you were living in an unstable environment.

Signs of emotional and physical abuse were evident." He holds up a crayon drawing for me to see. "But, when asked, you refused to say anything. In fact, you drew a perfect picture of a happy, loving home. In the final evaluation, the doctor said that she believed you were protecting your mother. You feared they would take you away and she would be left with him. How very self-sacrificing of you." He closes the folder and lets it slap to the ground. "In fact, almost every single assessment makes a note of your protective nature. You can't help yourself. It's who you are."

"What's your point?" I snap, tired of whatever he's doing.

Anger flashes in his eyes. His tone sharpens. "Did he used to call you Sammy?" He moves behind me, closes his fingers around my neck, and yanks my head back. "Did he?"

"Yes." I can barely whisper it.

His grip eases and he softly touches a small scar on my back. I flinch and attempt to pull away. "No matter what you do, how far you run, it's always with you, isn't it? Your past?"

I know it's what he wants, but I begin to lose control of my emotions. He's striking too deep, too close. My hands wrap around the bands holding me to the floor and squeeze tightly.

"He used to come home drunk and smelling just like this. Didn't he?" He raises his voice. He wants an answer but I look away. "He used to stumble into the house, drunk, loud, calling for your mom ... or you. Looking for someone to beat, to take his daily stresses out on. Tell me—would it matter who he found, or was it a first-come-first-serve kind of thing?"

"Enough," I bark. "What is this? Some sort of sadistic counseling session? Some twisted way of tapping into my daddy issues? Why don't you just ask me what you want to know?"

"Oh, we'll get to that," he smiles and continues. "Were you the brave one, Sammy? Did you give yourself up like a sacrificial lamb for slaughter in order to protect her? I bet you did."

"So you read through my files. Good for you. Classic sad story—poor welfare family, drunk, abusive father. Doesn't mean you know me."

"Nobody really knows you, do they, Sammy? He used to hit you, maybe throw you into a wall or two." Slowly, methodically, King starts to undo his belt buckle. "But that wasn't his favorite thing to do, was it?" As he removes his belt, folds it in his hands, and walks behind me, every muscle in my body tenses, readies.

"Where is Wright?" He knows I'm not going to answer—he's counting on it. "Where. Is. Wright?"

I close my eyes, clench my jaw, and prepare for the first blow.

SNAP! The leather whips across my back. The sting, the smell—for a split second I'm that scared little girl back in the kitchen with my father—but only for a second.

"Where is he? What did he have you working on?"

SNAP! Another blow across my upper back.

"Oh, that's right," King kneels down to my level and whispers in my ear. "Your file says they he sometimes liked to use the buckle end, didn't he?" He steps back and puts all his force into the swing. I feel the metal strike next to my rib cage and let out a sharp exhale of pain. He hits me again and, with this one, I feel the metal cut through skin. I try to hold it in, not give him the satisfaction, but a reluctant cry of pain seeps out.

"You know what?" I spit at him.

"Enlighten me."

"You think using some memory of my fucked-up childhood

is going to break me?" I'm not sure if it's the lack of sleep or the amount of pain I'm in, but I laugh. "It's like you said: it was his beatings that taught me how strong I can be. Go ahead—I've survived worse." I get ready for another blow.

King walks back in front of me with a different look on his face, inquisitive and malicious at the same time. It's unnerving. "The police report said your father came home one night, drunk as usual, and that he passed out in the snow just feet from the door. It wasn't until the next morning that your mother found him. Frozen to death. A tragic accident ..." He gauges my reaction. "Or was something left out?"

I look away.

"He did come home that night. But you were still awake ..."

"Stop."

"It says in the reports that you were usually awake, waiting for him to come home. It was no different that night, was it? You saw him walking up to the house ..."

"I don't know where Wright is. They'll have moved him by now, anyway ..."

"You knew what was going to happen when he got there ..."

"I DON'T KNOW ANYTHING ..."

"So you locked the door, didn't you?"

"Stop!" I'm looking down, shaking my head, begging for this to end.

"Look at me. Look. At. Me." I give in. "You locked the door. Refused to let him in ..."

"I didn't lock the door." My voice comes out in a whisper. "I just didn't unlock it." King waits for me to continue. And I do. I don't know why, but I do. "Sometimes, he would just stay out there, sleep it off on the porch swing."

"But not that night. It was too cold." He leans closer. "What happened?"

I can see the bitter dark of that night before me. My mother had told me to go to bed and then she'd fallen asleep on the couch. As usual, I couldn't sleep. I waited by the window—watching, waiting. An earlier blizzard had left a blanket of fresh white snow covering the entire front yard. Now the snow fell gently against a faded pinkish-blue backdrop. It was quiet, peaceful—giving a false sense of calm. Maybe, I thought, maybe he wasn't going to make it home that night. It had happened before. He had chosen to sleep it off in the bar or the seat of his truck.

But I was fooling myself. A puffy lump of green and orange awkwardly lumbered into view, tumbling over the white mounds in the distance. I covered my mother with a blanket and waited by the window. He was struggling to get to the front step. The snow was up to his waist and, with each tired step he took, great puffs of breath billowed out and dissipated into the cold night air. When he got within feet of the door, his powdered white face peered out from under his hood.

"Helloooo, Sammy." He smiled.

I smiled back—it was a reflex, nothing more. I hugged my knees tightly and watched his shaky hands fumble through a pocket in search of his keys. That sound—the jingle of keys— made me shiver. Maybe it was the cold of the night, the amount of alcohol in his system, or divine intervention—whatever it was, something caused him to drop the keys into a mound of snow. He mumbled a few swear words and tried to recover them. After a couple of minutes, he gave up and fell into the door.

"Open the door."

I hugged my knees tighter.

"OPEN. THE. DOOR." He knocked furiously.

I looked over at the couch but my mother never moved an inch. She must have taken something to help her sleep.

He backed up and looked at me through the window. "SAMMY, OPEN THE FUCKING DOOR."

I didn't move.

"When I get in that house you're dead. DEAD—YOU HEAR ME?" He was backing up as he spit out his threats. The snow had covered everything, making it impossible to see where you were walking, and, without warning, he backed up and fell off the edge of the porch.

It wasn't a big fall but he didn't move, didn't even try to stand.

I watched and waited. There was no movement except the falling snow that eventually covered his tracks and then his body with a new blanket of white—making things peaceful again.

"I didn't open the door." My eyes are fixed on the grinning purple devil. I had never told a soul about that night. Not one.

"But you could have," King says and waits for a response. "But. You. Could. Have."

I look away. "But I could have."

"And you thought that things would be better without him. But they weren't, were they? Your mother ended up caring more about her pills than she did about you. And you've had to carry the weight of what happened ever since."

"Why are you doing this? I thought this was an interrogation.

What does any of this matter?" My voice is hoarse.

"It's who you are. It all matters. Everything about you matters, don't you get that?" King seems pleased with himself. "You know they didn't want me to meet you. I was advised to stay away, almost like they're afraid of you and me being in the same room together. O'Brien wanted to be the one. I'm sure you've heard about his tactics. A tad brutish, if you ask me. Physical torture is not how I like to go about things. It's ineffective and, besides, it's the mind not the body that intrigues me. Just trying to understand."

"Well, understand this. You can read every file you want on me. You can play your little mind games, torture me, try to break me, and maybe, eventually, you will. But you will never understand me, you got that? I'm not something to figure out. I'm just Sam. And I'm going to fight you every step of the way. I don't care what you do to me."

He grins, revealing all of his perfect white teeth. "Well, I have always liked a challenge."

The sound of a throat clearing pulls King's attention from me to the back of the room. O'Brien's dark figure steps out of the shadows. It's unclear how long he's been there, but it's evident from King's annoyed expression that he's not pleased about being interrupted.

He drops his belt to the ground in front of me and meets with O'Brien at the back of the room. They probably think they're far enough away that I won't hear their conversation, but the acoustics in the empty changing room help me to focus on the echo of their lowered voices.

From where I'm kneeling, I can see their outlines and I watch for their body language to reveal something more.

O'Brien waves his cane in the air. "Are you quite done with your little experiment, infatuation, or whatever this is? While you're spending all this time with your little girlfriend there, we're losing this war."

"What are you overreacting about?"

"Wright has addressed the people, asking them to take to the streets and demand Samantha Smart's immediate release. We've taken control in most of the central cities but some riots are still raging. We've received word that mass demonstrations are being planned two days from now. This is exactly what I warned you was going to happen. The Collective is upset. That little stunt she pulled on stage has given the Resistance renewed energy and we need to respond. We need to make a statement now to let them know that this administration will not take dissent lightly."

The Collective. I had come across this term before. Working with Aaron, Maya, and a few others, we were searching out a theory that a higher power was pulling the strings behind King's government. Until now it was only a working theory. The quick rise in power of the Elite, media control, world food shortages, and medicine regulations: everything seemed too big and too neatly orchestrated for any single government.

"I'm doing everything they've asked. This was what they wanted."

"A little dissent, yes. Hell, a little dissent works in our favor. But they're worried that this could get away from us."

"What do you propose?"

"Make a statement. And make it public."

"Is that what they want?" King asks.

O'Brien nods.

"I thought it was too early for any of that."

"They're moving up the timeline."

"No. I can get her to turn on Wright. At the very least, use her against him. We take her out too soon and this could blow up in our face."

"Leave her to me, then. Stop playing with her. Leave her to me and get yourself to one of those demonstrations with the Elite. Stop it before it even starts. Make a clear warning to others that public displays of defiance will not be tolerated. No mercy on this one. We're too close to have it all come crashing down now."

"And what about her?" King nods in my direction.

I quickly look at the ground and make it appear like I am in more pain than I am.

"The longer the girl is here, the more her martyr status grows. I'll get from her what we need and be done with it."

King takes a minute to respond. "No. You won't get anywhere doing it your way. Not with her. Samantha Smart is the key and I'm getting to her. Soon she'll be telling me everything she knows and doing whatever I ask. We can still use her."

Although King's words send a shiver up my spine, I feel more relief than fear. As sadistic and cruel as King is, I prefer him to O'Brien.

"Samantha Smart is nothing anymore." I can tell that O'Brien is looking down the corridor at me. "Whatever this girl has got over you, deal with her and let it go. Don't make this personal. There is a war to win and a country to restructure. I'll go with the Elite and handle the riots. But the C5 want you to say something, make a statement. They are not asking."

The C5? The Collective.

O'Brien limps out of the room and King turns back to me, unmoving in the shadows. I can't make out his face but his silhouette stands, dark and sinister, his gaze fixed on me. His words run through my mind: *Samantha Smart is the key* ... the key to what?

18

THEN

TRISHA WEATHERS—MEDIANET NEWS FLASH

Good evening. In our top story: the worldwide energy crisis continues to spread and has cost more lives as hundreds unable to heat their homes have frozen to death in northern areas.

While President King assures the country that we are not in a critical zone yet, he asks citizens to be prepared, as Encor Power will be instituting roaming blackouts throughout the country in a national effort to conserve. President King is also encouraging any and all citizens to turn off your lights and power down any unnecessary devices.

The energy crisis is having far-reaching effects, and experts believe that there will be a worldwide food shortage of disastrous proportions in the coming years. Countries have already begun to stockpile their own resources. Here at home, President King says that measures have been and currently are being taken to ensure that this country is well prepared and well provided for.

Also on the home front, while clashes against the Guard have subsided in many cities around the nation, there continue to be targeted attacks against Guard-controlled facilities. In the last few days, two separate protest marches became riots as citizens demonstrating both for and against President King began fighting one another in the streets. On both occasions, the Elite forces moved in with water cannons and riot gear to subdue the rioters.

In light of these events, King has announced he's decided to keep the countrywide curfew in effect. Until further notice, people without a GAP (Guard Approved Pass) are asked to stay off the streets between the hours of 8 PM and 6 AM. For the time being, it is asked that those planning any and all organized gatherings seek approval from local Guard authorities. Any unscheduled meetings of three or more people will be treated as a threat to the government.

For a full list of curfew rules, please visit the King's Guard Medianet site.

And now to the image that continues to stir controversy and circulate the Mediaweb. While Samantha Smart's fame grows, the girl at the center of the O2 stadium attack appears to have gone into hiding and remains a mystery, leaving many asking the question, just who is Samantha Smart? Is the girl, seen in this now famous photo, a hero or a terrorist? We take to the streets to hear your opinion ...

Brent Hanson: Yes, I've seen the photo. Who hasn't seen the photo? What do I think? I think she's a victim, like everyone else. Honestly, I just feel bad for her and I think people need to leave her alone.

Sheila Brown: Like President King said, the girl is clearly troubled. I think she and everyone like her are what's wrong with this world. I hope the Guard finds her. I hope they find all the rebels and terrorists who think they can go after our President and attack us, and I hope they kill them all. I always said Wright and his radical side was no good. I said it but nobody believed me. Well, who's right now? I tell you what, she better stay in hiding, because if I see her, I'll shoot first and ask questions later—you better believe it.

Woman *(asked to remain nameless):* Look at the photo. She clearly loved that girl. I don't blame her for running. I think she was scared. We're all scared. Elite members showed up in my neighborhood and took my neighbor's son away for questioning. That was a month ago. No one has seen or heard from him since and the Guard denies taking him. If I were Samantha Smart, I would be running, too.

Young man: I don't care if she's a terrorist or not, look at her—with that painted face, looking all Braveheart and (BLEEP)—the girl's hard core.

Greg Anderson: She's guilty, plain and simple. Innocent people don't run. The Guard needs to find her, arrest her, and give her what she deserves.

Jane: I don't care what the Guard says about her. I know that Samantha Smart is a hero. My family was at the stadium that day and, during the commotion, my daughter was pulled from my hand. I thought I'd lost her. Samantha Smart picked her up from underneath a pile of bodies and took her to safety—she saved her life. Samantha, if you're out there somewhere, I just want you to know that Annie is fine and I can't thank you enough. Samantha Smart is a hero—A HERO!

Group of teenage girls: Samantha Smart? OMG, we love her ... WE LOVE YOU, SAM!

19

THEN

For the final twenty minutes of my fourteen-hour journey, I had been watching the first droplets of rain slowly collect and streak down the tinted bus window. Thick clouds made mid-afternoon seem like night and, as the bus pulled to a stop, the rain pounded down with enough force to cover the outside pavement in a half-inch of water.

The doors opened and I stepped down, thanking the driver who didn't care to look at me or any of the other anonymous faces scattered throughout his bus. I barely had both feet on the pavement when the doors snapped shut and the wheels rolled on. Aaron emerged from under a yellow umbrella, his face widening into a warm greeting when he recognized me peering out at him from under my hood. After the past few days, I was relieved to see a familiar face, but he seemed awkward, unsure how to greet me.

I didn't wait for him to make a decision. I dropped my backpack on the rain-soaked sidewalk and hugged him. It didn't matter that a torrential downpour was soaking through to my skin—I held tight and didn't let go.

After a brief embrace, he quickly ushered me to the closest shelter we could find, a rundown fifties-style roadside diner complete with red vinyl seats and mini-jukeboxes on each tabletop. With the weather outside, the restaurant was nearly empty—I say it was the weather but it could have been any number of the factors being spouted on the Medianet outlets: the failing economy, the constant threat of potential terrorist attacks, the fear of virus outbreaks, or the growing number of King's Guards patrolling the streets. Even with the lack of customers, Aaron chose a booth in a secluded corner and I kept my face hidden under my hoodie.

He watched in amazement as I downed a giant vanilla milkshake, grilled cheese, onion rings, and a side of wilted dill pickles. I had wanted a cheeseburger, fries, and a real salad, but with the food shortages and half the menu crossed out, this was as close as I could get. After the gas station junk food that had been sustaining me for days, it was still extremely satisfying.

"Hungry?" he asked with a laugh.

"Starving," I answered with a mouth full of food.

Aaron had grown his sideburns and goatee into a well-trimmed beard. He looked older. He noticed me inspecting him. "What?"

"The beard. It makes you look like a legitimate revolutionary."

"Well, that's the look I was going for." He winked. "Do you like it?"

I smirked and took another bite of grilled cheese. "It suits you." Now it was his turn to inspect me. "What?"

"Nothing ... I just missed your smile, your conversation. I missed ... you."

I felt my face heat up and hoped he couldn't see the flush in my cheeks. He patiently waited until the sandwich had disappeared before getting right down to the reason I had come. "So, are you all right?"

I nodded—unconvincingly, I'm sure.

"What happened?"

"I don't even know. One minute Kay and I were watching the game, the next ..." I paused, taking myself back to the stadium "... she was right beside me. Right beside me. I never saw her get shot. I only saw her lying on the ground. One second she was here and then ... I knew there was nothing anyone could do, but I had to get her to an ambulance just in case there was a chance."

"You did everything you could."

"It wasn't enough." I pushed a soggy onion ring around my plate. "It still hasn't settled in. None of this has. I just can't believe she's gone."

"What happened after? The news feeds all say you ran from the Guard."

"I was watching the paramedics trying to bring her back, and looking around for this little girl we picked up—Annie. She was separated from ..."

"I know the one," he interrupted.

"What?"

"Her mom was on a Trisha Weathers newsflash."

I perked up. "What? She was?"

"She said you saved her daughter's life, and that you're a hero."

"Really? She's okay?" I slumped against the diner seat, relieved. Ever since I'd run from the paramedic van, I'd felt guilty for leaving her.

Aaron nodded. "Have you had a chance to see the Medianet lately?"

"Not really. I know there's a couple pictures of me out there, that the Elite's been looking for me."

"*A* picture? Out there? Sam, you're all anyone is talking about. And the stuff they're coming up with ..."

"Like what?" I said uncomfortably.

"That you're a terrorist. You were a part of the attack. That you and Kayla were ..."

"Were what?"

"Together."

"*Together* together?" He nodded. I started to laugh, not at the idea of Kayla and me being together, just at the idea of it all. "She'd love that. Lesbian terrorists, everyone beware!" I continued laughing, alone. I guess Aaron didn't see the humor that I did in the situation.

"What happened after you got to the paramedics?"

"They took Kayla and Annie. Someone sprayed me in the face with water, told me to wait where I was. Like I was going to go anywhere, anyway." I took a deep breath and closed my eyes. "Two Guards came up to me. They started asking for my name, Kayla's name. They wanted my ID."

"Did you give it to them?"

"No. And as soon as they turned their backs, I ran. I'm not even sure why I ran. I wasn't thinking about trying to get away from them. I just needed to get away. I went back. Things were crazy. There was fire, smoke ... Guards everywhere, roughing up everyone—young, old, it didn't matter." I paused. "I needed to find Brady."

"Brady was there?"

"With the Guard."

"What?" Aaron leaned on the table.

"He and Ryan joined up over the summer. He told me to meet him at Gate 7 after the game. I wanted to find him. Tell him about Kayla. I figured maybe he would be there ... looking for me." I gazed out the window at the falling rain.

"And ...?"

"He was there. I saw him with a group of Guards, rounding up people from the stadium. They were forcing people to kneel on the ground with their hands behind their heads. Cuffing them. Throwing them into vans. They were beating anyone who didn't listen or act quickly enough."

"Brady as well?"

"No. At least, not while I was watching. He was just there, helping with others to corral people together. Mostly just standing guard to make sure nobody moved or tried to get away."

"And you ran?"

"Nope. I just stood there. Like an idiot. Eventually, someone shoved me in the back, told me to put my hands behind my head and get over with the others. Brady must have spotted me. I don't know how he did it without being seen, but he pulled me away from the group. He was so angry with me. Asked me what the hell I was doing there. Told me to run. I was just so relieved to see him. I tried telling him about Kayla but another Guard, one of his commanding officers or something—I don't know how they work—yelled at him. Asked him if he needed help with me. He yelled back that he was taking care of it ... of me," I said bitterly. "He shoved me behind a car. Yelled at me to get away, to run. I yelled back. Told him they shot Kayla, that she was dead. And I know he heard me. I could see it in his face. He said he'd find me later, at the practice field, and then he asked me again, pleaded with me to run and get away from him. So I did."

Aaron was literally sitting on the edge of his seat. "Shit. And did you see him later?"

"Much later. I had gone back to the dorms, showered, changed. At some point during that time, that picture of me hit the Medianet."

Aaron held up his phone. My image was saved as his screen shot. "It's a great shot. I think I spit out my soda when I first realized it was you. Although, I have to say, something about it didn't surprise me."

"Yeah, well, it shocked the heck out of me. I started getting tons of texts. I thought it was Brady trying to get hold of me, but it was everyone else sending me that picture. Asking if that was me. If it was Kayla. If we were all right. They said the picture was all over the Medianet. The mystery girl. I knew I couldn't stay in the dorms. That they would eventually figure out who I was and come for me. So I packed a bag. Took all my pictures, my computer, journals—I even went online to delete my email and public profiles, thinking if they linked me to Kayla that way, that they could link others to me, but ..."

"They were already deleted."

"Ya ... how did you know?"

"We did it. Well, our tech-heads did. The second I confirmed it was you and Kayla, I knew they would be after you. It's all I could do to help—give you somewhat of a head start. We've been closely monitoring the Medianet feeds and posts. When pictures of you pop up, posts appear about your whereabouts, or if people think they've seen you, we get to them first and erase what we can. We've also planted false intel about where you've been, in order to divert the Guards' attention."

"Wow. When my information was gone, I just figured it was them. I thought they were already erasing my life ..." I looked down.

"What's wrong?"

"It's just everything happened so fast, I never had time to really think about the fact that I left the dorm. The university. That place was my home. My life. It's all I've known for almost four years. It's silly, I know. It's just I wasn't ready to go yet. Not like that." Aaron reached his hand across the table and tried to give a comforting smile.

"I had it in my head that all I needed was to see Brady, and that if I was with him, everything would somehow be okay. I left the dorm and waited at the practice field for him. The whole time I was waiting, I kept thinking that he and I would run away together. We'd just go. I don't know where. I was so stupid. Fuck, I've been so naïve about this whole thing."

My fist hit the table.

"When he finally did show up, he was still wearing his uniform. And seeing him, in that uniform, I knew things were never going to be the same again. And I'm not just talking about him and me. I'm talking about everything.

"He hugged and kissed me but ... something was different. He apologized for being so rough with me at the stadium. Said he had no choice; it was the only way to get me out of there. I told him what had happened with Kayla. He told me that after the first explosion, he tried running in to find me, but that they were all ordered to wait, stand down, that they had received intel suggesting that the ones responsible for the bombs were still in the stadium. They were ordered to question and arrest anyone they deemed suspicious." I stopped.

"What?" Aaron asked. "What is it?"

"He showed me the picture. *The* picture. It had gone out to all members of the Guard, the police, everyone. They didn't have a name yet but they were told to arrest and bring me in on sight ... that I was ... *am* considered a conspirator to the bombings."

"He didn't think ..."

"No, he didn't believe it for a second. But he told me how serious this was. That I should go with him to clear my name. Tell my side of the story. He was worried that if I ran, it would confirm my involvement. Maybe he was right. Maybe I should have turned myself in at the start."

"Sam, you did the right thing. There's no way the Guard would have listened to anything you had to say."

"That's what I said. I told him I was going to run and that he should come with me. I almost had him convinced that we could just disappear somewhere, get away from all this."

"But ...?"

"But the Guard. He's not only one of them now, he actually believes in what King is doing, defending it. When I told him about Kayla, about how she died in my arms ... all he said was how she shouldn't have been there in the first place. Like it was our fault for being there."

"Wow."

"I don't think he meant it. He couldn't have."

"So how'd you leave it?"

"He told me to lay low for a while. Wait till he could figure things out with his superiors. Maybe try to clear my name.

"I don't know why I believed that he might be able to do something, but I did. I couldn't just stay in the dorms, so I left and went to Kayla's. I felt like I had to see her parents, tell them what happened.

"It took me a couple of days to get there. I guess at some point that's when the Guard figured out my name, because I went into a grocery store to buy a sandwich or something and I could feel people looking at me. At first I thought I was being super-paranoid, but then I went to pay the cashier and I saw a newspaper with my face on it, and not the stadium picture, but my school soccer photo with my name underneath. The headline read: *Mystery Girl Identified as Samantha Avery Smart—Wanted for Questioning by the Guard.* The person at the register recognized me. They picked up the phone to call someone and I just ran out of there. I didn't even pay for my sandwich. So apparently now I'm a terrorist and a shoplifter."

"Did you get to Kayla's parents?"

"Yes. I messaged her brother but he never responded. I would have called her parents but I didn't have their number, and I wasn't sure if the Guard was still watching them, so I waited until it got dark and then I snuck around back.

"Her mom was in the kitchen. She looked so tired, so broken. Her eyes were raw from all the crying. When she saw me she practically collapsed into a chair. She let me in. Hugged me. Cried some more. She said that they had just seen the footage of the bombing and riot on the newsflash when Guards showed up, banging on their door. They didn't know what was happening and the Guard didn't tell them anything—they just came in and took her son away.

"It was later when she saw the picture of me holding Kayla. A neighbor showed her. I told her what happened—what really happened and not what everyone on the Medianet was saying happened. She kept crying and going on about how she should have listened to Kayla from the beginning."

I stopped and looked out the window. It was now night and all I could see was my own reflection staring back.

"We all should have listened. I gave her Kayla's championship soccer ring. I had taken it off her hand as they were pulling her away …" I shook my head, frustrated with myself.

"What?" Aaron asked.

"I was so stupid. We heard the vans pull up. We both knew it was them. She shoved a bunch of money and food at me and told me she would distract them. I ran as fast as I could. I heard them coming after me but I just kept running …"

"What?"

"There were gunshots. Back at Kayla's house."

"You don't think …"

"I don't know. But I just left her there. I left her and took off without even thinking that something might happen to her."

"Sam, there was nothing you could have done."

"I could have stayed. They were there for me. They'd probably been there the entire time, waiting …"

"But you don't even know if …"

"I don't know because I ran and I kept running. I don't even know how long. I found a spot to hide at this park. I took out my phone and thought about calling Brady—a reflex. I was about to dial, and that's when I realized they must have tracked me through my phone. I mean, it had to be. They were probably still tracking me at that moment. So I threw it in a pond. I had so many pictures, contacts—my life was on that phone. Thank God you put your number into that book you gave me because I never would have been able to call you."

"I'm glad you did."

"Me, too. I had nowhere else to go."

Aaron leaned forward, "So, you and Brady ..."

"I don't know," I said bluntly. "I managed to get a disposable phone at a gas station. We've talked a couple of times. He told me that after they figured out my name, they turned the dorm upside down looking for me. They found Kayla's things. They know she was staying with me—that I was housing someone on the Watch List. They found our T-shirts, the ones we wore to the student protest." I rested my elbows on the table and let my head rest in my hands. "Three years. Three years we've been together and then this. The last time we spoke was right before I got on the bus to come here. He asked me ... more like accused me ..."

"Of what?"

"O2. He and Ryan let us in a side door. Ryan thinks we played them. They didn't check our bags ..."

"They actually think ..."

I nodded at Aaron before he could finish the question. "He says he doesn't want to believe it but the media, O'Brien, King, Ryan ... they've made us sound pretty fucking guilty."

"Okay, but Sam, he can't believe you were a part of that bombing."

"I don't know what he believes anymore." Aaron leaned back in his seat. I could tell by the intense way he was examining me that there was something else he wanted to ask. "What?"

He smiled. "Nothing ... it's nothing."

"Aaron. What?"

He shifted uncomfortably and took a breath. "Well, it's just the stuff they're saying about you, about your past …"

"Like what?" A tight ball formed in my stomach and it wasn't from the greasy food I had just scarfed down.

"That you spent time in juvenile detention for stealing, lived on the streets, did drugs …"

"I never did drugs."

"But the rest of it?"

"It's true."

"I thought your grandfather raised you."

"He was around as much as he could be. After my mom … eventually I did live with him, but there were periods, let's call them blips … I wasn't the easiest kid."

He leaned back in his seat and his eyes scanned me up and down. "Well, shit, Sam. I never took you for a badass."

"Badass is pushing it. I was just a messed-up kid with a chip on my shoulder. What can I say? People change."

I waited for him to say something more but he just looked at me. I hated that *look*. That apologetic-sympathetic-concerned look. Having my picture floating out in the Medianet was uncomfortable enough, but having my past talked about and dissected by the media and public made me feel exposed … vulnerable. And vulnerable was an emotion I promised my younger self I would never feel again.

"Why didn't you ever say anything?"

"Because of this." I waved a hand at him. "Because of how you're acting right now."

"Ya … but …"

"Aaron, what they're saying—I may have done some of it but that's not who I am. It's my past, yes. I'm sure it's part of me, but I've spent most of my life making sure that it's not who I am. Please. I know you're only asking because you care, but I hate talking about it and I really hate that look on your face."

He relaxed and did his best to smile. "Okay. I get it. No more looks, and we don't have to talk about it—unless you want to."

"I don't."

"I mean in the future. If you ever want to talk ... you know ..."

"Thanks."

The waitress came over to the table. "Can I get you two anything else?"

"No, thank you," Aaron replied. "We're fine."

She leaned down to clear the plates, speaking in a whisper. "It took me a while to realize who you are." She was stacking the plates and looking out the window, but it was clear that she was talking to me. "And I should tell you that I'm not the only one here who has figured it out." She nodded at a table with three men. One of the men was peering back at me. "If I were you two, I'd make myself scarce pretty quick."

I reached for my wallet but the waitress stopped me. "Don't worry about it, sweetie. This one's on the house. I think what you did was ... well, you just keep on doing it, okay?"

I nodded. "Thank you."

She smiled back and then went over to the table with the three men and spoke loudly. "What else can I get you gentlemen?" As soon as the men looked away, Aaron and I slipped out.

Back under the umbrella, he turned to me. "Come on. There's someone who wants to meet you.

Why do you think the photo became as popular as it did?

Sam: In the chaos of the O2 bombings, there were probably hundreds of amazing moments that could have been captured on camera. For some reason, someone pressed a button and captured mine. And for some other reason, they pressed send, and then someone else pressed share, and it went on from there. It could have been anyone. In the end, it wasn't about me; it was about what people needed to see.

Okay, but in the end, it was the photo that led you to join the Resistance.

Sam: Is that a question?

Maybe. Just trying to piece things together.

Sam: And that's what this is really about, isn't it. That's why you're here, aren't you? To know more? Not about me, but about yourself. You ask these questions about how I became a revolutionary but what you really want to know, why you're really here, trying to piece together my story, is to find out if you've got it in you.

I can't answer that. No more than I can answer it about myself. I can look at it and I see the pieces fitting together—the election, the bombings, Kayla, Brady, Aaron, the picture, my past, the fact that I had nowhere else to turn—I see it all. My puzzle. My path. If you take away even one of those things, maybe I wouldn't have ended up here, or maybe it just would have taken me longer. To be honest, I don't know. I can only understand it when I look back at it and see the moments that pushed me one way or another.

Do you have it in you? Only time will tell.

20

"Life can deal a bad hand sometimes.
It's up to you whether to fold or bluff."
~ Grandpa Smart

THEN

I looked down at the phone in my hand and contemplated dialing the number. Finally, after a few attempts, I pressed the send button and waited nervously for a response.

"Sam?" Brady sounded out of breath on the other end.

"Yeah. It's me."

"Oh, thank God. How are you? Where are you? Are you okay?"

"Do you have a minute to talk?" I paced back and forth.

"Yes. I'm just leaving my parents', actually."

"Your parents? You mean the Guard lets you have time off?" Try as I might, I couldn't hide the bitterness in my tone.

Brady's tone was equally sharp in response. "My group just happened to be in the area. Sam, where are you?"

"I'm ..." I hesitated. I had never lied to him before. I had omitted things but never lied. "I'm safe."

"What? You don't think you can tell me?" I didn't answer. "Sam, I'm sorry. I know you had nothing to do with the bombing.

I just … with everything they were saying, and then that picture of you … they know that I know you, that we were dating and I …"

"We were *dating*? Dating? For three years? Is that what you told them?" I hadn't called him to argue. At that point, I couldn't really explain why I had called him. To hear his voice, maybe. To see if we meant anything to each other anymore.

"Sam, I … I couldn't tell them. They questioned me … accused me …"

"What did you tell them?"

"Nothing important."

"I shouldn't even be talking to you. They're probably listening to us …"

"Do you hear yourself?" Brady barked. "You're paranoid. And besides, they don't know I have this phone."

"What did your parents say?"

"About what?"

"About the weather, Brady," I snapped. "What do you think?" Seconds ticked by before he responded.

"My mom wanted to know if that stuff about your past was true. I told her that some of it was."

"And your dad?" I asked, already knowing what his response would be. I can't explain why I cared so much. I wish I didn't.

"He … it doesn't matter what he thinks."

"Do they believe I'm guilty?"

"No, of course not. They're worried about you."

I knew him well enough to know the tone of his voice when he was lying.

"Sam? Sam? You still there?"

"Yes," I said softly.

"I miss you."

"I miss you, too." It was the truth. Given everything, I still really missed him. But the him I once knew, not this new Guard version.

"It's not too late, you know. I could come and get you."

"And then what?" Even though it could never happen, I wanted him to say that we should go away together. Leave. Run. I just wanted him to say it. But his response, although expected, was the one soul-crushing thing I was hoping not to hear.

"If you come in with me, tell them the truth. I know they'll understand that it was all a big misunderstanding."

"A *misunderstanding*?" In that instant I knew why I had called him. I hadn't wanted to admit it, but I knew. The only misunderstanding was the one between Brady and me. I knew that he and I had come from different backgrounds, but how had I not seen how different we really were? How could I have misjudged him so completely? How could I have been so stupid?

"SAM." Aaron's voice called for me. "It's almost time."

"What's going on?" Brady asked. "Who's that?"

"It's nothing, no one. I have to go, Brady."

"No, wait," he pleaded through the phone.

"What?"

"I ... well, you called me. Why?"

To tell you it's over. That I don't know you and don't know how I could ever have been with you for so long. But I couldn't bring the words out. "I guess I just wanted to hear your voice." I kicked at the ground. "And to tell you that ... umm ... whatever happens from here on ..." But I couldn't finish.

"SAM?!" Aaron called again.

"Sam? What do you mean, whatever happens? And who is that? Who are you with?"

"I have to go. I ... uh ... just ... you take care of yourself, okay?"

It was the closest words to "goodbye" that I could bring myself to say. I could still hear his voice calling out my name as I hung up. Immediately, his number tried to call back, but my finger slid over the decline button. It didn't feel like that long ago that we were contemplating forever, and now ...

"Are you sure you're ready for this?" Richard Wright walked up behind me.

I tucked my phone away and nodded. "I think so."

He walked me over to the bottom of a set of stairs and I looked up at a waiting wooden podium.

"Are you scared?"

I shook my head. "No, not scared."

"Nervous? Maybe I pushed too hard. Maybe it's too fast. If you're not ready to do this ..."

"It's not that. It's just ... up until now, I've only been a picture, an image. What if I'm not who they think I am? What if I'm not *that* girl? What if I can't do this?"

Wright stood in front of me and softly put his hands on my shoulders. "I'll be honest. I wasn't sure what to expect when Aaron brought you to me. He'd talked you up a lot and I didn't believe anyone could be as brave as the girl in the photo."

He looked up at a billboard-sized poster of my now-famous shot. The poster was one of many images and pro-Wright slogans lining the back of a makeshift stage. Where we were standing was private and hidden, but I knew that a few feet away, thousands of Wright supporters were waiting for me to make my first public appearance. Wright looked back from the poster to me.

"Now I've met you and you've turned out to be more than I expected, Samantha Smart. I know you're nervous. That's normal. Just try to remember what brought you here. Look at the photo, but don't look at yourself; look at Kayla. She's what this is all about. Remember that. Use that."

One thing was for sure: Wright certainly could be persuasive. I looked up at the poster and at Kayla, but I wasn't thinking back to that day; I was remembering our pre-game routine. I used to get nervous before every home game, so Kayla came up with a silly "Salt and Pepper" song and dance that could always make me laugh and calm down. Just thinking about it made me smile.

Aaron stepped up beside Wright. "You got this, Sam. I know you do. The people need this. They need you."

I clenched my jaw and nodded. I was ready. Turning and starting my ascent up the stairs, I thought about my conversation with Brady. It was the end of something—the end of something bigger than us. I may not have been able to say goodbye, but I had gotten the closure I needed. And it wasn't about Brady. It was about me.

As I reached the top steps, my thoughts returned to Kayla. If only she could see me now—she'd never believe it. She'd probably make fun of me, have some snappy comment about public speaking. Or she'd say that this is what she always saw for me. That somehow she knew.

"Sam." I stopped mid-step and looked back at Wright. "I think you're about to discover that you're not the girl in the photo, but that the girl in the photo is you." He smiled. "If that makes any sense at all."

"Kind of." I took a deep breath. "Thanks."

I took the last step slowly, carefully, using the railing to steady my shaking hand and body. I knew where the steps were leading me, and yet, I had no real understanding—I couldn't.

When I reached the platform and stood behind the podium, I looked out at a sea of people standing in an open park. For a second it was quiet, every face in the audience looking up at me. It all felt surreal, like I was in a dream at that pivotal moment just before waking. A small part of me hoped I would wake up any second; that this and everything leading up to it had all been one big nightmare. But ...

"IT'S HER."

"IT IS HER."

"SAMANTHA SMART!"

Someone pointed, someone yelled my name. Then came other fingers, more voices, confirmation it was me. A cheer erupted from the crowd like a tremor from the earth; first slow, then gaining momentum. Anti-King flags waved in the air. Signs with my image bounced up and down. Fists were raised and the voices began chanting something. At first I couldn't make it out, but then it became clear ...

"STAND UP .... STAND UP ... STAND UP ... STAND UP ... STAND UP ..."

I was overwhelmed. My voice caught in my throat. I wasn't ready for this. I looked back down the stairs at Wright and Aaron, wanting one or both of them to come and rescue me, but they just stood at the bottom, waving their hands, encouraging me to say something.

I waved, but that only encouraged more cheers and chanting, so I changed tactics, pushing my hands down, trying to calm the crowd the way I had seen leaders do in movies and documentaries. It worked. When it was quiet enough for me to begin, I swallowed a ball of nerves that had been collecting in my throat and stepped toward the microphone.

"Hi ... umm... I'm Samantha Smart and ..."

Upon hearing my name, the crowd erupted with more cheering and chants. It took another two minutes for them to settle. I wish I could say the same for my nerves.

"... I am Samantha Smart, and yes, the girl in that photo was ... is me. I was at the stadium when the O2 attack occurred. I was there when the clashes began and lives were lost. I lost my best friend that day.

"We, as a country, all lost something that day. President King wants you to be afraid. He wants to use that fear against us. Declaring martial law, granting himself, General O'Brien, and the Guard absolute power, using the Elite as a secret police, initiating protocols that take away some of our everyday freedoms. And we are letting it happen. Agreeing to third-party communication taps and social media restrictions because they tell us it will keep us all safer, that it's better for the nation.

"I say, no. And I stand against it. I stand against a government that would create a 'No Chance' policy, allowing this government to arrest and convict suspected troublemakers without so much as a trial. I stand against a regime that asks neighbors to turn on their neighbors. I stand against King. I stand against the Guard. I stand up for free speech. I stand up for living without fear. I stand up ... for you!"

"STAND UP ... STAND UP ... STAND UP ... STAND UP ..."

21

THEN

Trisha Weathers seated at her desk. The famous image of Sam is seen in a small box in the corner of the screen.

Trisha Weathers: Hello? Samantha, are you there?

Samantha Smart: Yes, Ms. Weathers, I'm here.

Trisha Weathers: Thank you for agreeing to this interview. I understand and appreciate the danger that it's putting you in.

Samantha Smart: No more than I already am. And I think it might be putting you in just as much danger.

Trisha Weathers: The media has a responsibility to report the news from all angles.

Samantha Smart: Does it? Because lately it seems pretty one-sided.

Trisha Weathers: We would have loved to have you on earlier, Miss Smart, but you are one elusive woman to get hold of. However, you're with us now and, as I understand it, our time is short, so I will get right to it. The question that many would like answered. Are you or are you not directly involved with the terrorist group responsible for the October 2 attack?

Samantha Smart: First of all, Ms. Weathers, despite what the King Government wants people to believe, there has still been no proof linking any terrorist groups to the bombings. And no, I am not involved with any terrorist organization. Then or now.

Trisha Weathers: But you and your friend Kayla Marchette were there?

Samantha Smart: We were. You know that, and it feels like the entire world knows as well.

Trisha Weathers: Why were you two at the game?

Samantha Smart: Like everyone else. We were there to watch, have a good time.

Trisha Weathers: The Guard claims to have footage of you two walking through a restricted hallway, anti-King paraphernalia was found in your possession, and Kayla Marchette was on the Watch List. Do you deny any of this?

Samantha Smart: No.

Trisha Weathers: *(Surprised)* Can you comment further?

Samantha Smart: We were there, yes. Should we have been there? Probably not. Retrospect is everything. I never should have agreed to go but she—Kayla—wanted to go. She knew the Guard was looking for her but we thought we'd blend in—safety in numbers, or something. She didn't know, we all didn't know how bad things already were. It's no secret that I don't support King or the Guard. But neither Kayla nor myself had anything to do with the attack. We were just two stupid, naïve girls who wanted to watch a game.

Trisha Weathers: Just to be clear. Are you saying that Kayla Marchette was a victim?

Samantha Smart: Aren't we all?

Trisha Weathers: Were you and Kayla in a relationship?

Samantha Smart: I shouldn't need to define what we meant to each other, but for you and everyone else who think that this matters: no, Kayla and I were best friends. Period.

Trisha Weathers: Do you think you deserve all the attention you're getting?

Samantha Smart: No.

Trisha Weathers: And yet you're playing a key role in helping Richard Wright lead the Resistance.

Samantha Smart: Am I?

Trisha Weathers: You wouldn't be talking to me if you weren't.

Samantha Smart: I suppose that's true.

Trisha Weathers: How does it feel being hailed as "The Voice of the People"?

Samantha Smart: Weird.

Trisha Weathers: I assume that comes with a lot of pressure?

Samantha Smart: I think you of all people would know, Ms. Weathers. Is this something I ever imagined myself doing? No. But the people need a voice to remind the country and the leaders that this is what it's all about—the people. The ones displaced, starving, and living in tent cities. The ones who tried to speak up but were killed or taken by the Elite. The ones who have lost loved ones. The ones too scared to speak up themselves. I'm still having trouble understanding my role in all of this, but if it's to be a voice for ordinary people ... all I can do is try.

Trisha Weathers: The things being said about your past, how true are they?

Samantha Smart: Some of it is true and some of it is being deeply embellished. It's mostly true and, although King is trying to exploit it, I don't feel like there's anything I have to be embarrassed about. We all come from somewhere. We all have a past.

Trisha Weathers: There are rumors flying around that you once dated a member of the Guard, but are currently in a relationship with fellow rebel leader Aaron Mahone. Pictures circulating of you two talking closely together at rallies and—

Samantha Smart: What? Wow. First Kayla, then a member of the Guard, and now Aaron? I don't see how my relationship status has anything to do with anything.

Trisha Weathers: Well, these are the things that the people want to know. So, do you deny being in a relationship with Aaron Mahone?

Samantha Smart: I'm not even going to comment.

Trisha Weathers: But you are friends?

Samantha Smart: Yes.

Trisha Weathers: And you knew each other before all this started?

Samantha Smart: I knew a lot of people before all this started.

Trisha Weathers: What is it the Resistance wants? How do you see this ending?

Samantha Smart: Ultimately, what we want is a new election. At the very least, we want King to be honest and tell the public exactly what General O'Brien and the Guard Elite are up to. He keeps talking about some grand future and the power of this country, but he's always evasive, talking around the issues, avoiding what exactly he means by restructure, rehabilitate, unity, and values. I don't know how this is all going to end, but I do know that there shouldn't be special privileges for some and none for others. That we shouldn't be restricted with our ...

Trisha Weathers: Hello? Hello? Samantha, are you there? Sam? Well, I'm very sorry, but it appears we have lost the connection.

(Putting her hand to her ear and listening) As we try to reconnect with Samantha Smart, I will move on to world news where foreign conflicts, fleeing refugees, and the threat of food shortages continue to worsen as …

22

NOW

A Guard holds my head under the ice-cold water for the ninth time … tenth? No, ninth—not that it really matters, anyway. I begin to experience a strange feeling that I have been here before. Well, not exactly here …

When Aaron had finally scared me into attending the talks on interrogation tactics, I often imagined what was happening now: my head being held under water, someone yelling at me to talk, to tell them something they wanted to know, and me refusing to give in. It was a scene I had seen played out countless times in movies, television spy dramas, and music videos. Maybe that's why I'm less scared and more amused that something like this is actually happening, that it isn't just something they do on TV.

Stick Bitch, however, is less amused. As I cough and sputter water from the last dunk, she leans over me with an evil smile. "You know, with your hair all matted to your face like that, all wet, skinny, and pathetic, you look a bit like my dog after he's jumped into the lake to fetch a stick."

Although I'm gasping for air, I still manage to get out a defiant, "Woof."

She looks at the Guards. One of them responds by kicking me hard in the side, and I let out a grunt of pain as I fall awkwardly on my shoulder.

"Get her up," she orders.

"Yes, get her up." King seconds the order as he enters the room.

"Mr. President." The Guards stand at attention.

"Anything?" King asks.

Stick Bitch looks at me with irritation and shakes her head.

The Guards lift me to my feet as King closes in. "I thought I told you to greet me on your knees."

He waits for me to comply but I stand as tall as I can and stare him down. A hard stick strikes me on the back of the legs and a Guard pushes me to the ground.

"Why are you making things harder for yourself?"

"I can't help it. I like it when Stick-up-her-ass gets all hot and bothered." I wink at her.

She raises her arm and lunges forward, but King holds her back and signals for her to stand down. "Go." He orders. "Bring the other one." *The other one?* "If you think this act of bravery somehow impresses me, you're wrong."

"That's too bad. I do live to impress you."

He ignores the sarcastic comment. "I know this is just a front for how scared you really are. Believe it or not, in one way or another, I've been in your position. Trying to fool my mind into thinking that I wasn't afraid … that I was somehow in control." He walks up to me and brushes the back of his hand across my cheek. I pull away sharply. "But I promise you, the mind will eventually betray you." He smiles like he is about to let me in on a secret. "If you're thinking that was the main event, you'll be disappointed to find out it was only a preview." He nods at the Guards.

They pick me up, undo my restraints, and then restrain me again so that my arms are over my head and I am half-hanging/half-standing from a bar secured to the ceiling.

King continues. "I'm sorry I couldn't be here earlier but I had to address the nation, give a press statement, warn the citizens that if they come out to protest your capture, which inevitably we both know they will, it will be considered an act of defiance and they will be arrested and contained just like their heroine." He stops. "How does it feel?"

I'm getting annoyed with these questions but decide to go along with his twisted game anyway. "How does what feel?"

"To know that you are the cause of it all. To know that their suffering and their deaths are ultimately your fault?"

"Why don't you tell me?"

"No. You see, I realize that in order to do what needs to be done, people are going to get hurt and lives are going to be sacrificed. I've come to terms with that. But you ... I don't think you can handle it."

Behind King, I see Stick Bitch re-enter the room. Two Guards come next; a beaten and gagged Maya is being dragged behind them. King grins when he sees the look of dread on my face. "I take it you two know each other."

Like many other rebels, Maya had sought me out. Telling me that my words and example inspired her to do more. As a daughter of Hispanic immigrant parents under threat from King's policies, Maya felt compelled to act against the government. With a background in computer science, she had been a key player in the

Truth Tellers cyber-hacking scandals. But it wasn't until she saw my image from the day of the O2 attack that she felt brave enough to do more than fight a revolution from the safety of a keyboard.

Maya had been so awkward and quiet when we were first introduced, even apologizing for acting a little star-struck. After a few minutes of staring, she explained that the reason it was so strange for her to meet me was because she felt like she had already been working with me from the start. She was one of the first people to push my picture to go viral, and she was the one who created the "Stand Up, Stand Against" phrase that had caught on so quickly. She felt like she had helped to create "Samantha Smart—the Revolutionary," and, in many ways, she had.

Only a couple of years older than me, Maya had gone to university, playing for a rival soccer school. Though the two of us had never officially met before, we quickly bonded over training and turf stories. Since Kayla's death and leaving everything I knew as home, I didn't really have another girlfriend to talk to. We both understood the reality of our situation, but having a friend to talk with, engaging in light gossipy conversations, felt needed.

One afternoon, a fun argument over who was a better soccer player turned into a challenge, and then evolved into our own version of intramural soccer teams that played in an abandoned shoe factory near our main base. From those who participated to those who watched, the games were a welcome distraction. Before the Guard took us, my team was leading hers, seven games to six.

I watch closely as they string her up across from me. When our eyes connect, there is a brief recognition and feeling of relief that we are happy to see each other alive.

But that relief quickly morphs into fear as we both understand that King is about to use our relationship to his advantage. Of all the interrogation scenarios I have imagined, this is the one I feared the most. The thought of it worried me so much that it was one of the questions I had privately asked the interrogator during training. "What do you do if they're torturing someone you care about in front of you?" At the time, I was thinking about Brady.

His response only fed my fears. "For many, seeing a loved one tortured is much worse than enduring the physical torture themselves. It's highly effective. There's really no way of knowing how you'll respond until you're put in the situation. Just hope that you never are."

"But what if I am?" I asked him.

"I don't know what you want me to tell you. The only way to get an interrogator to stop is to give them what they want. That's the only thing that made me stop."

"Just ... give in? That's your advice?"

"Or give half-truths."

"Half-truths?"

"Think about what's important versus what's less important and tell them what they want. It might keep you alive longer. But it's a dangerous game."

"Why?"

"Once you start talking, it's difficult to stop."

Now I can't hide my fear and anxiety from King.

"What? No clever comment?"

I tighten my lips.

He looks from me to Maya and then back to me. His right eyebrow arches and he smirks arrogantly, proud of his next thought. "I think I'm going to let you two alone. Give you girls some time to catch up." He nods to the rest of the room and, one after another, they turn and leave until only he remains. Pulling Maya's gag off her mouth, he winks at the two of us. "Don't get too comfy. I'll be back soon."

I'm not naïve enough to think that someone somewhere isn't listening in, but I'm so relieved to see Maya that I don't care. "Are you okay?"

She nods and then immediately breaks down into tears. "I'm sorry, Sam. I've said things … I didn't … I couldn't …"

"Hey, My … don't apologize. Please. I've said stuff, too."

She sniffs, "You have?"

I nod. Then I look at her black-and-blue face, the dark shadows around her eyes, and wonder if she's looking at the same image. On her arm above her head, I see her "Resistance" tattoo. Her hands look mangled, bruised, and broken. Her fingers turn and curve at unnatural angles. "What did they do to you?"

"O'Brien …" she shivers and can't finish. "He said the punishment should fit the crime. I think it's what they do to all cyber-terrorists. He only broke a few, I think. I can't feel them anymore. Are you okay?"

I do my best to shrug.

"King came to see me."

"What did he want to know?"

"Stuff about you."

"Like what?"

"Who your closest friends in the Resistance are. What you're like. What you do for fun. If you have any friends. If you dream. What you dream. If you talk about your past … anything."

Once again, without his physically touching me, I feel violated. "What did you tell him?"

"The truth. Mostly. That you keep to yourself and no one really knows you." Maya adjusts her wrists and winces from the pain. "This isn't going to end well, is it?"

"I don't know." I look at the ground. "I don't think so."

"They knew things about me. About my past. My family. And dumb things, too. My favorite books, music, where I like to vacation ..."

"Me, too," I whisper. "They'll use it all against you. Anything they can."

Maya looks away. "They threatened my family. Threatened to do things if I didn't ... Sam, I had to tell them."

"About what?"

Before she can respond, King and his crew come marching back into the room. "All right. Visit time is over."

Stick Bitch gags Maya again. Her usual wooden stick has been replaced with a thick steel rod. She flicks a switch and it begins to hum. I've never seen this device before, but it's obvious by the way Maya flinches that she's familiar with it.

"What is Project K?" King asks sternly.

My gaze shifts across the room. Maya looks down, almost apologetically.

King continues, "I know it's something you were working on together. What is it?"

"It's nothing."

He reaches for the metal rod. "As you know, I don't care for these new-fangled modes of torture. I find them less ... intimate. But I realize that I need to get with the times." He touches the end of the rod to my ribs. A sharp jolt of current surges through me and I groan from the shock of it. When King pulls the device away, I can still feel a stinging, tingling vibration where it touched me.

"It's quite effective, though. We're outfitting all of the Guards with them. I imagine it hurts." He hands the rod back to Stick Bitch. "I just wanted you to experience exactly what you're about to put your friend through. And just to be clear, it's you who are doing this to her. Please feel free to stop it at any time."

Stick Bitch moves the rod to Maya's body. Her eyes close and she jerks wildly from the pain.

"NO!" I shout helplessly.

"Then talk!" King demands. "What is Project K?"

"She doesn't know anything. It's nothing."

Maya lets out a muffled scream as they shock her again.

King can tell that his plan is working. "You couldn't save your friend Kayla but you can help Maya now. All you have to do is talk."

Hearing King say Kayla's name fuels an inner rage. *Half-truths.* "Really, it's nothing. We went out collecting supplies … food, clothing, anything we could find that we could use. But every time we went out, we kept running into people who wanted to tell us their stories. That's all it is. Images, videos, a database of people's stories … things that they've suffered through because of you … because of the Guard."

"A database?" he asks with interest.

Once you start talking, it's hard to stop.

"What were you going to do with it?"

"Vidposts on the Medianet. Let the people see and hear the real truth for themselves."

"You and your Medianet revolution. You actually think you can do any real damage to this government with the click of a mouse? This war is not going to be won by some social media campaign, no matter how well-crafted. The computer is not and never will be mightier than the sword."

"Is that why Intel Systems is trying to censor and control the Web? Why you're trying to control the Medianet? Because you're not worried about it?"

King scowls. "What else is on it?"

"Nothing."

He steps forward and inspects my eyes. I do my best to match his stare. "You're lying." He grabs the rod from Stick Bitch and shocks Maya again, holding it to her skin for a longer period of time.

"OKAY!" I give in.

Maya looks at me and shakes her head. King notices the subtle communication and shocks her again.

"Stop—OKAY—we were collecting evidence."

"Evidence of what?"

"Something ... anything. Evidence that your re-education facilities are bullshit. Information about who's funding your initiatives. Proof about who actually set those explosives and attacked the stadium ..."

"What?" King barks. "It was terrorists, the Truth Tellers ... you were—"

"Yes, I was there. I was a victim. I wasn't even involved in any of this until that day happened. And the Truth Tellers, they're all just tech-heads and data geeks. They know more about planting computer viruses than planting bombs. You can tell as many lies as you want to the public, but if they find out that there were ten times more Guards at Hickory Stadium than any other stadium in the country that day ..."

"For my protection," King argues.

"Yes, wasn't that convenient? As convenient as the bombs and shots going off nowhere near where you were located. Or how about the fact that pieces of the explosives have been tracked to Advantage Defence Corporation, the same company supplying the Guard with weapons—"

"They were stolen from—"

"Again, how convenient. You have all the answers. Do you have one that explains why the Advantage Defence CEO made a call to General O'Brien hours before the bombs went off—"

"ENOUGH!" King shouts. "How can you possibly know all this?"

I smile. "I think you'd be surprised about the effectiveness the click of a mouse can have if you know how to use it."

I can see him thinking. The entire room has fallen silent. Stick Bitch, the Guards, all wait for his next reaction. He quickly composes himself.

"Where is this information?" he asks with a hint of anxiety.

"Gone. Destroyed when the Elite came."

He pulls a gun from one of the Guard's holsters and aims it at Maya. "WHERE IS IT?"

"I told you ..."

King doesn't hesitate. BANG! The shot echoes loudly off the tile walls. Maya screams and bites down on her gag as she sways back and forth. Blood begins seeping through her jumpsuit just above one of her knees. He aims at her other leg.

"There's a USB. Maybe. It was probably destroyed!" I shout frantically.

"WHERE?"

Maya begins groaning loudly, trying to get my attention. She wants me to stop talking, but I know that if I do, King won't hesitate to kill her. I've said something that has him more than angry. I think he's scared.

"I hid it. In an old safe at one of the warehouses where they captured us. But I'm sure it's gone by now."

King motions to Maya. "Get her out of here."

The Guards untie her but, before they can restrain her hands, she pulls her gag off. "Don't give them anything else, Sam. Don't. Give them nothing ..." Stick Bitch hits her in the leg where she was shot and Maya collapses to the floor. The Guards bind her, gag her, and haul her out, leaving a trail of blood snaking out the door.

"Well, that was dramatic." King saunters back to me. "And telling. What else am I going to find on that USB?" I keep my mouth shut. He lifts the metal rod to shock me but decides to drop it, opting to punch me in the stomach instead.

"You really didn't know about the attack, did you?" I say between coughs for breath. "What else aren't they telling you? Who's really pulling the strings? Is it O'Brien? Is it the Collective? The C5?"

King's eyes snap and lock on mine. Now he has given something away ... and so have I. "Oh, Samantha Smart," he says carefully. "Quite possibly too smart for your own good."

"Who are they? The O2 attack was just the beginning, wasn't it? The game, the Elite, the bombing, the riots ... they were counting on all of it, weren't they? Systematic and controlled chaos."

"From chaos comes control," King replies robotically, almost as if he has said or heard the line many times before.

"You're just a piece of their plan, aren't you? A mouthpiece. That's why you're here, with me, not out there … you don't have any real power at all, do you?"

"Do any of us? You. Me. We're both just people cast in the same reality show. A reality show that everyone is watching but nobody realizes they are a part of. We're done here."

As King leaves the room, he stops at the door. "Project K," he says as though he realizes something. "It's not K like the letter. It's Kay, for your friend Kayla, isn't it?"

I don't respond. I don't have to.

23

THEN

In an attempt to protect as much of my skin as possible, I pulled a black knitted hat down over my head and ears. Zipping my jacket up to my chin, I caught a glimpse of the almost full moon in the reflection of my watch and flashed back to the night Brady gave it to me. At the memory of that night, our picnic on the field, I felt myself breaking into a smile. But as quickly as it came to me, I dismissed it, shaking it off and trying to focus my attention on the task at hand. I had been doing that a lot, remembering moments—ones with Brady, Kayla, my soccer team—from a past that seemed another world, another lifetime.

"Cold?" Aaron asked, his breath clouding in the night air.

"A little." I put my hands in my pockets and took a deep breath of what smelled like wet leaves. "I love it, though. Reminds me of the beginning of soccer season. Late night practices under the lights, the crisp air stinging my lungs and numbing my thighs." I stopped. Another memory. Soccer made me think about Kayla.

"You miss it?"

"All the time."

"Can you pass me the tape?"

I opened a backpack of supplies and passed him a roll of silver duct tape.

"I never got organized sports. Wasn't my thing."

"I loved it."

"But why? I mean, it's all just a game. It's not real life."

"Well ... that's why. Because it was a game. During those ninety minutes, nothing else mattered." I looked across the river and into the distance. Nothing—a stretch of empty highway, a curving line of dimly lit street lamps, and darkness. I lifted a radio to my mouth. "Anything yet?"

"Negative," a male voice responded. "Only a raccoon crossing the road."

"Keep me posted." I went back to Aaron. "You didn't play sports but you surf."

"Oh, yeah. But surfing is like ... Zen. It's just you and the water. There's no yelling from the sideline, no winners or losers, it's just ... *awesomeness*. You should try it sometime. I could teach you."

I tried to imagine a future where Aaron and I could actually relax by a beach, surf in the ocean, play Frisbee on the sand. It was such a stark contrast to the present moment where we were carefully positioning a bomb—a very dangerous and very real, exploding, killing bomb. My brain still could not fully comprehend the reality—I was about to blow something up that wasn't a balloon or bubble-gum. "I think I'll stick to soccer. I'd probably drown or get eaten by a shark or something."

Aaron stood up and looked me over. "Well, you do look pretty tasty."

I hit him on the arm. "Are you done?"

"I think so." He inspected his work. Two rudimentary explosives set strategically under the pillars of a small country bridge.

"Where did you learn how to do that?"

"On the Net. Before all the restrictions, you could find anything. Instructions on how to bake a chocolate cake to constructing your own homemade explosives."

"Are you serious?"

"Totally. You could find anything you wanted there."

"Not about that. About how you learned to make this?" I pointed at the device.

"Nah ... only a little. I got a few lessons from some of the ex-military guys."

I looked under the bridge at a grenade taped to the side of the pillar. A thin piece of twine was tied around a pin that led to a spool in Aaron's hand. "Okay. But where did you get the grenades?"

"My uncle's farm. He has a stash of military-grade weapons."

"He just has grenades lying around? Is he a veteran or something?"

"No," Aaron replied casually. "Just a collector."

I shook my head. "Do you ever think that ..." I paused, stopping mid-thought.

"What?"

"Well, that some of the stuff King is doing might not be so bad? I actually kind of agree that things need to change. School shootings, bombings, the economy, substance abuse ..." I trail off, thinking about my mom. Thinking about how I helplessly watched a prescription turn into a dependency and finally a death sentence. "It's not like things were totally great before." I could see that Aaron was surprised to hear me say anything pro-

King. "I'm not saying I support everything they're doing. I just think things aren't so black and white."

"No. I hear you." He nodded. "Are you having second thoughts about this? Want to join the other side? Suit up with the Elite?"

"No and NO. You think it'll work?"

Aaron shrugged. "I guess we'll find out."

"You think they're actually coming this way?"

"I guess we'll find out." We started hiking up the steep riverbank. "Hey, how did you find out that the Guard is using this road for transport?"

For a second, I thought about telling Aaron that I was still in communication with Brady. It wasn't often, and our conversations happened so infrequently, they had almost stopped altogether.

Really, it was just about checking in. Seeing that the other was doing okay. It was during our last talk that he had told me he was on a team delivering materials south. He complained that it was tedious work and never mentioned what, where, or when, but I put two and two together and knew he was with a group delivering supplies for King's secret (and really not so secret) wall project. I might have crossed a line asking Maya to put a trace on Brady's phone, but it gave us strategic insight and allowed us to follow the routes the Guard were taking. It was how we got definitive proof that a wall to divide the country was being built. I felt guilty using Brady like this but the old cliché, "All's fair in love and war," helped me justify my actions. Again, I had to remind myself, this was bigger than us—the little that was left of us.

"I have a source." I finally said to Aaron, unwilling to say more.

"And is this source aware that he's your source?"

My look communicated more than words could have.

We walked to a waiting Jeep and knelt behind it for cover. "Well, I just hope your 'source' is right about this."

"Me, too."

"White two to White one," a voice called out from the radio.

"Go ahead," I answered.

"We can see the Guard convoy. They're coming."

"You're sure it's the Guard?"

"It's them."

"You're positive? You have confirmation?"

"Yes. Positive. It's the Guard."

"Blow it," I ordered Aaron.

Aaron pulled on the twine and ducked his head. We braced for the explosion but nothing happened. He pulled harder. Again.

"Shit. It must be caught on something."

I looked over the hood of the vehicle. In the distance, headlights from a large truck were emerging over a hill. Others were following behind.

Aaron continued to tug on the twine.

"Stop," I called to him. "Wait here."

"Sam, NO ..." Before he could reach out and pull me back, I jumped out and started to sprint for the bridge. "SAM!"

I could hear Aaron yelling at me, but I ignored him and slid down the muddy bank. The trucks were coming quickly, and all I could think about was blowing the bridge before the vehicles (and Brady) got too close. The goal was to disrupt the Guard and send a message to King that the rebels knew what he was building. It was not my plan for anyone to get hurt.

Halfway down the bank, I saw that the twine was snagged around a bush. I freed the line and looked across the river. The first trucks would be at the bridge in thirty seconds ... or less. I knew it was stupid; I knew I was probably too close—but we were running out of time. I pulled, heard the pin release, and felt the line go slack. With my shoes slipping and losing traction on the mud, I turned and started to claw my way up the bank as fast as I could. Based on the limited grenade knowledge I had from watching action movies, I calculated a few seconds before ...

BOOM!—BOOM!

The force of the blast thrust me face-first into the mud. The ground, the air, everything around me shook violently as the bombs blew and pieces of concrete started raining down. I curled into a ball and covered my head.

Seconds later, everything went silent.

The sharp ringing in my ears sent me back to the O2 bombing with Kayla. Vibrations from footsteps came crunching toward me. "Holy shit! Sam, are you all right?"

After a quick self-assessment, I said, "I ... I think so."

Aaron helped me to stand. He brushed off the dirt and debris and wiped streaks of mud from my face. "That was friggin' crazy. What the hell were you thinking?"

I looked over the river and saw the line of trucks and Jeeps stopped about ten yards from the now smoking and damaged bridge. Armed Guards started leaping out of their vehicles.

"Come on," Aaron pulled on me. "We gotta go. NOW!"

POP—POP—POP—POP—POP ...

Bullets whizzed by—and now I know why people say that, because they actually do *whiz* when flying past your head—and hit the ground as we started sprinting for the road. Once in the Jeep, I turned and looked back at the bridge. It wasn't completely destroyed, but a third of it had crumbled into the river below, leaving a gaping hole and no way for their trucks to drive over it. I saw Guards standing bewildered and frustrated on the opposite side. Their dark silhouettes looked like a line of those miniature green army figures found at the bottom of toy chests in children's playrooms. It wasn't a victory. They'd fix it or find another route. But it was something.

Even from a distance and through the darkness, I was sure I recognized the outline of Brady's head and powerful football shoulders, standing at the top of the bank. I knew every muscle in his toned upper body; his traps and upper back were especially appealing to me. It was the first time I had seen him in months and, instead of running to him, I was running away. Turning back around and settling into my seat, I noticed Aaron glancing over at me. He had a goofy smile on his face.

"What?" I asked.

"See. I told you that you remind me of Che. You're a badass revolutionary, after all, Samantha Smart."

Samantha Smart, revolutionary. With my entire body still trembling from the adrenalin, I thought about what I had just done and smiled. Actually, I laughed, almost uncontrollably. "Just shut up and get us outta here."

24

THEN

TRISHA WEATHERS—MEDIANET NEWS FLASH

King's Corporate Amalgamation Policy, the CAP, continues to receive backlash and criticism from the Wright opposition as well as some of the country's largest companies. Many have expressed concern over allowing Nutri Corp the ultimate responsibility of monitoring the distribution of food, water, and other essential items. Wright argues that the rationing program is flawed and has no measures to ensure fair and equal distribution of supplies: "We cannot allow one company, no matter how large, to dictate what, when, where, and how we eat."

In a released statement, King slams the criticism and defends the program, arguing that the CAP will allow for better oversight, cut down on wasteful practices, and guarantee the citizens of this country will not go without, unlike so many other nations around the world.

In the statement, he says, "The time for indulgence is gone. We face an uncertain future, where food shortages, access to potable water, and lack of proper medicines are a very real threat. Other nations ask for our help but it is time we start helping ourselves, preparing for our own uncertain future. The CAP will provide better monitoring of food and aid distribution, which will allow this country to sustain itself longer."

In other news, the Wright Resistance has claimed responsibility for damaging a bridge in the Neutral Zone last night. According to a brief viral video hacked into the Medianet, Samantha Smart admits that the Resistance blew up the bridge, saying that the access route in the Neutral Zone was being used to ship supplies for the building of a secret wall. Grainy images of the area appear to confirm the allegations that a structure is being built to separate the East and West Zones. As of yet, there has been no comment from King, but we have been told that he will address the nation concerning this matter later today.

And finally, tent cities in the Southwest Region continue to grow as thousands of displaced citizens flee from the escalating Guard raids. General O'Brien has defended the increased use of force, commenting that the raids are intended to control the growing number of insurgent factions hiding in the areas.

Meanwhile, Richard Wright has accused O'Brien and the Guard of using the threat of insurgents to continue King's "clear out" campaign, a movement he claims is designed to drive out the poor, the undocumented, and others living on the fringes of society.

King calls Wright's accusations ridiculous and continues to deny any allegations that a "clear out" campaign exists.

We turn to the public to hear your reactions to the latest events …

Hugh Morrison: The wall? I think it's a great idea. Look, I've worked hard my whole life for what I have. You want me to say it? Yes, I think I deserve more than others. Life isn't a free ride. There needs to be some regulation on things. If this keeps me safer, keeps my family safer, I'm all for it.

Woman *(asked to remain anonymous)*: Am I surprised? No. Nothing with this government surprises me anymore. If you want to know the truth, the wall has always been there. It may have been invisible, but it was there. I'm not for it but I think it's been coming for a long time.

Sandra Pearson: I haven't felt safe in years. I think a "clear out" campaign is not the worst idea ever. My cousin's friend heard that Guards raided a house on her street and arrested a whole family of Resistance supporters who were planning to protest or attack City Hall. Imagine, a whole family. I feel a lot safer with the Guard around.

Male Student *(anonymous)*: Please don't talk to me ... what? ... Hell, no, I don't agree with any of this. But can I say it? You better not show my face ... please, just leave me alone. No, I don't support the Resistance. I don't support any of this. I just want peace.

25

NOW

I sit on a green gym mat—the exact kind we once used for tumbling exercises in elementary school PE class—hugging my knees tight to my chest. There is a plastic cafeteria tray with a stale half-eaten cheese sandwich and an empty apple-juice box beside me. The room they are holding me in clearly is, or was, a kindergarten room at one time—or so I assume by the animal and alphabet wallpaper trim still stuck high on the walls. The windows are covered by the same metal shades that protect all the windows around the building. I have looked over every detail in this room, right down to the scuffs on the floor and the rudimentary crayon drawings of dinosaurs in one of the lower corners. Kindergarten graffiti. A young anarchist in the making. I find the room comforting, somehow.

Or maybe it isn't so much the room but the innocents who were once educated in it. Little minds learning how to read, write, and color; the world outside these walls still a mystery, offering endless potential and opportunities.

At this moment, my attention is only on one thing—a thin line of light shining through an open door. The room is unlocked. The door is open. *But why?* I vaguely remember being brought back here after my interrogation with Maya. I think I passed out for a few hours, and when I woke up, I tried to eat the food they'd left for me but I couldn't stomach anything. After that, I must have fallen asleep again, but for how long I don't know. When I opened my eyes, the door was open, the light from the outside shining through the crack like a welcoming exit sign.

This has to be a trick, or a game King is playing with me—leave the gate open and see if the rat will run through the maze.

But what if it isn't a game?

Maybe the Guard who delivered my food forgot to lock it. Maybe it is a game and King is waiting on the other side.

But what if he isn't?

There's probably a Guard standing watch outside, anyway.

But what if there isn't?

If this is a trap, am I risking more by staying put or by attempting to escape? Could there be a mole within the King Camp?

Possible.

Has some stranger risked everything to unlock the door—and now, here I sit, squandering the opportunity, not moving or doing anything to get away?

Or maybe it isn't a stranger. Maybe it's ... no, I don't want to think about him. But could it be that seeing me on stage did something to him? A change of heart? No. Brady's the reason I'm here. There's no way he unlocked the door.

But what if he did?

After more internal debate, I finally make up my mind. The

jumpsuit they put me in is a size too large, so I roll up the pant legs and sleeves to make sure that nothing can trip me up if it comes down to a sprint. Given my situation, my knee, I'm probably not going to make it that far, anyway.

But—and this is the deciding factor—*what if I do?* I have to try, because the one thing I do know is that if I don't at least try, King wins. I'm beginning to understand that's what this is about for him. For them. Control.

Making my way over to the light, I stay low and peer out through the crack. I see a long softly lit hallway with other closed doors. At the end, there's a camera perched high in the corner. Someone is definitely watching.

If years of playing sports have taught me anything, it's that I need a game plan. Taking a breath, trying to calm my pounding heart, I close my eyes and do my best to think of the layout of the building. Almost every time they have moved me, they put a black bag over my head but, even without visuals, I think I can sense and feel my way around. To bring me into this room, they had to take me up two flights of stairs, so my best bet at getting out is going down. But if this is a game—and it most likely is— King would expect me to go down.

I look up at the black eye of the lens and make sure that whoever is watching me on the other end gets a good hard look. I smile, give a wave with my middle finger, and then, mustering the courage to endure the pain to my knee that my next move will bring, I jump up and knock out the camera ...

... I've been spotted and they're closing in. Footsteps stomp behind me. Doors slam. Frantic radio calls announce my name.

I slip out of one room and quickly find another unlocked. As in the others, the windows in this room are covered, but I can see low gray light shining down from an adjoining room near the back. I hear yelling and movement from the hall and know I'll be caught soon. I'm not surprised. This little jaunt of mine has lasted a few minutes longer and has proven more rewarding than I thought it would.

I imagine how angry King probably is at this moment, how angry he is going to be when he finds out who I managed to contact. The satisfaction I get from that defiance, the fact that I didn't cooperate, gives me the energy to keep moving.

Crawling under a giant stack of dusty desks and chairs, I pop up in a small cloakroom. The space doesn't give me much room to stand, but above the cubbyholes and lockers is a small triangle-shaped window that isn't covered like the others. I stand on a desk and then try to maneuver onto a large stack of chairs, already dangerously close to falling over from their own weight.

It's incredibly unsafe. I feel like one of those circus acrobats but it's my only shot. Balancing with both feet on the teetering chairs, I reach for the top of the lockers as I hear the door to the room being kicked open. With all the stacked desks and chairs, there's no way they can see me from the doorway. If I don't move, maybe they'll move on to the next room.

Holding my breath, trying to remain still, I wait and listen as the Guards relay information about me over the radio.

"Room 523 clear."

"Room 525, no sign of her here."

Without warning, my injured knee starts to shake and the stack of chairs I'm standing on gives way. I leap for the lockers and just make it as chairs and desks come crashing down behind me. I climb up and, from my perch on top of the lockers, I can see the Guards' surprised faces as they call for backup. They begin to wildly throw desks to the side, creating a path to get to me.

"Stop! Stay where you are!"

Ignoring their shouts, I stand and am relieved to find that this window opens. It takes a few blows to crack the seal of paint holding it shut, but I manage to force it open and push it out just enough to squeeze through. Without looking to see how close the Guards have gotten, I pull myself through and drop a short distance to the rooftop below.

"Ahhhh ..." On impact, a jolt of pain surges up my leg and I crumple, reaching for my knee. *Suck it up, Sam.* Quickly getting up, I turn back to see if the Guards have made it to the window yet and then continue to limp away. It's a slow escape as the gravely roof surface cuts into my bare feet. I see blue sky but, from here, I have no idea where to go next. My only thought is to keep moving as long as I can.

Making my way to the edge of the building, I look down and can see the entire grounds of the school. It's more like a compound. All around, as far as I can see, are the tops of green fir trees and, further in the distance, some mountains. The school grounds are extensive. Elite Guards are hustling beside a gated parking lot with blue vans and Jeeps; a brick wall surrounds the entire perimeter of four brick buildings and a running track/ soccer field. To the side, I spot the top railings of a metal ladder, but just as I take a step ...

"SAM! Don't move."

My heart jumps at the voice. *Of course.*

"Hands on your head. Turn around."

Doing as I'm told, I turn around. Brady stands with his arm outstretched, gun aimed in my direction.

"Well, this feels very familiar," I say.

"Sam ..."

"Nice uniform, by the way. Elite. Good for you." The last comment sounds sarcastic but a part of me means it. It's absolutely ridiculous that I am still happy to see him succeed. "Was that promotion for bringing me in?"

"Sam ..." He looks almost apologetic, like he wants to say more, but behind him, King, Ryan, and other members from the Elite come running out. His eyes harden. "DOWN. ON YOUR KNEES. NOW ... DO IT NOW."

Defiantly eyeing Brady the entire time, I drop slowly to my knees. A Guard moves in and binds my hands behind my back.

"Good work, Smith." King acknowledges Brady with a pat on the back as he walks toward me. "What were you hoping to accomplish with this little charade?"

"What did you want me to accomplish? You're the one who left the door open. What's the matter? Your lab rat didn't go for the cheese?"

His fingers clench into a fist a split second before he hits me so hard that I see flashes of light and fall to the ground. "Did you think you were going to get away? Did you honestly think that this was the next plot development in your little *story*?"

There's something about the way he stresses the word "story" that makes me look up at Brady—pure hurt at his betrayal in my heart. At that moment, something sharp pricks my neck and Brady's face starts to distort and go fuzzy ... and then ... everything ...

26

THEN

Home had become an abandoned shoe factory that Aaron and I had scouted as a location for the Resistance. He (and many others) referred to it as our rebel base, but that sounded a little too Star Wars for me, so I just called it the "factory." It was well hidden, embedded among a handful of other vacant warehouses in a derelict industrial area. I assumed most had been deserted when the economy crashed.

Exploring the area further, I discovered an extra storage attic in one of the adjoining buildings that I managed to convert into a somewhat liveable space, with a withered plant and slightly used sleeping bag. It wasn't much but, in some ways, it reminded of my university dorm life.

I was putting a USB in a shoebox when my phone vibrated. I could see by the caller ID—Rebel With a Cause, something he programmed in himself—that it was Aaron calling. Just seeing his name brought a warm tingly smile to my face. I wasn't unaware that Aaron and I might have feelings for one another, but given everything going on, (and that it felt like a betrayal to Brady—even worse that it was Aaron) the thoughts just seemed trivial and I pushed them somewhere deep.

"Checking up on me again?"

"I wouldn't call it checking up. I'd call it more checking in." I could tell by his tone that he was in a good mood.

"Whatever you want to call it. I'm here and I'm fine." As I put the USB into the shoebox I picked up the tattered Che book that he had given me. A photo fell out of the pages and fluttered to the ground. It was a photo taken back during a spring break vacation—a tanned Brady, Ryan, Kayla, and me, sitting around a beach fire. All of us smiling, without a thought or care in the world of what lay in store. It was one of the few photos I had saved when I ran from my dorm.

"Sam? Sam, are you there?"

"I'm here," I said, lost in the memory of that spring day. I took a last look at the group of us and then tucked the photo back in the pages and hid the shoebox up in a loose ceiling tile.

"Good. I was just saying that I heard there was some Guard activity in the area, so I just wanted to ..."

"Check in?"

"Yeah."

It wasn't the first time we had been advised about the Guard patroling nearby. It was almost always a false alarm, so I didn't give it too much thought. Instead, I giggled and lay down on my sleeping bag. "What are you doing right now?"

"Driving. I just dropped off some blankets at tent city. How about you?"

"Nothing. I'm just about to head over to the office."

"Heading to the office—you make it sound so normal. Has Wright talked to you lately?"

"It's been a few days. Why?"

"He wanted to know if you're planning to speak at the O2 anniversary memorial."

I still couldn't believe that it had been almost a year since Kayla's death—a year since my world (everyone's world) had been turned upside down and inside out. "Is he asking or telling?"

"Sam."

"Of course I will. Kay would want me to. Has he picked a location yet?"

"There are three options. He won't announce it until the morning of."

"You think O'Brien and his Elites will do something?"

"I wouldn't put it past them. If they knew you and Wright were in the same place ..."

"And you."

"Yeah, well I'm not as important as Wright or as pretty as you, so I think I'll be fine," he said jokingly. "I am worried about you though."

"Well, it wouldn't be a normal day if you weren't."

"Ha ha. I'm being serious, Sam. The Guard will be on high alert. They're still pissed about our bridge stunt."

"Why? It's not like it did anything. The country knows about the wall and it's still being built. Most want it."

"I think the media is only spinning it that way. Anyway, they'll be expecting us to do something. I'm sure they want revenge."

"Well, I wouldn't want to disappoint them." I made sure to say it with a devious tone.

"Sssaaamm ..." Aaron said my name accusingly. "What are you up to?"

"I don't know. It may be nothing, but Maya and I have been gathering intel, putting some things together."

"Have you told Wright about it?"

"No. I don't even know what it is yet. In fact, I better go ... she's waiting for me. Says she has something to show me."

"What are you working on?"

I looked up at the area where I had just hidden the shoebox containing the USB. "You'll just have to wait and see."

"You're seriously not going to tell me?"

"Not on the phone. I will later. I'll show it to you."

"Okay, fine. I'll let you go. But I was serious about the potential activity in your area. Be careful."

"I will. You, too. I'll talk to you later, when you check in, again."

"You know I will."

I hung up the phone, smiling. Even though I felt he called and worried about me way too much, it was nice to have someone worrying about me, and I usually got off the phone in a lighter mood. With the state of everything, that was a rare feeling.

Everyone in the warehouse was hard at work when I walked in. They were huddled around desks, scanning through papers, and focusing on computer terminals. In another time, another place, someone walking in might actually think it was a typical functioning factory. Aaron had commented that I made "going to the office"—my rebel base—sound normal and, in many ways, it was. It had taken four months to come together, but the group of people in this space, people of all ages, all races, all from different backgrounds, were working with a common goal.

We were protecting and defending our basic rights to information and freedom of expression. And in a short time, this riff-raff room of King rejects and wannabe rebels had come to feel like family.

I had convinced Wright to let me form this base and construct it as a sort of information hub for the Resistance. People like Maya, who could have been running their own dot-com or software firms, were working to break through the restrictions on the Medianet, hack it for information, or plant media flashes intended for the public to hear. We all understood that this was where the real revolution was taking place, and it was a fight I felt comfortable leading.

A group huddled over a table of maps and loose paper jumped up when they saw me approaching. I still hadn't gotten used to the effect my presence had on some. "Hey, guys, what are you working on?"

"Uhhh ..." One of them grabbed a grainy map off the table and handed it to me. "We think we found some satellite images that could be a re-education camp."

"I thought that ever since they started constructing the wall, it was impossible to access the satellite maps."

"The current ones, yes. But Max discovered a site with some older archives."

Max looked up at me sheepishly and I winked at him. "I knew you'd come in handy one day."

Max was only thirteen. Maya and I had stumbled on him while on a scouting trip for supplies—food, medicine, anything we figured could be useful. We were scavenging in a deserted convenience store when he came out from the back with a shotgun aimed at us. He was so hungry and weak that it was difficult for him to hold up the gun. He threatened to shoot us but then dropped the weapon and started to cry when he saw my face and registered who I was.

His family had once owned and run the convenience store but, during the first Immigrant Reorganization Wave, the Guard had stormed in and taken his father and older brother away. They had also emptied out all the food and supplies in the store. Max had hidden in the back, and had remained there alone, living off what little he could manage to scavenge until we arrived. We couldn't leave him. And when I gave him the opportunity to join us, he jumped at the chance. For me, this struggle began with Kayla. For Max, this was about his family. We all believed in what we were fighting for, but it seemed like every one of us had our own personal reasons for getting involved.

"It ... it ... was nothing. I got lucky." His cheeks turned red and he stuttered nervously.

"My grandfather used to say that luck was simply dedication flirting with opportunity." I could see Max thinking about that one. "Let me know if you find anything." He nodded wildly and put his head back down.

Maya raised a knowing and suspicious eyebrow when she saw me. "Let me guess," she said. "You just got off the phone with Aaron."

"How'd you know?" I asked casually.

"Because you always have this look after you get off the phone with him."

"What look? I do not."

"Do so. You're ... happier."

I felt defensive. "I am not. And don't say it like that. We're just friends."

"Mmm–hmmm. Does he know? Cuz I think he'd like to be more than that."

"Can we just concentrate on leading a revolution, please?"

"Yes, sir." Maya gave me a mock salute. "All I'm saying is that in this current climate, we should be doing everything we can while we can. Live in the moment and all that. And I wouldn't mind living in the moment with that boy, cuz he is fiiiiinne. I mean, he's a little scruffy and brainy for my taste, but I think you two would make some nice-looking rebel babies. And let's face it, we could use more recruits ..."

"Okay," I laughed. "Enough. Like I said, Aaron and I are just friends. That's it. Can we focus, please?" I sat down beside her. "What did you want to show me?"

Maya turned to the screen, taking only a second to transform from a gossipy girl into her intense computer-hacker persona. "You know how we've been looking into Advantage Defense?" I nodded. "I've been trying to access their systems because, as you can imagine, they have some pretty amazing firewalls in place. But then I remembered that I saw their name somewhere else. Do you remember the 'Robin Hood' virus that I worked on with the Truth Tellers?"

"How can I forget? It was all over the Medianet."

"Well, the main banks we hit have all upgraded to an offline server, but I kept a copy of all the files we accessed when planting the initial virus." Maya was talking like she had just downed a whole pot of coffee. I had gotten used to it. She always talked fast when she was excited about something. She pulled up a page of files on the screen. "It looks like account numbers, initials, nothing important ... but look at this one." She pointed to a set of numbers:

3585612 AD – Transfer – 4688907 CCA – 25.000.000.

"What am I looking at?"

"I think you're looking at a twenty-five-million-dollar transfer from Advantage Defense to an unknown account. And look at the date. This was transferred months before the election. I would say it was a campaign contribution. Or an investment."

"Why do you think that?"

"Well, look what else I found." She scrolled pages of account activity, highlighting four other identical transfers:

5844389 NC – Transfer – 4688907 CCA – 25.000.000
1318506 BI – Transfer – 4688907 CCA – 25.000.000
8852291 EP – Transfer – 4688907 CCA – 25.000.000
6396421 IS – Transfer – 4688907 CCA – 25.000.000

"So if AD is Advantage Defense, then NC would be Nutri Corp?" I assumed.

Maya agreed. "And Biopharm Innovation, Encor Power ..."

"And Intel Systems." I sat back. "All the companies that are assuming control after the CAP."

"Coincidence?"

I shook my head. "Unlikely. And what's CCA?"

"I can't find CCA anywhere, but I think it could stand for Company Campaign Account or Corporation or Corporate Collective ..."

"Collective!?" I looked at Maya. We had seen this word pop up in a few other places—company policies, documents, emails—but it hadn't really meant anything before. I stood up and started pacing. "Advantage Defense controls weapons and defense systems, and supplies the Guard. Nutri Corp is food and water and, with the CAP, would also control things like essential items, clothing, and accessories. Biopharm is health and medical. Intel Systems is media and technology. And Encor is about to corner the entire continent's power grid."

"And," Maya added, "we already have evidence that Advantage Defense had a hand in the O2 bombing, that Encor orchestrated those energy shortages, and I am sure Biopharm is the reason our medical supplies are in short supply."

"Not to mention those Nutri Corp documents. Proof that they falsified their food and resource projections." I looked at Maya with stark realization. "I mean ... *collectively* ... they not only control but are manipulating everything that matters. Everything, all of it—it's all been orchestrated form the beginning. And everyone has played right into their hands."

"Soon they'll have total power," Maya nodded.

"*Absolute* power," I said. "And with what oversight?"

"The government?"

"Well, that depends. Who is overseeing who? Does this Collective work for King or does he work for them?"

"That's a scary thought."

"Why hasn't anyone else picked up on this yet?"

"Well, with everything going on, the focus isn't exactly on the corporate world. This civil war is all anyone cares about."

"Meanwhile, this *Collective* continues to gain more power and is slowly taking over. Convenient." I shook my head as I thought about something.

"What?"

"Kayla. I always used to make fun of her conspiracy theories, but she was always right about this. There is a bigger truth to what's going on here. Much bigger."

"Isn't that why we're working on Project Kay?"

I nodded.

"Should we tell Wright?"

"Yes. But let's do a bit more research. We should add this info to the Project Kay file. I'll get the USB and, when I get back, I'll help you look into these companies, see what else we can find on them and then ..." I stopped, turned, and did an abrupt double-take as a figure way at the back of the warehouse stole my attention. *No. It couldn't be.* The unmistakable shape of Brady's broad upper body stood in the shadows.

"Sam? What's wrong?" She followed my frozen gaze. "Who is that?"

The hairs on my body all stood at attention as a wave of emotion and nausea hit me. "It's no one. Do me a favor and radio outside. See if anyone responds."

She pressed her com-device. "Adam, Julie? It's Maya. Are you there? Anyone watching the gates, please respond." No voices answered back. She looked back at Brady's waiting figure. "Sam? What is it?"

A cold feeling of dread crawled over me. "It could be nothing ... but be ready ... okay?"

"Ready for what?"

"To run." The tone of my voice was enough to let Maya know I was serious. She turned and started frantically typing on her terminal's keyboard.

As I got closer to Brady, I could see that he was in civilian clothes—a pair of khaki pants and a black jacket. *Could he have left the Guard?* Within a foot of him, I stopped. My initial urge was to hug him—the casual way you hug someone you haven't seen in a while—but his hands were tucked defensively in his pockets and he seemed on edge. Something, everything about him and about the situation, felt wrong.

"Hey, Sam." He smiled half-heartedly.

"What are you doing here, Brady?" I approached him cautiously.

"I came to see you. Needed to see you."

I glanced behind him at an open door where there should have been a person standing watch. All my internal alarm bells were going off. "How did you get in?"

"Through the back. Your security kind of sucks."

"How did you know where to find me?" He didn't answer.

And then I realized. Of course. How could I have been so stupid? So trusting? Our conversations. The ones we had before riots became revolution, and then after, even when we were no longer the "us" we once were, we still checked in. Still needed to hear the other's voice. It was the one thing that gave me hope. Not that we would ever get back together, but that maybe this would finally blow over and things could go back to some semblance of the way they had been before. During those times, hearing his voice was the last tether to normality I had. Looking at him now, I knew the rope was finally about to snap.

"You tracked my phone." It was an accusation, not a question.

"Don't say it like that. You did it to me first. The bridge? I know it was you, Sam."

"I did it to you first? What are you, five years old?"

He didn't have or didn't want to give a comeback.

"*Why* are you here, Brady?"

"Can't a guy come see his girlfriend?" He could see that I was not amused. "Sorry, his ex. His friend? What are we?" he asked provocatively.

"Brady."

"I told you. I needed to see you. Needed to see for myself."

"See what?"

"You." He looked past me. "So, this is it? This is you now?"

"I don't know what you want me to say."

"I want you to say that you're not this. You're not the terrorist they're all saying you are. You're not the Samantha Smart I've seen on TV. That it wasn't you running from the bridge that night. I want you to say that this, ALL of this, everything that happened and is happening is all a big misunderstanding and that you're not standing on *that* side, and I'm not standing on this side ... that there are no sides. I want you to say that we're not over."

He seemed so angry and bitter. Had I done that to him? The heaviness in my chest was increasing, and I could feel my eyes starting to sting from the salty tears I fought to hold back. We stood in silence and stared at one another.

"There's so much you don't know. That you don't understand about King and ..."

Mid-sentence my attention was pulled away. Under the half-zip of Brady's jacket, I saw a recognizable blue. I stepped forward and put my hand on his chest. Pulling the flap of his jacket back, I saw the embroidered emblem of the Guard.

Before I could pull away, he grabbed my wrist and tightly held my hand to his chest.

"How did you get in here?" I had known it from the moment

I had seen him, yet the realization and disbelief of what was happening began to set in. It felt like I had received an emotional punch to the gut. I felt sick. "What are you *really* doing here, Brady?"

His voice dropped to a sharp whisper, "Look, Sam. You need to come with me. Right now. Walk with me out of here and no one will get hurt. I promise."

"Oh, Brady—"

"It's better if you just come with me. I'll tell them that you gave yourself up. They'll go easier on you."

I could see that he actually believed his own naïve words. "You don't know what you're doing. You don't understand who you're working for. If you only knew what we've found ..."

"No, Sam. It's you who doesn't get it," he growled. "You're fighting for the wrong side. You'll see—"

I stepped back and tried pulling away but he held my wrist tight. I looked down at his grip; our two watches were almost touching. "Let go."

"No."

"Brady, let go!" I used a defensive move I had learned in training and twisted my wrist toward his thumb. The move surprised him and forced him to release my hand. In the stairwell behind us, I heard the echo of heavy boots climbing in our direction.

"It's too late. You should have come when I told you."

"What have you done?"

"Me? What have you done, Sam? I never wanted it to be this way."

Turning back to the area where everyone was still working—unaware of the danger that was coming at them because of me—I starting yelling. "WHITE ZERO, WHITE ZERO, WHITE ZERO ... THE BLUES ARE HERE ... THIS IS NOT A DRILL."

Heads snapped in my direction. For a moment, it looked like everyone was frozen in time, and then ...

... Shots were fired from somewhere outside ... footsteps pounded up all the stairwells ...

... Everyone exploded into a fury of movement and panic ...

"RUN!!"

I turned back to Brady. His jacket was off and he was holding a gun on me. Two other rebels came to my aid.

"NO." I stopped and waved them off. "GO."

"But, Sam ..."

"GO ... Help everyone else. NOW!" Reluctantly, they turned and ran for the nearest exit. "Really?" I looked searchingly at Brady. "Is this the part where I say that we both know you won't shoot me?" I started backing away from him. "Brady, this isn't you. This is them. I have to go." I turned to run.

"SAM!" His voice was steady, steadier than I had ever heard it. "I can't let you do that."

I stopped and spun back to face him. Behind me, soldiers and Elites started flowing through the doorways, yelling and firing as people tried to escape. It was already too late. I raised my hands in surrender and put them around my head, staring directly at Brady.

Elites took no time to circle around me. A soldier used the butt of his gun to hit me in the stomach and then push me to the ground. It took about thirty seconds for my hands to be bound and a black bag shoved over my head.

Brady was right. I had done this to myself. I had trusted him.

Was there a specific moment when you knew it was over between you and Brady?

Sam: *(Thinking ...)* There was never just one moment. It's kind of the opposite of falling in love. Things evolve until, one day, you just look at that person and realize that this is it, you're in love. Then comes another day, you look at them and realize that this is it, everything's changed.

Is that what happened?

Sam: I guess. I don't know anymore. I'm starting to wonder if we ever really loved each other at all.

What do you mean?

Sam: Love is supposed to conquer all. Isn't it? Well, that's bullshit. How can a person know they love the other if they don't really know them? I mean, you can think you know someone but, until you're each pushed to your limits, put in those extreme circumstances ... I don't know. Love is complicated. I get that part. What I don't understand is how you can go from loving someone, if you truly love, to feeling nothing at all.

Are you talking about Brady or you?

Sam: I don't know. Next question.

27

NOW

Whatever drug they shot into my neck has worn off. The flashes of my mock escape, the adrenalin, everything feels so fresh, like I've been rudely pulled out of a deep dream. It takes me a minute to settle and gather my senses. I'm seated in a chair, wrists bound behind me, in a room I've never been in before. As my faculties start coming back into focus, I notice a large metal desk with restraints at one end. A shiver runs through me.

There's a shuffle behind me and I jump, realizing that someone else is in the room. Not someone. Brady.

"What is this?"

My throat is dry. Brady doesn't respond. He nods to a camera in the corner of the room.

"What? You don't want King to know about us? The real us? You're an idiot if you think he doesn't already. Why do you think you're in this room with me? They know everything. This is all a game to him, just like using Maya."

"Who's Maya?"

"Doesn't matter."

Brady moves so his back is to the camera and lowers his voice to a whisper. "I never told them about us. They knew some things about us, yes. But I never told them about what we meant to each other."

I roll my eyes and shake my head.

"You don't believe me."

"Should I?"

"That's not fair."

"Really?" I shake my bound wrists behind me. "You really want to talk about what's not fair here?"

"I swear, Sam. I didn't talk to him."

"It doesn't matter. He knows. Do you think it was a coincidence that it was you who found me on the roof?" I can see him thinking about my question, refusing to accept what I know is true. I nod toward the desk. "So, what ... is this the principal's office? I must really be in trouble now!"

"You think this is all a joke? How can you act so cavalier about everything?"

"Cavalier?" I shout back. "Look at me, Brady. Cavalier is all I've got right now."

He tenses. "Shhh ... Sam, lower your voice. Why can't you just cooperate? You're making this harder than it has to be. And for what? You won't win this."

"Win! You don't get it. You never have. It's not about winning."

His tone softens. "Sam, why did you go to the roof?"

"I don't know. I figured King wouldn't expect it." I can see the concern in Brady's expression. "What? You thought I was going to jump? Is that what they're saying?" His look confirms it. I squirm and try to move my arms again. "Might not have been a bad idea."

"Don't say that."

"What do you care, anyway?" I ask sharply. "Do you have any idea what I've gone through? What they've done to me? To my friends?"

I notice him cringe as he scans my welts and bruises. "It didn't have to be this way. If you'd just give them what they want."

"I can't do that, Brady. And you know it. You had to have known I never would. You had to have known what they would do ..." I can't finish.

He steps toward me. From his stance and expression, I can sense an apology forming. "Sam ..."

"Don't." I shake my head and look away. "Please, don't."

For the next couple of minutes, neither of us says a word.

Brady breaks the silence first. "Do you remember the first time we kissed?"

The question surprises me. "Brady, I ..."

"No, I'm not trying to mess with you or anything. I'm asking if you remember."

I hesitate, wondering if this is another mind game. A trap. I'm sure King is listening in somewhere. "Of course I remember. We'd just gone for ice cream at that stand on the beach. We were walking on the driftwood, trying not to touch the sand ..."

"You made it a game. Said the first one to fall off a log and touch the sand loses. Always so competitive ..." he trails off. "But I loved that about you."

I continue. "We came to a gap where a storm drain was flowing into the water. It was a big jump, but you made it."

"I warned you not to jump. It was too far and the log was

wobbly, but you had to prove me wrong."

"I made it, didn't I?"

"Yeah, and you rolled your ankle in the process."

"Put me out of soccer for two weeks. My coach flipped out."

"You fell right into me. Swearing something about hurting your foot. You got so mad at me for laughing at you, but then you looked up and I couldn't resist." He smiles. "You tasted like chocolate chip mint." We both go quiet, reminiscing about the moment. "That was real, right?"

I nod. "It was real."

"How did things get so messed up?"

The vibe in the room shifts. "Are you really asking that question?" I say.

"Are you really going to blame *me* for all of this?"

I shake my head. "No—not for all of it." The words coming out of my mouth are not what I want to say to him, but the floodgates have opened and I can't hold back the hurt and anger anymore. Neither can he.

"I saw you, you know. I was on one of the trucks shipping materials to the Neutral Zone. But of course you knew that."

I think back to the bridge. "Materials for the wall. Those trucks were shipping iron and concrete for construction of the wall that King is building to separate the country, dividing us."

"It's not a bad idea if you think about it. Let Wright and his rebels control the West and King can control the East. People can choose where they want to live. It would put a stop to all this fighting."

"Is that what you think? When has a wall ever been built to create peace? They're building it so they can select who stays and who goes. They're cleansing the East, sending prisoners, rebels, criminals, immigrants, poor people, no-chance offenders—anyone who doesn't meet their standards—to the West. They can say what they want about survival and a stronger nation, but what they're actually doing is playing God. Creating their own version of a perfect world, their world. Their own messed-up, dysfunctional, utopian-dystopian society."

"You don't know that."

"And what do you know?" I snarl back. "Ask yourself that. What do you really know besides the orders you have to follow?"

"I know that you used me to get information about the shipping routes. And I saw you with that TA of yours." His tone is bitter. *"Aaron Mahone.* It was you two leading the strike on the bridge that day. After it collapsed, I saw you running away together."

"Is that what this is about for you? You saw me with another guy and what ... you were jealous?"

He turns and takes a few steps away from me. "You used me, Sam. You betrayed me first." When he spins around, I can see the hurt in his eyes. "When I saw you on the other side, I just knew that it was never going to be any different—not for us."

"Not for any of us."

"There's no going back, is there?"

I slowly shake my head in response. "I saw you, too, you know."

"What?"

"In a security video. You and Ryan—with a group of Guards in this convenience store ..." Brady swallows. The look in his eyes is revealing. "There was this kid we found, hiding out in the back of a store his family used to run. The Guards took everything out of the store, but they left the security cameras—which is what we were really after—we needed the parts and materials. Anyway, when we went over the footage, I recognized you. Imagine my surprise. You, Ryan, other members of the Guard ..."

"Sam, I didn't ..."

"No, you didn't. But you were there. And you didn't do anything to stop them, either. When the owner and his eldest son protested, they were beaten nearly unconscious. Ryan actually looked like he was enjoying himself. You just stood there. Watching. Then you helped drag them away and take whatever was needed from the store. Did you know that they had run that store for twenty-one years? It was their home."

"Sam, we had orders. We were told to clear ..."

"Oh, *orders*." I repeat and emphasize the word back to him to make sure he knows how ridiculous an excuse it is. "Authority is just an illusion, Brady. It only holds power if you let it."

"That's not fair. We've both done things ..."

Before Brady can finish, the door opens. He jumps to the side and stands at attention. Two Guards, one of them Ryan, enter the room and violently lift me from the chair. They hold me tight.

Stick Bitch enters next, followed by King. He doesn't waste a second, striding straight up and backhanding me across the face with an echoing slap. "YOU MADE A FUCKING PHONE CALL?"

I look up, making sure to have a smirk on my face. Maybe it's the adrenalin from my escape, or maybe it's the drugs they've given me, but something makes me feel particularly confident and a little bit *cavalier*. "I was wondering when you'd figure that out. Imagine my surprise, hiding out on the fifth floor, seeing a phone sitting on a desk, picking it up on the off-chance it had a working line out, and then hearing that dial tone. I guess someone forgot to shut those ones off."

King glares at a remorseful Stick Bitch and then turns back to me with an icy stare. "You went too far this time. We're done playing games." He takes off his jacket and loosens the collar around his neck. There's a hint of desperation to his voice and movements. For the first time, I feel truly afraid of him.

The Guards pull me over to the desk. King walks up behind me. I feel his breath on the back of my neck. "My Guards are working on who you made that phone call to. It's only a matter of time before they find out."

He unties the restraints around my wrists. My whole body tenses as two hands slide around my body and over my front. King moves his hand up my chest and slowly slides the zipper down on my jumpsuit. His hands go to my shoulders. He squeezes, grabs the material of my suit in his fists, and yanks the top part down to my waist. Stepping into me, pushing me against the edge of the desk with his whole weight against mine, he speaks viciously into my ear.

"Every summer when I was growing up, my family used to send me to visit my uncle's farm. I learned pretty much everything I ever needed to know there. How to shoot, hunt, live off the land. How to survive. He once told me that you can only truly know that you've broken an animal if you can leave the gate open and they choose not to run away. Open or not, that animal knows where they belong. Of course, my uncle knew that some were more stubborn than others."

He pauses.

"Here's what we're going to do now. My Guards think they can find out who you made that call to before I can get it out of you." He violently slams me down on the desk. My arms are pulled out in front and my wrists are tied down. "Let's find out."

"I thought you said no more games?" I try sounding brave but my own voice betrays me.

"Maybe just this last one." King drops a metal watch, my watch, on the table in front my eyes. I can see the back inscription just inches away. He steps away and seizes the bamboo cane from Stick-up-her-ass.

"Smith." He orders Brady to his side and hands it to him.

This has been King's plan all along—to use Brady against me. I can see out of the corner of my eye that Brady is reluctant to take the stick, but he and I can both tell by the way King is acting that this is a test. Also in my periphery I see Ryan, watching intently. Brady positions himself behind me so that he can't see my face and I can't see him. I know he's looking down at my back, at the new bruises intertwined with old scars. He won't do this. Not this.

King walks to the front of the desk and leans over so we are almost face-to-face. "Who. Did. You. Call?"

I keep my mouth shut but raise my eyes to meet his.

He signals behind me ... to Brady ... I wait for the hit ... but it doesn't come ...

"Do it!" King growls. "And don't stop until she speaks."

Brady hesitates.

"Do it or I'll have you escorted out and let Marshal continue in your place."

I can see the anticipation in Ryan's gaze and I know Brady can see it, too.

"Tell him, Sam. Please ... just tell him."

I grip the edge of the desk and clench my teeth together. "You have your orders."

I can see the shadow of his arm reluctantly rise. SNAP. The thin but sturdy stick whips and stings across my back. SNAP! He hits me harder the second time. I shut my eyes tight and bite my lip, fighting back cries of pain. A steady stream of tears flows down and drips off the edge of my nose to the table.

"Harder," King orders.

CRACK! I whimper when I feel my skin open and know that he has drawn blood.

"AGAIN."

"Sam … please!" Brady pleads. He raises his arm to hit me again.

"Weathers." I say a little louder than a whisper.

"Wait! What did you say?" King prods eagerly.

I close my eyes and swallow. "Trisha Weathers," I finally concede. It's the athlete in me that registers the significance of my words. I know this isn't a game but I also know that whatever this is, King just won. And I know he knows it, too. I can't see, but I hear the door open and a new voice enter the room.

"Mr. President. We've located the recipient of the call."

King looks in the direction of the voice.

"Actually, we didn't have to." The voice hesitates. "There's something you need to hear. And there's an urgent call waiting for you."

"O'Brien?"

"No, sir. They said you'd know who it is."

I can sense a trace of fear in King. He straightens, nervously runs a hand through his hair, and quickly tucks in his shirt. With a sharp scowl at me, he leaves without a word.

The room is silent but I can sense that Brady is still behind me.

"Sam … I …" But he doesn't finish. I hear the stick drop to

the ground and the door to the room click shut.

Thinking I'm alone, I finally let it all go—Kayla, Maya, Brady, everyone.

In between sobs, I hear the faint scuffle of footsteps and I stiffen. A body leans over me and a harsh voice whispers in my ear.

"There, there. Don't be too hard on him."

"Ryan?"

"Hey, Sam."

"What do you want?"

"You know, the first day we saw you walking into the dorm, we were up in the window, rating all the fresh meat. I bet lover boy never told you that we played a game of rock-paper-scissors over who got first dibs on you. I wonder what would have happened if I had picked paper instead of scissors?"

"Nothing," I hiss back.

"Oh, I'm not so sure. You know, Brady didn't want to bring you in. I think we both know that he's too soft for this. He still holds on to some ridiculous fantasy that he loves you. I had to convince him it was the right thing to do. Although, it didn't take much—just a threat that if he didn't, I would. We suspected that you two were still in communication. I told him that if he didn't make a move, if he let you go any further, I was going to turn him in. I made him believe that if the Elite got hold of his phone, knew where to find you, well, they'd probably kill you." He laughs. "He brought you in to save you. How twisted is that?"

"What do you want, Ryan?"

"That's Elite Officer Ryan to you." He presses down on one of my fresh welts. "I don't want anything. Thanks to you, I already have everything."

28

TRISHA WEATHERS—MEDIANET NEWS FLASH

This is Trisha Weathers streaming live over the Medianet. It has been an incredibly eventful day, perhaps the most eventful since the initial days of the Wright Rebellion.

(Pausing)

You'll have to excuse me—I'm not quite sure where to begin.

Mere moments ago, I was about to broadcast a recorded statement from Samantha Smart, who managed to reach me during an attempted escape from the Elite facility where she is being held.

But now that recording will have to wait as I have just received information, confirmed by General O'Brien himself, that Richard Wright, leader of the Wright Resistance, has been shot and killed ...

Again, this is breaking news ... Richard Wright has been shot and killed. The event occurred during a rebel attack in the Neutral Zone. General O'Brien and the Elite were at the wall to stop a rebel protest that turned into a rebel attack. While I question its validity, a report I have been given says that heavily armed members of the Resistance charged a gate at the wall with the intention of attacking. An armed conflict ensued, and the Elite, having no other options and fearing for the safety of the eastern citizens, returned fire. It was during the mayhem that Wright suffered a fatal gunshot wound to the head. General O'Brien has sent us this recorded message:

O'Brien: The Resistance thought they could attack the innocent civilians living east of the wall. And even though the wall is far from completion, the defense system in place worked to keep the armed rebels at bay. Let this be a warning to all Resistance factions and anyone who plans to attack the wall, break the country-wide curfew, or demand the release of Samantha Smart: The Elite will not hesitate to use lethal force against you or any suspected enemies of the state. You've been warned. Your leader is dead. Samantha Smart will be tried and found guilty of treason. This revolution is over.

Trisha Weathers: Those words coming from General O'Brien. And now, at the risk of losing my job and possibly my life, I am going to play you that earlier recording of a conversation between myself and Samantha Smart in its entirety.

(Noise of someone fumbling with a recording device)

Trisha Weathers: Can you say again who this is?

Sam: It's me, Sam.

Trisha Weathers: Samantha Smart?

Sam: *(Frustrated)* Trish, yes. It's me, Samantha Smart.

Trisha Weathers: How are you calling me right now?

Sam: I don't have time to explain ... they're coming for me.

Trisha Weathers: Where are you?

Sam: Some school, maybe a boarding school. I don't know.

Trisha Weathers: Are you all right?

Sam: Listen, I don't have a lot of time. Can you get a message to Aaron and the Resistance?

Trisha Weathers: I'm recording you now, so anytime you're ready.

Sam: Oh, okay ... ummm ... well, I just want everyone to know that I'm okay and I ... umm ...

Trisha Weathers: Sam? Sam, are you there?

Sam: Yes, I just ... I'm just realizing that this could be the last message that you hear from me and that ... ummm ... okay ... I wish I had more time to think, say something epic and inspiring to keep the hope alive ... but the truth is, I'm not feeling all that hopeful these days.

There's a darkness coming. I've seen it. Maybe it's already here, and maybe it's only just beginning. Some people call me a terrorist, others a hero ... maybe I'm both. They say history is defined by those who win the war, and if that's true, then I could end up being the villain in this story.

But I have to believe that what I'm fighting for is right and just. Because if I lose sight of that, if we lose sight of that, then we won't just lose, we'll be lost. Change is inevitable ... it's how we adapt that's important. I guess what I'm trying to say is that King and the Collective might win, but that doesn't mean the Resistance has lost. We only lose if we accept defeat and fall to our knees. I don't know what the future holds. I'm not sure I'll live long enough to see it, but I hope that if it becomes a future we've been fighting to defend, there will still be those out there who can find the strength to stand, and it's to them I leave this message.

I don't know who you are, I don't know where you are, I don't even know when you'll be listening to this—but I want you to know that I'm just like you. I'm scared and terrified, and there are times when I feel it would be easier to just give in. There is no shame in wanting to live. But if you can't stand up and fight for what you value and believe is right, then you're not really living anyway ...

(Noise of yelling in the background ... shuffling ... the line goes dead)

Trisha Weathers: Sam? Sam?

Trisha Weathers *(Live)*: I have a feeling that in only a few minutes, the Elite will come storming in and seize control of this station. As this will likely be my last broadcast, I am going to leave you with a looped recording of this conversation and these clichéd yet fitting final words ... "Vive la résistance" ... I'm Trisha Weathers, standing up and signing off.

10 Minutes Later ...

General O'Brien: "This is General O'Brien. Anyone found rebroadcasting or listening to a Samantha Smart speech will be considered Resistance and detained on the spot.

If you know of anyone rebroadcasting or listening to a Samantha Smart speech and do not report it, you will be guilty of association with the Resistance and will be detained on the spot. A state-wide curfew is still in effect. The Medianet and media airwaves are now under full control of the Elite. Do not try to hack the Medianet. You will be found. You will be caught. You will be punished."

29

NOW

I'm lying on my side, hugging my knees close to my chest in a tight fetal position. My tears have long since dried up but my eyes still feel raw and irritated. I hold out my arm and examine the RESISTANCE tattoo, slowly running a finger over the letters burned into my skin. The thin raw welts on my back are still throbbing from where …

Brady hit me.

The emotional sting of that reality hurts far worse than any damage done from Stick Bitch's favorite toy. Physical pain I can handle. I've always been able to tolerate pain. Suffering it from the hands of someone I love—loved—is something else. It puts me right back into a place I have tried to bury. No, I know Brady is nothing like my father, and I know the circumstances can't be compared. Yet here I am, feeling the same level of resentment and disgust.

This is what King wants. This is all a part of his twisted game, and my anger should be directed at him, but all I can focus on is Brady—his voice when he pleaded with me to give King what he wanted, the sound of that stick snapping on my back when I didn't. He made me feel like it was my fault. If only I had told King what he wanted to hear, he wouldn't have had to do that to me. I hate him. Not for hitting me, but for asking me to do something that he knew I couldn't do.

I hate him. No—I don't.

What was he supposed to do?

If he hadn't gone through with it, King might have done much worse ... to both of us. He did the only thing he could. If the roles were reversed, I might have done the same thing. No. That's just it ... I wouldn't have. I couldn't have. But he did. As angry as I am with him, I'm angrier with myself. I may have given King something that he was going to find out anyway, but I still gave it to him. I gave in. I let him use Brady against me.

I hear the lock on my door click open. I jump at the sound, still clutching my knees but moving so my back is to the wall.

O'Brien's hunched-over silhouette is framed by the doorway. "No need to restrain her. Just close the door behind me."

I swallow nervously as O'Brien limps into the room with his cane. The door shuts behind him.

"Get up," he orders me.

I stand, trying not to let him see the pain and stiffness in my body. I keep my back securely against the wall. Just being in his presence makes my knee throb.

O'Brien moves so he is standing inches away from me. He leans forward, letting his cane support his weight.

"I make you nervous."

I don't answer.

"Good," he says. "I should. I can tell that my reputation

precedes me. That's the way it should be. That's what King doesn't get. He likes to play these games behind closed doors. Doesn't like showing his whole hand. I'm the opposite. It's not about the hand, it's about the person holding the cards. I think it's much more effective getting straight to the point. Don't you?"

He waits for me to respond but I keep my mouth shut. His knuckles whiten as they tighten around his cane and I take a breath, preparing myself for a blow.

"How long has Trisha Weathers been Resistance?"

I don't move or take my eyes off his.

"Not that it really matters anymore. I'm just asking out of my own personal curiosity."

I give away nothing.

"I suspected her five months ago but my Elites found nothing. By how chummy you two sounded, I assumed you would know."

I try to contain a smile. Weathers must have released our conversation over the Medianet.

"At this point, you've figured out that your little phone call was broadcast on the Medianet. Weathers managed to loop it on air ... right after she announced that Richard Wright had been assassinated."

My eyes open wide.

"No games. It's true. I was the one who pulled the trigger," he says with satisfaction. "He had the misguided notion that he could take his little 'Smart Protest March'—that's what they called it, by the way, in honor of you—he thought they could march right through the wall." He can see my anger building. "Like you, he let his arrogance guide him, blind him. Shame, really. All those people ... dead ... because of you."

Is this another trick?

As if can he read my mind, O'Brien reaches into his pocket and pulls out his communication device. He hits a play button and holds it out for me to hear the earlier broadcast ...

"... mere moments ago, I was about to broadcast a recorded statement from Samantha Smart, who managed to reach me during an attempted escape from the Guard Elite facility where she is being held ... but now that recording will have to wait as I have just received information, confirmed by General O'Brien himself, that Richard Wright, leader of the Wright Resistance has been shot and killed ... Again, this is breaking news ... Richard Wright has been shot and killed."

He stops it. "I'm sorry to be the one to tell you."

"No, you're not," I say. All I can think about is Aaron. Is he dead, too?

"No. You're right. I'm not." He grins. "I have to tell you, though, I didn't count on your little speech hitting the Mediawaves right after. I knock them down and there you go, picking them right back up again."

A cockroach scurries along the floor. O'Brien uses his cane to squash it. "You're like one of these cockroaches. No matter how many times I step on you ..." he lifts his cane and the bug starts to run, "... you just keep moving along."

He steps forward and stomps down on it. Turning his foot left and right, he makes sure the bug is dead before lifting his shoe to see the brown goo staining the floor.

"The thing is," he continues, "your little speech has given the people hope again. And I gotta tell ya, hope is a dangerous thing right now—especially for your kind."

"Does King know you're here?"

"King?" He half laughs. "The time for King knowing things is coming to an end."

"I thought you two were friends?"

"As you well know, Miss Smart, in these trying times, all kinds of relationships are put to the test. King and I have served well together, but all good things ..."

"So, are you using him or is he using you?"

"Sweetheart, we're all being used in some way or another. It's just that some of us know when to use that to our advantage."

"So, what? You made a deal with the Collective or whatever they're called?"

"You do like to push it, don't you?" O'Brien grins. "Okay, seeing as your time is also coming to an end, I'll humor you. The Collective has plans. I happen to factor into those plans, and King, well, he's the pretty face we needed. Handsome, intelligent, smooth, we just had to stroke that ego and let his hubris allow for easy manipulation. Every cause needs a face ... as you well know."

He looks at me and I can tell he's calculating what to say next. "I respect you, you know that. You've earned it. You've put up a good fight. And that's why I'm here—not torturing or playing the mind games that King likes to play, but conversing with you—appealing to your rational side. Everybody thinks that I'm this ruthless tyrant, but the truth is, I just do what needs to be done in order to get things done. Don't get me wrong, there are lots of things I could do to you or your friends. Things you couldn't even imagine. Things you don't want to imagine."

He pauses to let the hidden threats sink in. "You and I both know this is over. Wright is dead. You're here. The Resistance is scattered and on the run. All those years of playing sports must have taught you to know when you've been outplayed; to recognize when it's time to be a good sport and let the clock run out."

"What are you asking of me?"

"To do what you do. Speak to the people. Help them to realize that it's in their best interest to stop fighting and let their government lead." He stares at me, searching for something. "I believe that there is a part of you—even if it's a small part—that understands and agrees with what we're trying to do."

"Even if I did, they're not going to listen to me. That's what free will and free choice are all about."

"*Free* will and *free* choice. It amuses me that you ever thought they existed. Not everyone will listen to you, but I expect many will."

"And for what? So we can all blindly follow you into whatever totalitarian future you have planned?"

"A safer society. Assurance that there will be enough for those who deserve it, that our country will stay strong when others go weak. Did you ever stop to ask yourself if this is the future people want? There's an understanding that change has to happen."

"What does any of that even mean? The people don't want this. A world of hate, control, dividing us in two."

"You don't think that the divide was already there? How do you think we've gotten this far? All we're doing is making it concrete. And as far as the people wanting it, people want what they are told to want. Survival is human nature, and our future doesn't just guarantee that this country will survive, we will thrive."

I am so sick of hearing that line. "At what cost?"

O'Brien smirks. "Have you ever had to clean or reorganize

anything? A storage shed, a closet, perhaps?"

"What?"

"We've all had to do it at one time or another. Purchased or collected too many useless things that we stuff into one space, hoping to forget about them, until one day we realize that we just can't stuff anything else in. What do we do? Do we shut the door and leave it alone, hoping it won't one day come tumbling down on top of us? Or do we deal with it? I've always been a man who deals with things, Miss Smart.

"Now, nobody actually likes the task of reorganizing. It's messy, and there are decisions   that we have to make, things that have to be dealt with or thrown out. Things we might be attached to. But are they necessary?"

He pauses and bangs his cane on the floor. "So, we set to the task. And we don't do it by pulling one thing out at a time. No. We pull everything out at once—making a bigger mess than we first started with. Then, after we deal with everything we need to—assess, sort, throw out, what have you—we set to the task of reorganization. We start putting things back. Things we need, that we deem important, of value. And we don't just throw them back in, we organize and calculate where each item should go so we don't end up with the mess we had in the first place. And when we're all done, we step back and look at our work. Tired but pleased with what we've accomplished." He smiles. "Now ... Miss Smart, I ask you. Is that space better or worse off than when we started?"

"You can make all the twisted analogies you want. I'm never going to agree to help you *reorganize* this country's future. To deal with people like they're some form of clutter. Tossing them aside the way you would an old pair of shoes or favorite childhood toy. I'll never join your side."

"I'm not asking you to join our side. Unlike King, I don't believe we need you for anything. You are that old pair of shoes—once popular and in style, could still be functional, even, but really just taking up space. What I am asking is that you do one last useful thing. Help to stop the killing and set progress as a priority. You're not just losing this battle, you've lost. How you accept defeat is up to you now. Do you continue to lose more lives or do you let the recovery process begin? One side was always going to lose this revolution. It's how all revolutions must end. It might not be the end you want, but there is a part of you that understands it needs to end at some point." He pauses again. Giving me time to think. "How many more lives are going to be lost, Samantha Smart? How many?"

He walks to the door and taps on it with his cane. It opens. "You know, I can understand why King and everyone else is so taken by you. It's a shame you're on the other side. I've enjoyed this little chat. I'll give you some time to think about what I said."

30

SHERMAN ROGERS—MEDIANET NEWS

Good evening, everyone. I'm Sherman Rogers, host of the Medianet News link.

The dust has begun to settle on what many in the social Medianet circles are calling "The Wall Brawl." The Guard Elite have taken full control of the Neutral Zone, surrounding both sides of the wall with a 24/7 patrol. President King has urged all citizens needing to cross the wall to apply for a Neutral Zone Pass card. NZ passes can be obtained at your local Guard Authority.

President King has expressed condolences to supporters of the Wright Rebellion, saying that Richard Wright was a fierce competitor and intelligent leader. He honored the rebel leader with a moment of silence and has ordered a twelve-hour ceasefire to allow for a proper memorial.

Amidst protests and general concern, President King's Corporate Amalgamation Policy is nearing completion and final implementation. Intel Systems has assumed control of all telecommunication services and, in a few days, will be allowing unlimited restricted access to the Medianet. This comes as a relief to the majority of the public that has been without Medianet access for over a week. A spokesperson for Intel Systems has sent us the following statement:

"We at Intel Systems are happy to work with our one-time competitors as a team. Where once people saw bidding wars and feuding advertisements, they will now see one corporation united with a collective goal. Intel Systems understands the responsibilities that come with overseeing such an important sector of society. We are not autonomous.

"Intel Systems will be working together with other leaders in the corporate sector: Encor Power, Biopharm Technologies, Nutri Corp, and Advantage Defense, all of us committed to serving the public and to growing the industries that we now oversee. While the rest of the world struggles with an economic crisis, the CAP is designed to help us systematize, which has allowed us stability and the power to create more jobs. We look forward to working with the other heads of industry as a Collective 5 to create a coherent, connected, and cohesive organizational system. Together, unified, we will grow and build a model of public, economic, and environmental sustainability that we hope will extend into other countries around the world. The C5—Securing our future through Innovation. Opportunity. Progression."

And finally, on the eve of Richard Wright's memorial, and just days away from the one-year anniversary of the October 2 bombings, the fate of terrorist Samantha Smart has been decided. She and other members of the Resistance have been found guilty of treasonous activity against their government and conspiring to destabilize the Collective Command. All will face execution by firing squad. Fittingly, the public executions will take place in the ruins of Hickory Stadium on the anniversary of the notorious bombings that ignited the now defunct revolution. Intel Systems will be broadcasting the executions as they occur over this Medianet link. However, if you would like the opportunity to attend the live event, tickets can be obtained through your local Guard facility.

In other news, Biopharm Technologies believes it has made a breakthrough with the T8 virus that was spreading from the Western zone into the East. Those in the East seeking a vaccine are encouraged to go …

31

Eight corners, four walls, one ceiling, and one floor. I pass the time pacing in my cell. Sometimes, just to spice things up, I lunge around in a circle, touching the ground with my fingers as I dip low or walk backwards with my eyes closed to see if I can guess when my back will hit the wall. Every few hours, I stretch and do exercises to try and strengthen my knee.

It's been days (I think) since O'Brien came to visit. Days inside my cell with no contact with the outside world—except when the door opens and a voice orders me to stand facing the wall, and then a Guard enters to exchange my portable toilet and leave a tray of stale food. Each time the Guard asks if I have considered O'Brien's proposal, and each time I answer with a "Tell O'Brien he can go ..." but the door always slams closed before I can finish. Sadly, it's the most exciting part of my day ... or night. With no natural light, living in a constant darkness lit only by the fluorescent glow that seeps in through the bottom of the door, time has become irrelevant.

I'm relieved to have a break from King and his games but it bothers me that they're leaving me alone. Why? What's going on? They're doing this on purpose. Trying to break me by making me go crazy. Wondering when someone will come and get me. What King or O'Brien has planned for me next. What they're going to try and get me to say or do. How long they're going to leave me like this. If what O'Brien said is the truth. Is Wright dead? Is Aaron? What's going on out there while I'm in here?

I let out a frustrated growl, punch the wall, and then let my body slide to the floor. Hugging my shins tight, I rest my chin on my knees and wonder how long it takes for a person to start going crazy. Because I think I might be. It wasn't long ago that I began to hear voices. First they were just whispers. I thought someone was talking in the hallway or in the room next to me, but then the voices became clearer and more familiar— my mother, father, grandfather, Kayla, even Brady—asking me questions, talking to me. At first I ignored them, tried to cover my ears and tune them out. But then I started to find them oddly comforting. They made me feel less alone, and now I welcome them.

Well, not all of them. My father still has some pretty degrading things to say ...

"Look at you now, Sammy. Always trying to be the hero. Defender of the helpless. Fighting for a lost cause. Look where it's gotten you. No one cares about you. Your boyfriend is right—you're on the wrong side, sweetheart. Or maybe you're exactly where you want to be, with the weak. You always were good at taking a beating ..."

"SHUT UP!" I yell out and hide my head in my arms. "Get it together, Sam."

"*Sam?*" It's my grandpa. "*You don't have to listen to him. You don't even have to listen to me or anyone but yourself. I'm proud of you, Sam. No matter what they do to you, stay true to yourself. You will never be lost if you follow your own direction.*"

Kayla jumps in next. "*Listen to your grandpa, Sam. Always full of things you need to hear. You need to stay strong. I wish I could be there with you. Just think of the cute revolutionary outfits we could have worn together.*" I giggle. "*We made a good team, you and me. I miss you.*"

"I miss you, too."

The door lock clicks open. Without being asked, I stand up and turn to face the wall. It's too early for dinner, I think. Or is it? Maybe it's King, finally back to finish what he started. It could be O'Brien, here to ask if I'll do what he wants.

I hear the door shut, then another familiar voice. "Sam?" At first I think I'm imagining it, back to the voices again, but then a hand touches my shoulder. I cringe at the touch and jump away.

Brady.

"Sam?" His voice is soft as he takes a step toward me.

I don't even realize that I'm backing away until I hit a wall and there's nowhere else to go.

He watches me recoil and lowers his head. I can see the remorse in his eyes. "I don't have much time. You were right. They know, have always known about us. They used me to get to you. And I let them. Did exactly what they all wanted from me. Ryan's been a part of it from the beginning. Made a deal to get the Elite uniform. You should see him … he's become O'Brien's personal little lackey. But Sam, you have to believe me. I didn't say anything. I wouldn't do that to you."

"I used to think there was a lot you would never do." I mean for it to sting.

"Sam ..."

I don't like the way he's looking at me. It makes me feel even more vulnerable. "Why are you here? What do you want?"

"If I didn't ... Ryan would have ..." He stops. "I'm sorry. I'm so sorry. For what they made me ... for what I did to you. For everything." I can see that his apology isn't just words. He reaches for me. "Sam, I understand if you can't, but I need ..."

"I forgive you," I interrupt. "But not because you need me to. Because I need me to." He nods. I know he wants me to say more but I can't. Looking at him up close, I see a purple welt on his cheek. "What happened to you?"

"It's nothing. Ryan and I had it out. Sam, I have to tell you something. They've decided ..." he can't get the words out.

"What?"

He hangs his head so he doesn't have to look me in the eye.

"They're going to execute you."

I know his words are true. I've known it for days. I can't say I'm that shocked or surprised, and yet it takes all my strength to keep my knees from buckling.

"It's all over the Medianet. It's disgusting. They're ... making it public. You and a couple of others. It's supposed to symbolize the end of the Resistance, marking the O2 anniversary."

"When?" I whisper.

"Tomorrow. At Hickory Stadium."

I can hear Brady talking about the details, I know he's saying something important, something that I should know about, but the only thing I can focus on is the word that hits me like a wave crashing down and engulfing me—execute. He takes a tentative step forward and I can feel that he wants to touch me, hold me …

The door opens and a head leans in. "Time's up, Smith."

"Sam, I know this is my fault."

"It's not. I don't blame you for this. Not anymore."

"I'm going to make it right—I promise." He turns toward the door.

"Brady? Is … do you know … Is Aaron dead, too?"

I can see the hurt in his expression. "No. He's on the run, but the Elite are tracking him down."

I can't hide my relief and I know that Brady sees it. He wants to say more but, instead, gives me one last look, nods, and leaves. When the door closes, I let my knees give in to the weight and I crumble.

Execute.

I'm going to die.

Everyone dies.

But I'm going to die tomorrow.

I listen for the voices. But they don't come again.

32

TRISHA WEATHERS—MEDIANET HACK

This is Trisha Weathers, reporting to you from an undisclosed location. Our Medianet hack allows me to speak to you for only four minutes.

The Resistance survives. The "Wall Brawl" was not a planned attack. It was a peaceful protest with women, children, and people of all ages. O'Brien and the Elites opened fire on innocent and unarmed civilians.

I repeat, the "Wall Brawl" was not an attack; it was a massacre. Aaron Mahone is encouraging as many of you as possible to keep the hope alive—fight for Samantha Smart. Fight to stand up. We don't have much time but, on the eve of Samantha Smart's execution, I want to leave you with this footage obtained from a hidden USB recovered by members of the Resistance.

Sam is on screen. She's alone, seated in the warehouse, taping herself with a computer camera.

"Hi ... I'm Samantha Smart, but many of you already know that from this image."

(The famous picture of Sam holding Kayla in her arms at the stadium pops up.)

"The one some of you don't know, or have chosen to forget about, is the girl in my arms—Kayla Marchette; I called her Kay."

(The image switches to another video—handheld-camera footage of a locker room full of sweaty, mud-covered girls, in soccer uniforms. There's music blaring, and the girls are all taking turns dancing in the middle of a circle with a large trophy in their hands.

Kayla does a moonwalk into the circle and then begins to do the "running man" dance move. She's laughing and celebrating with everyone else. At one point she looks up at the camera. "Come on, Sam, get in here."

Sam's amused voice is heard off-camera. "No thanks, I'm having way too much fun watching you."

Kayla takes the cue and starts doing another crazy dance move. "This one's for you, Sam." She points at the camera, smiles, and continues dancing ...

The screen changes back to the image of Sam holding Kayla's body. The effect of the two extremes is powerful. Sam, sitting in front of the computer, flashes back on screen.)

"Kay wasn't a terrorist. She was a daughter, a soccer player, a student, a bad dancer ... she was my best friend. I've been searching for the evidence to clear her name. Going around, trying to prove that she had nothing to do with the O2 attack, thinking that if the truth of that day came out, it could change something.

But I've come to realize that it doesn't matter. It still

happened. She's still gone. And finding out who really did it isn't going to change where we are now. In my search for the truth, I've met hundreds, maybe thousands of you out there, who've been telling me your own stories. You say that I inspire you, but it's you who inspire me. Every person I meet, every story you tell, gives me the courage to keep going.

Kayla once told me that this revolution will start and end with people ... I didn't get it then. My hope is that if you see these faces, hear their stories, that maybe we won't see each other as the other anymore. Maybe we'll start to realize that we all feel, laugh, fear, hate, love ... we're all just the same."

The video ends.

33

One last time, I'm taken out of my cell. One last time, my hands are bound behind my back. One last time, I'm brought in front of King. Brady, Ryan, Stick Bitch. Everyone but O'Brien is here.

King nods and waits for me to kneel before him. And one last time, I stand tall and refuse.

"Defiant until the end," he says to me.

"A girl's got to have something."

"You know, believe it or not, I'm going to miss you. I was hoping we'd have more time. I believe there's still much to learn from one another. But with Wright gone and the Resistance down to a minor annoyance, it's time to take this country into its new era."

There's something different about King. It's subtle, but he seems more controlled.

"Sorry I'm going to miss out on your Brave New World."

"Oh, don't be bitter. Just because you're going to be executed in a few short hours doesn't mean you'll be gone. You, Samantha Smart," he reaches out and strokes the side of my face, "had an important role to play in all this. Don't you forget that."

I pull my head back and look away.

"The people certainly won't forget it. Do you know that tickets for your execution sold out in less than an hour?"

"You're disgusting."

"I'd love to take credit but it was O'Brien's idea. Personally, I think we should keep you around a bit longer. There's still a use for you. But he's right; it's what the people want and it's time to move on. I have one last question for you, though. And I really do hope you answer it truthfully."

He turns and motions to Brady.

"Smith came to you yesterday and told you about the execution. That's not the question, it's a fact. I wanted to give you two some time together. Call it a final gift."

I look at Brady. His jaw is clenched so tight I can see the tendons and veins in his neck popping out. He doesn't move or look my way.

"What I'd like to know is how you felt the moment he told you that you were going to die?"

I think about all the smartass comments I could make, anything to make myself sound braver than I'm feeling. But I'm tired of keeping up the brave facade. I'm just tired. "Scared." It's a simple word but it's the truth.

"And now?" He steps closer. "Knowing you have hours left?"

"Still scared," I say with a hint of irritation.

He gives me the same look he had during my interrogations when he didn't believe me. When he knew I had more to say.

"Relief," I finally admit. "I feel relieved." It's a surprising truth, even for me, but a truth nonetheless. I'm not sure why I give it to him.

King gives a satisfied smile. "You see, you and I really aren't that different. We understand each other. The burdens and expectations placed on us by others. To accept a role thrust upon us. It starts to get away from you ..."

He pauses as if he just now realizes that the rest of the room is listening. Appearing to collect himself, he turns to Stick Bitch. "Roberts ..."

Stick Bitch stands at attention. She has a name? Not that it really matters, but learning her name makes me feel strangely content. Like I finally have something on her.

King continues, "... you will go with the other detainees in one transport. Smith, Marshall, you two will accompany me and Smart."

Making Brady go with me all the way to the execution—is this another "gift" from King, or his own sadistic way of making me suffer one last time?

I'm taken outside and toward a waiting helicopter on the soccer field of the school. They don't bother to put a hood over my head. What's the point? Everywhere I look, there are Guards and other faces watching intently as I'm led away. Across the field, being loaded into a second helicopter, I see Maya—limping on her bad leg—with a couple of other familiar faces, all linked together. I wonder if they've been told what's about to happen. Is it better or worse to know? At the last second, before stepping into the chopper, Maya turns her head and meets my gaze. She gives me a quarter-smile and nods—a goodbye, maybe. I do my best to return it.

The noise from the helicopter makes it too loud for anyone to talk. Not that we have anything to say, anyway. What does one say when on the way to her execution? Nice weather we're having? Good day to watch people die and humanity falter?

For most of the ride, King keeps his eyes on me, watching as Brady and I exchange quick glances with one another.

I have been with Brady long enough to know giveaways and tells. A bouncing left leg means that he's excited about something. Holding his right hand in his left while he strokes and massages his right thumb means he's nervous—really nervous. He used to get this way before playoff games when he knew the team was counting on him to perform. He notices me looking at his hands and quickly stops. He meets my eyes for just a second and then turns his attention out the window. His evasiveness gives everything away—he's planning to do something. But what? Things are too far gone. There's nothing he can do to stop the events that have been put in motion—nothing without putting his own life in danger. I want him to look back at me. I want to give him some shake of the head, some look that tells him to leave whatever he's planning alone. But he won't turn away from the window.

I focus my attention on Ryan. He's sitting across from me but his casual glances fall on King. Of the two of them, Ryan has always been the calm and collected one. He never seemed to care about anything enough to let it get to him; but I can see by the way he's incessantly tapping his fingers on the weapon in his lap that something has him nervous and fidgety, too. If anyone should be nervous, it should be me, but I find myself unusually calm. Instead of thinking about my own impending death, I can't help but wonder what it is about King that has Ryan so on edge.

The ride to Hickory Stadium doesn't feel long enough. Not for me. King reaches over and puts his hand on my shoulder. His touch makes me jump. He points out the window and I look to see the stadium coming up quickly. I can see the giant gaping hole left from the bombing. The H, I, and O have fallen off the top of the structure—a modern-day ruin. There's a sea of people both outside and in. The people are what King wants me to see.

Lines of Guards form a blue wall around the perimeter of the stadium. The closer we get, the more I can see clearly that the masses outside the stadium walls are waving protest signs. It's an all too familiar sight and a chill crawls through me as I remember the chaos of that day ... remember the shock I felt the moment I looked down and saw the blood saturating Kayla's shirt. Maybe it's fitting that this ends where it all began.

The helicopters hover and then land on an open section of turf inside the stadium. I'm taken out and, as the propeller noise from the helicopters shuts down, I am overwhelmed by another deafening sound, this one coming from the thousands lining the stands, cheering at our arrival in the same way they used to cheer for a scoring drive.

Up on the big stadium screen, they flash a close-up of my face as we exit the chopper, and the crowd responds with a mix of cheers and boos. The screen changes to show the cheering faces in the crowd, those that have been lucky enough to purchase tickets to watch me die. Just like outside the stadium, a wall of armed Guards circles the inside of the field. There's a military-style canvas structure with a long tunnel leading to the edge of a large rectangular platform built on the fifty-yard line. One side of the platform is lined with armed Elite—the ones, I assume, assigned to shoot me—while on an adjacent side stands a lone microphone, obviously placed to allow King to address his public.

I take in the reality of this spectacle and I'm confronted with the realization that the world I have been trying to fight against, trying to prevent from happening, is already here. I'm living it.

With all the distractions around me, I have failed to notice O'Brien approaching the group. I also can't see Brady anywhere. How could he leave me now?

The noise from the crowd is far too loud for me to hear what O'Brien is saying to King, but I see him point to a glass spectator box, and I follow his finger up to a tinted window with five shadowy figures outlined behind it. The glare off the glass makes it impossible to see their faces, but I guess I'm looking at them, The Collective, come to watch my execution.

King walks forward into the tent. Maya and the others are led from their helicopter and are forced to stand in a line. They place me at the back with her directly in front. She tries to turn and face me but an Elite uses his gun to give her a hard nudge in the ribs. As they lead us into the tent, I glance over at O'Brien speaking with Ryan and two other Elites. Whatever he's saying makes Ryan and the others nod and then start jogging toward one of the stadium tunnels. Again I look around for Brady but see nothing. As much as I don't want him to see me die, I also don't want him to leave me like this. A hand on my back nudges me to move forward. I snap my head around and am confronted with O'Brien's menacing face.

"Let's get this show on the road, shall we? No time like the present to control the future."

Once we're inside the tent, things start to move quickly. A woman looks King over, adjusting his hair and straightening his jacket. When she's finished and King looks his presidential part, he walks directly into the tunnel leading toward the podium. O'Brien walks behind him. The crowd erupts at their appearance and begins to chant King's name. My line is maneuvered toward the entrance to the tunnel. Guards with machine guns and stoic faces surround us.

I want to turn to one of them and scream: "Do you know what the hell you're about to do? DO YOU KNOW? DO YOU GET IT?" But it won't make any difference. Outside, the crowd quiets and, through the loudspeakers, I hear King begin his speech.

"We are gathered together today for two reasons. First, to commemorate those who were lost one year ago today, right in this very stadium. Brave lives, tragically taken too early due to the senseless acts committed by individuals who tried to attack us from within. Those acts drove the citizens of this country against one another. Neighbor against neighbor, friend against friend, and even loved ones turned on one another as we fell deeper into a destructive revolution. Was it dark times? Yes. Are we through those times yet? I'm afraid to say, not quite.

"Change two letters in revolution and you get revelation. Through this dark time, we have seen our darkest selves and we know what has to be done to move forward. The change that this country needed is happening, and it's starting with you. It's happening in this moment, and it will continue to happen after we have laid to rest the demons from our past.

"The second reason we are here is to address those demons. Today, the executions of Samantha Smart and her rebel conspirators will mark a new beginning for this country. A beginning that will require discipline, sacrifice, and faith. Faith in your government and faith in one another. We are working to create a nation that will survive the problems plaguing the world. Where others weaken, we will strengthen. Where others merely survive, we will thrive." (I can't help but roll my eyes.) "We will grow strong together, and together our strength will be a message to others that we are the greatest nation in the world."

The crowd erupts. The Guards surrounding us are so taken by King's speech that they don't notice or don't care when Maya leans over to me. "I still think you give a better speech."

I smile. "I don't know. The revolution/revelation thing was pretty good. But thanks."

"I guess this is it."

"I guess so."

"The only regret I have is not getting to know you better. I think we could have become good friends."

"We are," I say back.

She nods. "If by some miracle you survive this, I've been wanting to tell you that right before the Elite stormed in, I dropped all that banking information I found into our offline K-box. And if not you, maybe someone will find it one day—know what to do with it."

"Maybe." I'm inspired by Maya's urge to keep fighting until the very end, and I find myself envying her strength and optimism.

O'Brien's voice sounds over a soldier's com-device: "Bring them out."

We are taken into the tunnel. At the end near the opening, I see a soft blue light. Not exactly the white light I was expecting, but not many expectations I've had for my life have worked out the way I thought. The group is stopped and the first prisoner is led out, met by a noise of subdued cheers.

Is this actually about to happen?

I hear them announce his name, followed by a list of alleged crimes against the government and Collective Command. I half-expect a drum roll or something announcing the moment to come, but the only thing I hear is the deafening silence of the crowd and then multiple shots firing. In front of me, Maya's body shudders with the shots. I wait to hear the cheers continue but only silence follows.

The next couple of prisoners are led out, one after the other, and the same process is repeated. Introduction. List of offenses. Silence. Shots. A thud from a body hitting the platform. Silence.

Maya's next.

Two Guards grab her by the arms and lead her out. She looks back at me just before disappearing through the flaps in the tunnel door. It's a goodbye. I want to shout something out to her ... something ... anything ... but there's nothing to say.

As it did with the others, my heart begins to beat fiercely while King reads the list of offenses. My chest starts to ache; it feels heavy and I have difficulty breathing. Maybe I'm having a heart attack. Maybe I'll die before they can kill me—a final defiance. But my body betrays me. I close my eyes and wait. In my mind, I see Kayla standing up on the platform and, no matter how hard I try to picture Maya's face, Kayla is all I can see. Where is the rescue party? Where is the miracle that's going to stop this and save—

Guns fire.

A thud.

Silence.

I'm next.

34

*"In the end, the only thing that anyone
can really take from you
is what you let them have."*
~ Grandpa Smart

Two sets of hands seize my arms and walk me the length of the tunnel. Without their support, I'm not sure I'd be able to stand. My legs feel like cement pillars in four feet of mud, each forward step a bigger struggle than the last. I'm not trying to get away or stop them from taking me out; it's just my mind working against my body. They stop me at the exit. Through a crack in the flap of the tent, I see King standing in front of the microphone.

"And now, for what I guess you could call our main event. The reason many of you have come here tonight—the reason many of you are tuning in to our live Medianet broadcast—Samantha Smart."

At the same time King is introducing me, one of the Elites standing at my side leans close to my ear. I expect a nasty comment but instead he whispers, "Aaron's here."

"What?" I try to turn but the Guard tightens his grip.

"Eyes forward." He stands at attention, avoiding eye contact and looking like a perfectly well-trained member of the Elite. But I know what I heard—I think. Maybe my mind is playing tricks on me again, trying to give me something to hope for. I want to ask him again, but the flaps of the tunnel door part and I'm pushed onto the field.

Aaron's here? I'm positive that's what I heard. Why would he say that to me? Did he say that to me? If so, what does it mean?

I anticipated cheers and angry shouts but, as I'm guided forward, the crowd becomes eerily silent. All the lights in the stadium have been turned off except for a few shining directly on the platform where King is standing. I look out into darkness. If I hadn't seen the crowd when we came in, I wouldn't believe anyone is here now.

I'm led down the field and up a flight of stairs. I'm dizzy. I'm going to be sick. Everything is a blur of images. King glares down from his podium. The big screen zooms in on my gaunt and bruised face as the Guards take me to the end of the platform. I hardly recognize myself. There are no bodies, but dark red bloodstains are splattered over the ground and wall. It reminds me of an old gladiator movie I saw when I was little. I never could understand the idea that humanity allowed people to kill and die for sport in a stadium and yet, here we are. History repeating.

They make me stand above a taped X on the floor. The Guards let go and move off to the side. I guess they're not afraid of me running anywhere at this point. I could run. I could try to get away. But I can't move. I look at the Guard who I'm sure had spoken the words "Aaron's here" for something else—a nod, a wink—anything to let me know that he actually said those words. And what did he mean by it? Aaron is here with others to rescue me? Or Aaron is here to watch me die? That's probably it. Aaron got a message to me so I would know I'm not alone.

I'm numb. A voice commands me to kneel and, this time, I follow the order without objecting. Looking up, I see King standing in front of me, armed Elite soldiers on either side of him, awaiting their order to fire.

Then, just behind King, something catches my attention. A speck of bright light waves in the air. Then another comes on. And another. One after another, the light from peoples' cell phones flashes on and begins to slowly wave—a tiny little sea of stars—scattered around the darkness. I'm confused. I don't understand. Is this for me? They came here to watch me die. Now they're ... what? What does this mean?

King witnesses the silent protest and steps up to the microphone, speaking quickly.

"Samantha Smart." His voice is directed at me. "You have been convicted of terrorist and treasonous acts against your government. Your words fueled a revolution and your actions have directly led to the deaths of innocent civilians. Let your execution give justice to those you've harmed, and serve as a warning to those who would try to emulate your ..."

King's voice abruptly cuts out. He taps the microphone, trying to get the audio back. Suddenly, the sound of a recording cuts in over the loudspeakers. I recognize it instantly.

"... Yes, I just ... I'm just realizing that this could be the last message that you hear from me and that ... ummm ... okay ... I wish I had more time to think, say something epic and inspiring to keep the hope alive, but the truth is, I'm not feeling all that hopeful these days. There's a darkness coming; I've seen it ... maybe it's already here, and maybe it's only just beginning ..."

A confused mumble rises from the darkened stands. O'Brien,

King, and every Guard on the podium frantically scan the stadium.

"SHUT IT DOWN. NOW." King shouts from the stage. Guards scramble but the recording continues.

"... *Some people call me a terrorist, and others a hero ... maybe I'm both. They say history is defined by those that win the war and, if that's true, then I could end up being the villain in this story. But I have to believe that what I'm fighting for is right and just, because if I lose sight of that, if we lose sight of that, then we won't just lose, we'll be lost ...*"

Is that Aaron? I look in the direction of the Guard who whispered in my ear, but he's gone. Shots ring out, causing me to jump and flinch. But I'm not hit. King and the Elites have their eyes turned to the opening in the stadium, toward a rising rumble of shouts and chants. The overhead lights flare on, revealing a large mass of people starting to push through the opening. They wave protest signs, battling with the Guard to get through and into the center of the field.

King spins toward me with shock and fury in his eyes. For some reason, I want to defend myself, tell him this isn't me. I didn't do this. He opens his mouth, raising his arm and finger to point at me and, in that moment, another loud shot rings out and echoes from the stadium walls.

Once again I cringe and react to the gunfire, thinking someone is shooting at me. But it's King who stops. It's King who clutches his chest. And it's King who falls to his knees. He looks at me with disbelief—maybe a hint of relief (meant just for me)—and collapses forward. Screams resonate from the stands as people realize that the President has been shot. In those screams, I hear a familiar voice and my name. Up until this point, my brain has been registering my surroundings through a muffled slow-motion lens, but as I hear my name again, everything switches, like someone has just turned up the volume and pressed "play."

"SAM!"

I look in the direction of the yelling and see Brady running onto the stadium platform. "SAM." He waves wildly at me. "RUN ... RUN ..." He continues signaling at me to run, and then I realize I haven't moved. I'm still on my knees, frozen in place.

"SHOOT HER. SHOOT. HER. NOW."

O'Brien stands in the middle of a crowd of people pushing their way to get down off the stands and out of the stadium. He reaches for his gun. "SHOOT HER!" he yells at the few Guards still standing at the edge of the platform. They acknowledge his instruction and raise their rifles.

It's too late. I know it's too late, but I get up off my knees and start to run anyway. I hear the shots—this time, there's no doubt that they're directed at me—I feel something sharp stab into the flesh under my shoulder, someone tackles me, and the ground disappears from underneath me as I fly off the platform. With my hands still bound behind my back, there's no way of protecting my body from the force of the fall. I fall through the air and hit the ground with a bone-crunching thud. The full weight of whatever or whoever forced me off the stage comes down on top of me, knocking the wind from my lungs.

I struggle for breath, but something heavy is constricting my chest. I am surrounded by yelling, shooting, hostile sounds of fighting.

"Sam ..." A voice wheezes. I turn my head to see Brady's face. He tries to lift himself off but his arms give out, letting his full weight slump down on top of me. "I told you ... I'd make this right. I'm sorry it took me so long ... I'm sorry."

"Brady?"

I cough his name between breaths. "Brady?" I cry out, unable to move from underneath him. He doesn't respond. My breath shortens as I continue to gasp for air. I cough and sputter, tasting the metallic flavor of blood in my mouth.

"Brady ..." I say, hoping he can still hear me. I struggle for a last breath. His arm lies limply on the ground, his watch around his wrist, and mine lying loosely in the grip of his fist. It's the last thing I see.

35

SHERMAN ROGERS—MEDIANET NEWS

President Marcus O'Brien, commanding members of the Guard Elite, and delegates from the Collective gathered today to commemorate former president John King. King was assassinated five days ago during the anniversary ceremonies of the O2 bombings. After the commemoration, President O'Brien gave his first public interview since assuming his new Presidential role.

"This is a sad time for me as I not only honor the death of our great President but also mourn the loss of a close personal friend. It is with a heavy heart that I accept the role of President. While I may not be the leader that everyone voted for, I hope the people will allow me to lead them through this trying time in our country's history and carry on with President King's vision toward a stronger future.

"In light of recent events, I have decided to open the gates in the wall for an amnesty period of three days. This will allow all rebel supporters the opportunity to relocate from the East into the West. Anyone choosing to cross from the East into the West during this amnesty period will not be questioned or detained by any members of the Guard.

"As we have all witnessed, and certainly some have experienced, there has been enough fighting, and I hope that both sides will be able to settle our differences, begin the healing process, and move forward.

"I must warn that after this three-day period, the Guard will begin routine ID scans and arrest those suspected of anti-government activity. I want to make it clear that at the completion of the wall, we will still remain one united country.

"The wall is in place for the safety of everyone—the East and the West. It does not divide us. It is merely part of a system that will allow the Collective 5 to better assist citizens in all areas of society. Those that are less fortunate can find more work, access to better support, and aid programs in the West zone. I know the public has many more questions about how the wall will function, and I will address all those concerns after I meet with the C5 this coming week."

In other news, many have turned out to a designated area on the western side of the Neutral Zone, lighting candles, spreading flowers, and leaving commemorative messages to remember the life of Resistance leader Samantha Smart. The polarizing revolutionary was shot and killed last week during an attempted rescue by the Resistance.

The nation was shocked at the discovery that the Elite soldier seen tackling the Resistance leader was not trying to attack her, as first speculated, but rather protect her. President O'Brien has confirmed that the soldier in question was in fact a rebel spy.

Hours after the story of their deaths, images of the two popped up on many Medianet sites, revealing that Samantha Smart and Brady Smith attended the same university and were an athletic power couple. As family and friends come forward with more stories of the pair, we have begun uncovering a Shakespearean-like love affair that the Bard himself would have been captivated by.

When asked his thoughts, President O'Brien made a comment referring to the event as a "tragic loss of life." He went on to say that he "hopes supporters on both sides of the revolutionary conflict will learn from their deaths and stop the fighting before more lives are lost."

We'll have more news after we listen to a message from our C5 sponsors and a quick check-in to see what the weather holds for your region of the country. How's it look out there, Bob?

Bob: Thanks, Sherman. Well, the storms in the Midwest have finally settled and we are beginning to see sunny skies in …

36

I wake to the sound of O'Brien's voice and, for a brief moment, think I am back in my cell. It takes a few hazy seconds to realize I'm listening to a Medianet broadcast from a real bed. Slowly, the fog leaves my brain and I start to focus on my surroundings—white sheets, yellow curtains, dated flower wallpaper—it looks like some kind of hotel or motel room. My right arm is bound in a cast and there are heavy bandages wrapped around my knee, chest, and shoulder.

If I understood the Medianet news report correctly, I'm supposed to be dead. But the uneven mattress and the sharp pain pinching my ribs every time I take a breath contradict that report—unless heaven is a tacky rundown hotel with lingering aromas of old smoke and cheap cologne.

"Sam?" Aaron's scruffy head peeks into the room. His face lights up when he sees me. "You're awake."

"Aaron?" My voice is weak. I try to lift my head but a sharp pain in my shoulder pulls me back down.

"Don't try to move. You have a fractured collarbone; you broke your right wrist and arm in two places; you cracked four ribs; and a bullet punctured your lungs. You were almost dead when we brought you in."

"Brady?" I ask, hoping that if the Medianet news had gotten my death wrong then maybe … Aaron's silence and solemn expression confirm what I suspect. I turn my head as hot tears form.

"He saved your life. One of the bullets made it through both of you but he … stopped the rest of them."

I let the information fully settle. "A Shakespearean-like love affair?" I finally respond, quoting the news report.

"That's the spin. We're not disputing it. We think it works for us more than them."

"And I'm dead? Does that work for us, too?"

"Well, we haven't …"

Two faces peer in the door. "She's awake!" I recognize Max's enthusiastic expression. The other takes me a second to place, but then I flash back to the stadium, the voice—the Elite who whispered to me before I was led out to the platform. "Can we come in?" Max asks.

Aaron looks at me to see if it's okay.

I wipe a tear and nod.

"Sam, this is Justin. He's the one who carried you out of the stadium. He saved your life."

"Thanks." It sounds simple and stupid, but I don't know what else to say.

Justin smiles. "Anytime."

I look back at Aaron. "What the hell happened? I hardly remember anything after I was led out of the tunnel."

Aaron sits on the edge of the bed. "I'm not sure where to begin."

Max jumps in excitedly. "I found your USB drive. The one with Project K."

"You did?"

"After the base was attacked and you were captured," Aaron says, "a few of your crew managed to hide out."

Max talks over him, proud to tell the story. "The Elites were shooting at everyone, but I ran and hid up in the storage attic. I stayed there for a few days until Aaron came. I found a shoebox with a book, your picture, and this USB. I knew it was important so I kept it hidden."

Aaron continues, "We were able to release a few things on it, a video of you, but we haven't been able to access the rest. There's a solid firewall. I assume it's Maya's work."

At the mention of Maya's name, the room goes silent.

"Is it true about Wright?" I ask.

Aaron confirms it. "O'Brien shot him at the wall demonstration. In front of everyone."

"That's when Justin joined us." Max takes over again. "He's an Elite soldier and ..."

"Ex," he corrects Max. "I'm an ex-Elite soldier."

"Right."

"You really are Elite?" Coming out of my mouth, it sounds more like an accusation. Looking at him now, his haircut, how arrogantly and straight he holds himself, I can see it. His presence makes me feel edgy, uncomfortable.

"Was."

"But now you're working with us?"

He begins to open his mouth, but it is Aaron who jumps in

to answer. He seems defensive, like he needs to vouch for Justin, and only then do I realize how distrustful I must sound. "He was at the wall that day. O'Brien ordered his Elites to open fire on the crowd. Some of them resisted ..."

"I just couldn't do it," Justin says. "There were children. When O'Brien realized that a few of us wouldn't pull the trigger, he ordered the others to start shooting at us. I signed up to be Elite from the beginning. Hell, I helped design that wall. But not for this."

I know Justin sounds sincere but I give Aaron a skeptical glance.

"He's legit, Sam. Really."

"Really," Max chimes in. "It was Justin who had an idea that we could break into that school and get you out of there. We didn't even know where you were until he came along, and we were working on a plan, but then King announced your execution and ..."

"And we had no plan," Aaron finishes. "Until Brady reached out."

"What? How?"

"Your phone. I guess he kept it or got hold of it after they took you. He told us to rally a group of Resistance and mix in with the rest of the crowd outside the stadium. He said he would unlock and clear a door at Gate 7 ..."

"That's how Justin got in," Max adds.

"I still had my Elite uniform, so it gave me an in to the stadium. No one questions an Elite. I ordered the Guard who was supposed to lead you out to another post and I took his place."

"I wanted him to get a message to you that we were there and to be ready." Aaron takes over. "Brady told us that he was going to create some distraction so we could force our way into the stadium. After he took you out, Justin snuck back and unlocked other doors for us to enter through. He ordered Guards standing watch to different posts and confused them long enough for us to push through."

"That's when everything went crazy," I say, trying to make the sequence of events correspond to what I recollected.

"Pretty much."

"Who shot King?" I ask. Aaron and Justin look at one another.

"We don't know," Aaron shrugs. "Might have been Brady. No one knows. O'Brien is blaming the death on the Resistance. Maybe it was. But it wasn't something we had planned."

I think back to the way Ryan was looking at King in the helicopter. The way he'd been nervously tapping his fingers on his gun, and then about the moment I saw O'Brien order him to do something.

Aaron can see me thinking. "What is it?"

"O'Brien. I think he had King shot. It would have been the perfect opportunity. Let everyone blame the Resistance for the assassination while he slides into the position. It's even better than a coup. I think he has been working with the Collective and planning all of this from the beginning. We all just played right into their plans. What happened next?"

Justin continues. "King got shot and, at that point, the Resistance was infiltrating the stadium. Aaron was leading them and I tried to get back to you. I thought you would have been running at that point but you were still on the stage."

I think back to that moment. That was when I heard Brady calling my name. "It was all happening so fast. I had been taken out there to be executed ... and then everything ..."

"Went crazy?" Aaron confirms.

"Yeah."

"Well, while you were just hanging out on the stage watching it all go down, your boyfriend Brady ..."

"Justin!" Aaron snaps and shakes his head.

"What?"

"A little sensitivity."

He looks at me. "Oh ... right. Sorry. Anyway, O'Brien ordered the remaining Elites to shoot you, but Brady got to you first. He jumped in front of their shots; you both fell off the side of the platform and he landed on top of you. I got to you about a minute after you hit the ground. I have to admit, I thought you were dead. But we had come to get you out of there, so I picked you up and carried you to Gate 7 where Aaron and others were fighting with the Guard. They snuck you out from there."

"And we got you out and brought you here." Aaron completes the story.

I take some time to think about everything they've said, to sort out the mix of emotions storming inside my head. Brady called Aaron. He sacrificed himself. For me.

Why am I so shocked? Why do I feel so guilty? Because I don't think he is ... was capable? Because, given everything that's happened between us, it's impossible to accept that he still loved me enough to die for me?

No, I can't believe that it was love that made him do it—guilt, compassion, a shared history—but not love. Brady was "making it right" the only way he knew how. But there's nothing "right" about any of this.

"Sam?" Aaron's voice snaps me out of my thoughts. "Are you okay?"

"Yes." The neck of my hospital gown is soaked with tears.

"Are you sure?"

"Why does everyone think I'm dead?" I ask, hoping to change the subject.

"We carried your body out of the stadium. In all the videos and images, you ... appear dead. O'Brien told everyone that he let the Resistance take you as an act of good will. He sent a private message to us, saying that we should acknowledge we've been outplayed and accept our defeat—something about letting the clock run out. He was showing mercy. Letting us have you in exchange for peace."

"That's what his message said?" I lean in with interest. *"Let the clock run out?"*

"Yes. We still have it. You can hear it if you want."

I shake my head. I don't need to. It's a message for me. I'm sure of it. "How many people died trying to get me out?"

Aaron looks away to avoid my question.

"Aaron? How many?"

"Twenty-three," Justin answers. "Twenty-four if you count Brady."

"Twenty-nine, if you count Maya and the others." Max adds.

I turn my head away. "And how many people know I survived?'

"Us three. And the four doctors and nurses who worked on you."

"We didn't want to tell anyone in case ..." Max trails off.

"In case I didn't make it?" I look at Aaron and he nods in confirmation. "So ... I'm dead, then."

"But you're not." Max smiles. "And just wait till everyone hears that ..."

"No." I snap sharply. "No. Kayla, Maya, Brady, King ... all the others. O'Brien's right about one thing. The killing, this violence, it has to stop. One side has to give in."

"Sam," Aaron says gently, "maybe you should take some time to …"

"I don't need time." I think about O'Brien's message. It was a warning. "It's better this way."

The room goes silent. Aaron, Max, and Justin all exchange glances.

"But this can't be the end," Max pleads, looking at me and then back to Aaron. "It can't be. This isn't over. They can't just win."

No one responds.

Aaron points to my left arm, to the Resistance marking. "Just so you know, the doctors that worked on you said they could probably remove that. Or at least make it so it's harder to see."

"No." I rub my hand over the elevated skin. "That can stay."

He pats my blankets. I think he must be reading my mind, or understands that I need some time and space to process. "Okay, we should let you rest."

"But …" Max starts to protest.

Aaron lifts his hand to stop him. "No, we should go. Sam's been through a lot."

"Come on, kid, let's go." Justin starts to push him out of the room.

"Oh, fine. But we'll be back to see you soon."

Aaron waits for the others to leave. He opens his mouth to say something and then stops, changes his mind. We do have things to say to one another, but they can wait. "How are you feeling? Do you need anything?"

I flinch at his question. "Do me a favor," I say. "Please don't ask me why, and also don't take this the wrong way, but can you not ever ask me how I'm feeling, like, ever?"

He looks hurt, opens his mouth to say something, and stops himself again. "I hope sometime you can talk about it. What you've been through."

"Sometime. Maybe."

He pulls a USB out of his pocket. "What do you want to do with this?"

"It doesn't really matter now."

"It might." He waits for a response. Realizing it isn't coming, he sets it on the bed beside me. "You never know; it could come in handy someday." He squeezes my arm before turning to leave. "Oh, I almost forgot." He stops, pulls the Che book from his back pocket, and throws it on the bed beside me. "The kid gave me that. I thought you might want it," he shrugs. "You never know."

"Aaron?" I call out. Now it's my turn to open my mouth and stop. "When they led me out to ... to be executed. It was dark but the people in the stands ..."

"Turned their lights on."

"I didn't dream that?"

"No."

"But they bought tickets. They came to see me die. They watched others—Maya. Why me? Why would they ..."

"Because it was you, Sam. I think it was out of respect." He glances down at the USB and the book. "I know how you feel about it now but I think, where you're involved, there's still hope. Don't give up on the people, Samantha Smart, because they won't give up on you."

"Aaron?" I call to him before he disappears out the door.

"Actually ... can you stay with me awhile?"

He pulls up a chair and rests a hand on my leg. "As long as you want." Together we look over at the TV and listen to a broadcast message from the Collective 5.

"The Collective has begun working closely with your government to better serve you. A new ID implant, designed in a collaboration between Intel Sytems and Biopharm Tech, will sit just underneath the skin's surface on your left palm, allowing us to monitor the vital signs and medical needs of each collective citizen. In a few short weeks, representatives will be visiting your house to offer this obligatory service. We assure you this beneficial procedure is virtually painless and takes only a brief moment to complete. The C5—Innovation. Opportunity. Progression."

As the Collective Medianet message continues to play, I reach for the Che book and, from the pages, I pull out the spring break photo of Brady, Ryan, Kayla, and me. I gently touch their images, letting my finger rest over Kayla's. My hand falls to my inner forearm, running a finger over each of the letters burned into my skin.

R-E-S-I-S-T-A-N-C-E

Wait ... that's it?

Sam: I wish I could say it wasn't but, yes, that's it.

They win?

Sam: One side had to.

But ... So ... What happens next?

Sam: You're the one turning the pages. You tell me.

"I knew that if someone out there was reading my story, then everything was going to be okay, because stories always have a happy ending. And if it wasn't happy, that meant it wasn't the end."

~ Samantha Smart

ACKNOWLEDGMENTS

Thank you.

Thank you to all my fellow revolutionaries in life. Over the years you have listened to my numerous ramblings as the initial ideas for this novel formed, added your thoughts, and encouraged me to write, keep writing, and pushed to get this story published.

Thank you, to you, the one reading these words. Truly. Sincerely. Thank you.

Thank you to my students. Your inquiries, passions, and enthusiasm constantly teach me new ideas, inspire my writing thoughts, and give me hope for the generations to come.

Thank you to my editor Peter Carver and publisher Richard Dionne at Red Deer Press for seeing the potential in *Samantha Smart*, and in me. You have allowed for my stories and characters to run free and for that I will be eternally grateful.

Natalie, I don't think it's a coincidence that the year I met you the pages in my writing world started to turn. Thank you for having patience to put up with the fluctuation of my writing moods, having ears to bounce ideas off, having a mouth that tells me to focus, having a wild spirit that reminds me to pause, breathe, and enjoy the world we are in, and for having a heart that supports and loves me.

Grandpa Green, thank you. Even though you are no longer here, your words and guidance continue to have an impact in my life. You taught me to read, write, and believe in myself.

AUTHOR INTERVIEW WITH DAWN GREEN

What was it that compelled you to write this story? Was it events occurring in the real world, or a wish to create speculative fiction about events that probably would never occur?

I'm a fan of all kinds of fiction. I've read many dystopian novels and series but what always intrigued me about them was the story before the story – how did a society let itself get to a place where the dystopian governments could emerge and exist? For me, that's the most interesting and terrifying piece. *How Samantha Smart Became a Revolutionary* is something I have had in my brain for well over fifteen years. In fact, the initial seed was probably planted by my own grandfather who (like Sam's) used to casually joke each time the price of gas or housing rose, "One day there will be a war between the haves and the have nots."

In setting the plot and doing the research I examined historical examples of the formation of real totalitarian governments. All over the world, through the last century, from Europe to the Middle East, South America (and many other areas) there were similarities and patterns of events, attitudes, votes, coups etc. … societies that had had peace and stability but fell into chaos. How? And is this a pattern we are destined to repeat? And why? And what would it take to happen here? So many questions I wanted to examine with this story.

I wrote my first draft of *Samantha Smart* about four years ago. At the time this was completely speculative fiction but it was all too easy to read headlines about advances in technology, terrorism concerns, governments spying on citizens, laws banning religious symbols, immigration debates ... the list goes on. As I was polishing the final drafts of this novel intense votes and elections were underway in Europe and the United States. While many people were shocked with certain outcomes, I was less surprised and more nervously wondering if I had some unknown and previously untapped psychic abilities. It is easy to read this now and see mirrorings of events, slogans/statements, talk of building walls, and certain leaders, but that was not my intent when I first put pen to paper. I'm not about to leave writing and set up shop with a crystal ball, and I am also not saying that what I have written will come to pass; I truly hope it doesn't.

Can you explain why you chose to tell the story in two different times—the Then and the Now—in Samantha's life?

Personally, I am a fan of stories that move back and forth through time. I enjoy when certain details are revealed slowly and things take time to fully connect. As much as this novel is about the rise of a dystopian world, it is a story seen through Samantha's eyes, that follows the steps of how she becomes a revolutionary. And just as the reader is connecting the events, examining, and reflecting on how all of this could occur, so is Sam.

Why was it important to you to include the Trisha Weathers segments in the novel?

There are a couple of reasons for the Trisha Weathers news segments. Throughout this novel I really wanted to convey the role that the media (and social media) plays in everyday life and I was hoping to demonstrate how the media, a main source for information, one that should be objective, can be a contributing factor when it comes to building fear and terror in the public domain. News is big business. The more shocking a headline, the quicker a story breaks (even if the facts are not totally correct), the more people will tune in. And as much as more people are tuning in, we are bombarded with so many headlines and so much information, more people are just as quickly tuning out. Events that should rock us to our core, should be paid attention to, are quickly swept aside as soon as the next story breaks.

Currently, many of our media outlets seem to be under attack and the value of journalism has been seriously undermined. Journalists are there for the public. They are supposed to investigate, challenge, and ask the difficult questions that average citizens either can't or are too afraid to ask. I wanted Trisha to be that voice, and while it is a journalist's job to remain objective I also wanted to show that they are people and when faced with something like a revolution, their moral values and beliefs will sometimes pull them to one side or another.

Some readers might find it difficult to read descriptions of the brutal treatment of Samantha and others in the Resistance. Why was it important to you to include those scenes?

Yes, as much as those scenes may be difficult to read, they were much more difficult to write … and still at times (based on research and reading real life accounts) I feel like I could have gone further. I wish I could say that we live in a world where torture and evil do not exist, but as has been proven throughout history through stories like Abu Ghraib Prison, and psychological studies such as the Milgram Obedience experiment and the Stanford Prison experiment, the truth is that when humans are challenged with taking sides and put in roles that involve being authoritative or submissive we classically fall into these roles with very little effort or objection.

I am not saying that we are all intrinsically evil, because I believe in the inherent goodness of people; however, I don't think I would be doing justice to those who have suffered torture, and who have fallen victim to authority, if I were to sugar coat what would happen to someone in Samantha or Brady's position—it is important to remember that wars and revolutions ultimately have victims on both sides and they are not just those who endure torment and torture, but also those who inflict it.

Sam suffers physical, emotional, and psychological torture. The power play between her and King is less about information gathering and more about control. Through her suffering I wanted to show her strength and also show the lengths that those in authority can and have gone to gain power over others.

What was the purpose of the interview with Samantha, pieces of which occur throughout—and which in fact begin and end the novel? Who is the interviewer?

The purpose of the interview is to get an authentic voice from Sam—as authentic as we can get. I deliberately made the time frame of this interview ambiguous. This novel is about how Samantha Smart becomes a revolutionary and how civilized society can fall into ruin. I would hope that the reader is picking up this novel because they are questioning how and why this can happen. The interviewer—like Sam, like the reader—is searching for responses that get to the bottom of those questions. Unfortunately, they don't all come with an easy answer.

I think there are a couple of answers as to who the interviewer could be, but I am going to leave that up to the reader to decide.

As a teacher of high school students, you have been asking your classes to read George Orwell's *1984*. What connection, if any, do you see between your novel and Orwell's?

I will not pretend to compete or even come close to touching what Orwell and other great dystopian writers have written. What I do hope is that, like 1984 and others, this novel makes the reader think, reflect, and critically examine themselves and the society in which they live. I want Samantha to serve as an inspiration, but I also want her story to challenge and make the reader feel uncomfortable; some of the best novels I have on my shelf have done just that.

By the end of the book, it appears that General O'Brien and the Collective have won the long struggle against the followers of the Wright Resistance. Why did you choose to end the story on such a disheartening note?

This is meant to be a pre-dystopian novel, describing what happens when a society allows a totalitarian-like government to come into place. It should come as no surprise that the ending is not exactly happy. Although it is important to remember that, for those who are on King and the Collective's side, this is a happy ending. It's all a matter of perspective. But for those die-hard Wright supporters, and those rooting for Sam, have faith: "... if [the ending] wasn't happy, that mean[s] it wasn't the end ..."

You are an author whose three published novels (*When Kacey Left, In the Swish,* and now *How Samantha Smart Became a Revolutionary*) cover a range of themes and styles—each one quite distinctive. Why is it you like to experiment with new storytelling approaches in each project?

At times it is hard to fathom that I have been lucky enough to have one novel published, let alone three! When I set out to write a novel I am setting out to tell a story. As much as I am hoping to grow and consistently challenge myself as a writer, I don't intentionally set out thinking about writing in a style or theme different from what I have done before. I just try and write in whatever style I think will best tell each particular story. I really can't say where these stories and characters come from; they're just there, running around my head, poking, prodding and pushing at me to release them. Each time I complete one (as terrifying as it is to let it go out into the world alone), I feel a certain sense of relief ... briefly ... until the next one comes knocking.

Thank you, Dawn.